A WORLD OF TROUBLE

A WORLD OF TROUBLE

TROUBLE

FATEFUL DECISIONS

Jacky Renouf

This is a work of historically based fiction.
The days and dates of critical events in Guernsey are accurate. Most other events in
Guernsey occurred within the periods covered in the chapter headings.
The main characters in the novel are entirely fictitious and any likeness to persons
alive or dead, is co-incidental.
Reference is made to some key figures, during World War 2. The roles played by
King George VI; Prime Minister, Winston Churchill; Home Minister, Herbert Morrison;
and the Bailiff, Mr Sherwill, are based on real events. Other notable people played
fictitious parts.

Matador
9 Priory Business Park,
Wistow Road, Kibworth Beauchamp,
Leicestershire. LE8 0RX
Tel: 0116 279 2299
Email: books@troubador.co.uk
Web: www.troubador.co.uk/matador
Twitter: @matadorbooks

ISBN 978 1838595 005

British Library Cataloguing in Publication Data.
A catalogue record for this book is available from the British Library.

Printed and bound in Great Britain by 4edge Limited
Typeset in 10.5pt Adobe Garamond by Troubador Publishing Ltd, Leicester, UK

Matador is an imprint of Troubador Publishing Ltd

The ultimate measure of a [wo]man is not where [s]he stands in moments of comfort and convenience, but where [s]he stands in times of adversity and controversy.

*With apologies to **Martin Luther King Jnr.***

This book is dedicated to my mother Joan, grandmothers Ida and Mary, great grandmother Leah and my many aunts, whose lives were beset by unbelievable turmoil after June 1940.

The title of this book refers to a song from Gilbert and Sullivan's comic opera The Mikado entitled 'In a World of Trouble – Wondering what this world can be.' This popular opera includes another song 'Three Little Maids from School' which underscores the naivety of three young women, when war encroached on their youth.

This book is a work of fiction but is based on real experiences. I grew up with the stories of family members who stayed in Guernsey and the different stories of family members who evacuated. I believe some of these stories need to be told.

I hope they will be of interest, particularly to my daughter, Nicola; granddaughters, Miro, Lauren, Daisy and Livia; and great-granddaughters, Isla and Veda.

AUTHOR'S NOTES

1.   Guernsey Patois

The phrase '*À la prochaine*' is a Guernesiaise version of the French phrase, 'Jusqu' à la prochaine fois'; meaning 'until the next time' and is a typical Guernsey farewell, for someone leaving for an extended time. In German it can be rendered as '*bis zum nächsten mal.*'

2.   Bailiwick of Guernsey

Guernsey is a self-governing British Crown Dependency. Like Jersey, it is a remnant of the Duchy of Normandy, with its judicial and administrative arms having their roots in Norman feudalism.

In 1559 Queen Elizabeth 1 granted a Charter confirming the neutrality of the Channel Islands and approving all existing laws and customs practised in the Islands. This preserved the judicial and administrative autonomy of the Bailiwick, with a Governor as the Queen's Representative. In 1660, with the restoration of Charles 2, all the previous rights and privileges lost during the Civil War, were given back to Guernsey. Its allegiance has belonged since to the English Crown, not the Parliament of the United Kingdom.

3.   Secondary Schooling in Guernsey

While free state secondary schooling for girls and boys was first discussed in 1851 it did not eventuate for boys until 1883 and for girls in 1895, when 'Une Ecole Intermediaire pour Filles', opened. This school, then in Rosaire Avenue, became the Occupation School in April 1941, with 68 pupils aged 10-16. In January 1942 the Germans commandeered the site and the pupils were taught elsewhere in St. Peter Port. In September 1946 the Girls' Intermediate restarted.

4.   Vinery

Grapes were grown in heated glasshouses from 1792 for the domestic market. From 1870, with the benefit of a steamboat service to England, flowers, melons and tomatoes were grown for export instead of grapes. Large glasshouses continue to be called 'vineries' in Guernsey.

5.   Haybox

Boxes filled with hay were used for slow cooking to save fuel. A meal was first heated and then placed in the haybox overnight. By morning the dish was cooked.

6.   Dolmen

Neolithic people settled in the Channel Islands around 5500 BC. They left megaliths for a Mother Goddess and burial tombs known as 'dolmens' (derived from the Brèton, *dol* [table] *men* [stone]).

7.   Barnes Wallis's Bouncing Bombs

These were designed to bounce across water, unhindered by torpedo nets, to reach their target.

PART ONE
INVASION
17TH JUNE – 1ST JULY 1940

PART ONE
INVASION
17TH JUNE – 1ST JULY 1940

CHAPTER ONE
MONDAY 17TH JUNE 1940
GUERNSEY

WHAT COULD HAVE HAPPENED TO RACHEL, WHO WAS always punctual? Marion, typically the latecomer, was surprised to find herself the earliest arrival at the coffee shop for the monthly lunch meeting with her former school friends. It was an occasion all three looked forward to.

Different in many ways, Marion Le Prevost, Stella Ferbrache and Rachel Dorey had been friends since they met, aged 12, at the Girls' Intermediate School. By their fourth year they had become inseparable, forming a special bond over their sporting and academic interests. As well, they enjoyed amateur dramatics and all three were key performers in the comic opera *The Mikado*, produced in their final year.

High spirited and happy in the limelight, Marion made the most of the lead role of Yum Yum, while Rachel and Stella played supporting parts.

'Three little maids from school,' they remained firm friends as their working lives began. Marion was the payroll clerk at De La Mare's department store; Stella had a good job with the Guernsey States Government; and Rachel, now a trained nurse, was working at the Victoria Hospital.

There was always much to discuss at their lunches together, Marion reflected. She and Stella had the added excitement of being bridesmaids when Rachel and her artilleryman fiancé John set a wedding date.

Choosing an upstairs table overlooking the harbour of St Peter Port, Marion thought how peaceful and picturesque it looked. Small fishing boats filled the marina. On the outer stone breakwater two British Naval ships were tied up; the Guernsey mailboat was at its mooring on St Julian's Pier. Vehicles and pedestrians filled the waterfront esplanades as usual.

In many ways, Marion thought, it was as if Guernsey and the other Channel Islands were barely touched by the war that erupted nearly nine months ago. The rapid German conquest of France had surprised the Guernsey people, but they were British patriots and believed that the British forces would prevail, as they had in 1918. News of the rout of British troops at Dunkirk, had not shaken peoples' confidence.

Despite being able to hear the rumble of gunfire from the nearby Cotentin Peninsula, most of the Guernsey population felt safe and protected. British soldiers and heavy artillery were located at key points around the Island. Both King George and Prime Minister Winston Churchill had promised that Britain would always defend 'their dear Channel Islands.'

At last Rachel rushed in, out of breath, with her long blonde hair flying loose.

4

'I simply had to stop and listen to the radio before I left! The announcer said that last week the British Cabinet met about the future of the Channel Islands. While no decision appears to have been made, he said that the British don't think they can protect us if Cherbourg falls to the Germans. He said we may be demilitarised and if the British soldiers leave, they will take all weaponry with them. We would have no way to defend ourselves if the Germans then decide to come here! Everyone at the hospital is in a flap.'

Marion was unperturbed: 'The Germans won't come here! We're not important enough to invade. The Bailiff said they will want to attack England not us. My Uncle Harry believes this war won't last long. He says the British forces will regroup after Dunkirk and return to liberate Normandy. They will soon push the Germans back again. They are not weak like the French!'

Stella joined them, pulled out a chair and sat down, running her hand through her curly mop of auburn hair. 'Have you heard the latest? It's awfully frightening. We didn't imagine that we might ever be invaded, just like France was. But it now seems likely.' Her round face, usually crinkled with laughter, was serious.

'The senior staff at the States are being called to an emergency meeting this afternoon to meet a newly appointed Transport Officer and begin planning for vital supplies and a possible evacuation,' she continued. 'My father thinks the Islands will be the next to fall into German control. He says we are unprepared for any attack. Gas masks haven't yet been distributed, and there are no air-raid shelters.

'He said that some people have already made their own plans to evacuate the Island and have been slipping away on the mailboats. He's not at all optimistic about our general preparation for what might happen. He said the British have overlooked our vulnerability.'

Marion retorted: 'My mother says that the people planning to leave are being selfish. They might have the money to go, but they are not thinking about the rest of us who don't have that option.'

'It's not so simple,' Rachel said. 'John phoned me from his Airforce base at Swindon last night. He asked me to leave Guernsey and join him in England because he is likely to be sent abroad with his artillery battery within the next few months. He wants us to be together until then.

'I know that I could join the Allied Nursing Service, as part of the war effort. Two other local nurses have already got positions and they asked me to join them.'

'What do your parents say?' asked Marion.

'They oppose it. My mother says I am too young to be alone in England when John goes overseas. Also, my Dad insists nurses will be needed here, if we get invaded. He isn't confident that England won't be invaded as well. He says they are as unprepared as they were in 1914. He thinks our family will be safest living on our farm.'

Stella took Rachel's hand. 'You poor thing! You must feel pulled in two directions.'

Rachel nodded, 'I really don't know what to do!'

Marion interjected: 'Your mother is probably right, you know. It might be better to wait here until John comes back. When it's all over! I don't think it will last too long.'

Stella was not so optimistic. 'Everything is going to change for the three of us,' she predicted. A line from *The Mikado* seemed apt: 'It really is a world of trouble now.'

CHAPTER TWO
FRIDAY 21ST JUNE 1940
GUERNSEY

IT HAD BEEN THE STRANGEST DAY, STELLA REFLECTED. IT started in the familiar surrounds of her home in Guernsey and was ending somewhere on a grimy, crowded boat in the English Channel. She had been caught up in panicked decisions and was on her way to England, with no notion about her future.

She was cold and overwrought. She put on her winter jacket and wrapped herself in her raincoat, closing her eyes but her mind kept racing, denying her sleep.

Since her lunch with friends on Monday, when they had discussed their uncertainties about Guernsey's future, everything had changed utterly. On Wednesday, the Bailiff published a notice in the morning paper saying that the British would demilitarise the Channel Islands and immediately remove their troops back to England. The British Lieutenant Governor would also leave with the soldiers. The British intended to declare the Island an 'open town' once the last troops had left.

Later, on Wednesday morning, after days of indecision, the Bailiff proclaimed that all the school children on the Island should be sent to sanctuary in the United Kingdom, beginning tomorrow. After school, that afternoon, the children came home with a note asking parents to approve, by 7pm, their being evacuated with their classmates and teachers. The harried parents were given a list of instructions to follow on the following morning, when they left their children at school, to be taken down in their class groups to the wharves.

Yesterday, Stella's eleven-year-old brother, David, with his teacher and classmates, had left the Island, destined for Glasgow in Scotland. Stella knew it was a forlorn hope that she could persuade the rest of her family to take the mailboat to England. Her father, as sub-editor of the local daily paper, *The Press*, felt he could not abandon his job. Official notices around the town begged people in essential services to 'remain at their posts as a patriotic duty.'

On Friday morning, when Stella cycled to her job at the States Offices on the quay, she anticipated that it would be another stressful day. Staff were now busily preparing for large-scale evacuations of people from the Island; rushed plans had been made with shipping companies in England to ensure enough boats would be available on Friday morning.

While most of the young men on the Island had hurried to enlist when war was declared and had left soon after to join various regiments in England, today, all the remaining single men who were of military age, were required to report to the States Office. They were urged to leave immediately for

England. The remainder of the eight hundred places available on the ships in port on Friday were for more school children to be evacuated, along with pre-school children with their mothers. A long queue had already formed outside the office when Stella arrived. It continued to grow during the morning.

Stella was organising passages for women with their young children. These women were in a state of shock and deeply distressed at leaving their husbands and parents. She felt enormous pity for their predicament, but knew it was important for her to maintain a calm, unhurried manner as she made the arrangements for these part-family groups. She was secretly relieved that she had not been assigned to process the line of young men, many of whom she knew as school mates and fellow sportsmen.

To her surprise, around 11 am she was called to take an urgent phone call from her mother, who said: 'I've got you on to a boat going this afternoon, as an extra helper for Miss Parish who is accompanying the Amherst schoolchildren to Wales. Your father and I agreed last night that you should go to England now, while you still can. I will try to convince your father that we should follow you and David in the next few days.

'Come home right now to collect your things. I've arranged for Mr Webb next door to drive you down to St Julian's Avenue to meet the schoolchildren by 2 pm.'

Flustered, Stella ran to her supervisor, Mr Hollis, who said, 'Your mother told me that you have an offer of a passage out of here. You need to take it. We can find someone to replace you. This will be no place for young women like you. You will be able to help the war effort over there. Off you go quickly, and quietly, and good luck!'

On her way home, Stella just had time to call at Marion's house, asking Mrs Le Prevost to give Marion her love and say she would write. Mrs Le Prevost gave her a frosty reception.

Arriving back home at Rosaire Avenue, Stella found her mother and father busy organising for her departure. Her father had been to the bank and taken out the twenty pounds she could take with her and had found her birth certificate, matriculation results and her passport, which he placed in a black leather wallet.

Her mother was upstairs, where she was now packing as many of Stella's clothes as she could into a small brown cardboard case.

'I've made up the food parcel you need for tonight. I followed the list that they gave out for David to take on the boat yesterday. Now you need to have a good lunch, then dress in as many clothes as possible, since I can't get much more into this suitcase,' her mother said.

At the table, Stella asked her father to get a message to Rachel, who was on night duty at the hospital, knowing that she, like Marion, would be disappointed not to have spoken before she left.

'Well, I want you, as well as young David, off this island when the Germans come,' her father said. 'I saw what happened to villagers in France in the last war and it's not what I want for either of my children. I have things I need to do for the paper in the next few days to help with the evacuation. Perhaps your mother and I will be able to leave after that. It will be safer for you both in England and your mother and I will be happy knowing that.'

Her father added another piece of paper to her document folder. 'Here is Mark Webb's address in Cambridge. Mr Webb says you should phone Mark when you get to London and he may be able to help you find a job and a place to live. Yes, I know you don't like him much, but he is a steady lad. Remember?'

Stella grimaced as she thought about Mark Webb, who was three years older. They had played together as small children, but she had unhappy memories of the awkward time when he escorted her, as a teenager, to the school ball. After three years studying at Cambridge, he now had a rich girlfriend, and was in her view far too conceited to still be 'the nice boy next door.'

At her mother's urging Stella ate a large meal of beans and tomatoes with chunks of cheese and bread. 'We are drowning in tomatoes,' observed her father. 'It's been difficult for the growers to send them to England these past couple of weeks. You had better enjoy them as they may be the last you get.'

Feeling very full, Stella went upstairs to put on three pairs of knickers, two singlets, and a petticoat, followed by a skirt and cotton blouse and then a woollen dress and cardigan. 'I feel like Michelin Man,' she said to her mother. 'I will have to carry my jacket and raincoat. I will wear my heaviest shoes, though!'

Stella struggled downstairs and into the kitchen. 'Right young lady, it's time to go,' said her father rising to his feet and hugging her closely. 'We will see you in the by and by, so no tears.'

Stella saw her mother bite her lip, as she had the previous day when they said farewell to David in his school playground, obeying the instruction that families should be 'unemotional.' Stella knew her mother's attempt to keep a brave face was cover for an aching heart; she had heard her mother sobbing last night and knew she would be very sad again tonight.

'I must be brave for her,' thought Stella. Giving her parents a brief hug and kiss, she briskly picked up her case and coats and followed Mr Webb to his waiting car.

'Make sure you contact our Mark,' Mr Webb said. 'I telegraphed him to say you were coming and that he was to be your contact point. He is doing some secret war work with other men he knew at Cambridge. Not sure exactly what, but he says it's as important as joining the army.'

'You're not going to leave, Mr Webb?' Stella asked.

'No girlie. We need to look after Mrs Webb's mother and father, they are in their seventies and cannot leave here. Give our love to Mark. Goodbye and good luck, lass. Or perhaps, I should just say '*À la prochaine*'; till the next time.'

Stella walked down St Julian's Avenue, which was full of children clustered in groups. Each child had a large label, giving their name, birthdate and parents' address, pinned to their clothes. Each was clutching their bag of food and some cuddled a soft toy. Heaps of small suitcases were sitting by the rough signs indicating which school the children came from; St Martin's School, Catel School, then the Amherst children she was to accompany, who were sitting opposite the Boer War Memorial.

She quickly spotted her mother's friend, Miss Parish, who introduced her to the junior children, some of whom were still tearful and whey-faced after parting from their parents. She gathered a small group to sit on the pavement so she could tell them an improvised story of Peter Pan. Gradually the children relaxed and became absorbed in the tale, with even a rowdy group of little boys joining in.

It was over an hour before it was their turn to line up to board their assigned transport. The stone wharves were crowded with boats, many in various stages of dilapidation. Only days before she had seen a most unseaworthy-looking open boat, full of women refugees from Normandy, calling in on the way to England.

She hoped that her group would be better accommodated than that, but realised they had to take their chances. 'It's an adventure and I always hoped for adventure and travel,' she told herself.

The Amherst children, with Miss Parish leading the juniors, and Stella bringing up the rear, walked down to the White Rock jetty. It was eerily quiet: neither traffic nor pedestrians could be seen along either of the shoreline esplanades. The children, too, were silent and watchful.

A port worker directed their group to a small ferryboat, *The Pride of Kingston*. It had three decks with the second deck providing a large lounge area, some toilets and a galley. The blue paintwork on the boat was chipped and fouled with weed. As they went aboard Stella noted how scruffy it looked, with overflowing waste bins, dirty brass fittings, and littered floors.

As the children found places to settle, and the teachers worked out shifts to oversee them, the captain announced the boat was about to be untied from the dock. Some of the older boys cheered; other children joined in despite not really knowing what was being celebrated. As the captain outlined the emergency instructions, Stella realised it was unlikely there would be enough lifebelts and lifeboat spaces for all those on board.

When the boat pulled away, the headmaster got the children singing, so most were immersed in the hymn 'There's a green hill far away' until well out of the harbour. Stella, instead, watched the receding town – its tall higgledy-piggledy buildings, with their numerous rows of round chimney pots, climbing above the port – until it became a distant blur.

Much more comfortable after shedding some of her excess clothes, Stella joined Miss Parish to devise activities for the children until it was time for them to eat, and then settle down for the night. The sea was calm and as dusk turned into a still moonless night, many were quickly lulled into sleep on the gently rocking boat. Most were worn out by the turbulent day they had experienced, but in one corner a small girl still sobbed inconsolably.

Stella, who had long since eaten the lunch her mother had packed, was too hungry and thirsty to sleep. She made her way to the galley to ask for some water.

She found a man in a dirt-stained chef's jacket who told her, 'There's nothing available here. No food, no liquids. We had to turn around so fast we didn't get a chance to stock up. We've been running back and forth across the Channel as fast as we can. First it was Dunkirk and now it's Guernsey and Jersey. The crew haven't slept in nearly two weeks. We don't even know what day it is.'

Although the boat would arrive near Weymouth during the night, it would have to anchor offshore. 'We can't go into the port till morning,' the chef told her. 'There is a submarine barrage across the harbour at night. Lucky it's a still night, and its clouded over, so none of Jerry's subs will see us waiting offshore, like ducks waiting for slaughter. There are quite a few ships in tonight's convoy.'

Stella eventually fell asleep but awoke with a jolt to hear the anchor being raised, and stiffly got out of her chair. It was barely light, but her watch said 5 am. The boat must now be moving towards the harbour. Following Miss Parish down to the main deck, Stella helped the junior students as they woke, chattering away about the experience of sleeping on the floor or wondering when they would arrive and have breakfast.

Once the boat had docked, the passengers filed off and entered a large dockside warehouse. There the children, seated at large tables, were given a breakfast of porridge, fruit, toast and milk. Men and women in Salvation Army uniforms were running between the tables attending to the children's appetites.

At one end of the warehouse a Customs Officer was checking over the passports and lists of schoolchildren. At the opposite end, other government officials were preparing ration books and travel vouchers for the entire group. Realising her twenty pounds would not be enough to travel to Wales with the children, Stella asked the headmaster if she could finish her duties. He thanked her and wished her well.

Clutching her transportation papers, Stella followed the signs on the wharf to find the central railway station. She had a travel warrant to get her as far as Cambridge. The timetable indicated the first train to London on a Saturday was not until 9.30 am. As the station was almost empty, she lay down on a long, padded, station seat, with her baggage tucked around her whilst she waited.

Now she faced the adventure of fending for herself. For the first time in her nineteen years she was entirely alone, in an unknown place. She was anxious about finding her way around London knowing she had to change stations quickly to make her connecting train.

CHAPTER THREE
FRIDAY 21ˢᵗ JUNE 1940
GUERNSEY

MARION LEFT WORK AFTER 6 PM; LATER THAN USUAL. During the afternoon, the serving staff in De La Mare's Department Store heard a rumour that clothes were going to be rationed, and that everyone would need a coupon book before they could make any purchases.

Since Friday was payday, the salesgirls asked the manager if they could buy items from the store before they went home that night, and he agreed. When the shop closed at 5.30 pm the staff began rushing around to find various clothes, they, or their family, might need. Marion came down from the accounts office to join the excited fray.

Heavily laden with bags of clothing, she began to walk

down the High Street to the steps linking up with the harbour, but she was turned back at the esplanade by a policeman.

'No-one is allowed along the harbourfront right now,' he said. 'We are still boarding men of military age, who were meant to leave the port at 3 pm. They have to get going quickly.'

Marion, with tight shoes chafing her heels, and her arms straining with the weight of her parcels, turned abruptly around and retraced her steps. She wound her way back along the cobbled streets, past the shops, and was forced to climb the steep and lengthy steps rising off St Julian's Avenue.

Marion paused halfway up the uneven flagstones to catch her breath and take in the scent of wallflowers and fennel from the granite walls beside the steps. Out on the harbour she saw a thin skein of white water from the armada of boats heading out from the wharf into the shipping lane. She was shocked to see just how many vessels were leaving.

She topped the crest of the hill and wound her way back downhill again, to her mother's house at the base of the incline. By the time she reached home, after her lengthy detour, she was footsore and grumpy.

Her home was a narrow, terraced house, fronting onto the inner edge of the footpath. The house presented only one lounge window, covered in white net curtains, and a heavy black painted door at street level. On the first floor, two narrow windows also faced the steep cobbled street. Marion entered the front door and kicked her shoes off before going down the narrow, dark passageway beside the stairs leading to the lean-to kitchen at the rear of the house. Her mother was sitting at the kitchen table reading *The Press*.

'You're late!'

'Yes. Well...,' began Marion, but her mother interrupted: 'You will never guess who came here this morning? And you will never guess why?'

Marion pulled out a chair and sat down heavily, 'Tell me then.'

'It was your friend Stella. She turned up here around 11 o'clock. I was just finishing cleaning and I still had on my apron. She was all hot and bothered. She had cycled here, you know.'

'Yes, but why was she here?' queried Marion.

'Ah well, it's like this. You know her brother went off with his school yesterday, well, today Stella's mother arranged for Stella to go to England too. She's gone off as a volunteer with the Amherst children. Would you believe it? Just like that; she up and goes! Not a care for you or anyone else. I suppose just because her parents have money, they can buy her an escape. I told her that you wouldn't have that chance.'

Marion stared at her mother in disbelief: 'When is she leaving?'

'Oh! She will be well gone. She said she had to meet the children at St Julian's at 2 pm. Be out at sea by now, I shouldn't wonder.'

'I crossed St Julian's coming home and there were no school children there. I wonder if they are still at the wharf. A policeman told me they were still boarding passengers when I tried to walk along the esplanade. I could run down to see if she is still there.'

'And what good would that do?' her mother asked. 'Like I said she has just up and left us all to carry on as best we can. She did say to tell you goodbye.'

She went on, 'When I went out to do a bit of shopping this afternoon, I heard the public broadcast by the new Controlling Committee. They said we did not have to evacuate; it's not compulsory. We should stand 'shoulder to shoulder.' The Committee especially requested farmers and growers not to leave. It's a bit late though as there are now hundreds running off! There was a sign up in the butcher's saying, 'Don't be yellow! Business as *usual*.' Pity they didn't read it. It's not right for them to go. I don't know what they are afraid of. That Mr Churchill said he will be looking after us.'

'Well Stella isn't yellow,' Marion retorted. 'Maybe her parents wanted her to look after her brother. She did try to let me know what was happening. Did she indicate where she was going?'

'No. She said she would write. But what's the use of that? It won't be the same for you now without your posh friend.'

Marion sighed, pushed away from the table and got up 'I'm struggling to believe this. It's all so sudden. I'm just going up to change.'

She left the kitchen and slowly climbed the stairs to her room, shut the door, and lay down on her bed.

Marion, whilst she would not admit this to her mother, felt deflated and tearful. She was going to miss Stella greatly, as her confidante, but she would also miss the harmonious life of Stella's family. Marion had relied on Stella and the Ferbrache family, throughout the years they were at school together. They had provided her with some respite from her mother's often cantankerous behaviour.

Marion had always been a welcome visitor in their home and during their school days Marion had often done her homework at their house. Stella's father had taken the two girls to sports events and always taken an interest in their successes, which her own mother regarded as a waste of time. Marion wondered how she would cope without this refuge.

After half an hour, her mother knocked on her bedroom door.

'Are you asleep? Do you want some tea? I haven't got much in the pantry, but we could have a nice egg! What are all those packages you left in the hall? You haven't been buying more clothes, I hope? We can't afford that!'

'No! I'm not asleep, just thinking. Yes, an egg will be fine. Yes, there are some clothes for me. But there are some for you as well!'

Marion quickly changed out of her work dress into an old frock. She washed her hands in the basin in her room and brushed her bob of dark hair, pushing stray wisps back behind her ears. She renewed her lipstick, grimaced at her reflection in the mirror, and straightened her shoulders.

Once downstairs Marion said, 'It seems likely that the States are going to introduce clothing rationing soon. Since it was a payday, I brought us a few items to help tide us over.'

Her mother sniffed. 'I hope you haven't spent all your pay. I can't be sure that my pension will be paid out now, you know.'

'Why don't you see what I've got for you,' said Marion, passing two of the packages to her mother.

Mrs Le Prevost sat down and opened the first bag containing two sets of underwear, two pairs of socks and a warm night gown. She then opened the next bag containing skeins of royal blue knitting wool. 'They will be useful I suppose,' she conceded. 'What did you get yourself, then?'

Marion opened her bags to show her mother that she too had been practical, for once, buying underclothes, more feminine than her mother's, a cardigan and matching blouse and some lisle stockings. 'We might not be able to buy much in the future, so I thought we should stock up a bit,' Marion said.

'I suppose it might be eggs for the next few nights then!' was the tart response.

Marion forced herself to smile at her mother, who always needed to be teased out of her ill-humour. She went to the pantry to get out the eggs, milk and bread they would eat that evening.

After a tense meal Marion said she had a headache and escaped the heavy silence in the kitchen for the privacy of her bedroom.

CHAPTER FOUR
SUNDAY 23RD JUNE 1940
GUERNSEY

I HAVE JUST HAD THE MOST DISTRESSING WEEK.

It started out with my feeling guilty; guilty about not going to England when John had asked me to join him there. Sad too, because I have missed him during the six months since he went back to England to enlist.

I've been lonely without him and I've had no social life at all since the men in our group left. Now, with him about to be posted overseas, I am afraid that I might never see him again. We might never get married as we intended. I can't bear to think about that.

And I'm angry, too, for two reasons. I was angry with my parents; first, for not letting me get married to John before he left in

January and then again for not letting me leave last week, whilst I still had the chance to go. Now that is impossible.

Then yesterday Stella's father phoned to tell me that Stella had evacuated as a volunteer to accompany some of the school children. He said that she had made her way to Cambridge and was going to look for work there. He said Mark Webb was helping her out.

I'm so jealous that Stella's parents let her leave when mine wouldn't, but I'm also sad that my oldest friend has gone away. Over the past few days I heard of so many people, including my aunt and cousins, who have departed. We lost medical staff from the hospital as well. Mr Ferbrache said that 17,000 people left last week; which is almost half the population.

My parents decided that my brother would not evacuate with his school. I am not sure what will happen about his education once summer holidays are over. I am pleased, though, that my parents were consistent in their decision-making!

Planning on the Island has been frenetic this past week. There have been many rumours circulating, along with much speculation about our future. So, it's been hard to determine the facts. We now know that the British troops have left Guernsey and the Guernsey Militia has been demobilised. Not a soldier left on the Island!

The Guernsey mailboat, which has a large gun on board to protect it during Channel crossings, is the sole artillery weapon at Guernsey's disposal, to counter any possible German assault by land or sea.

We also know there are changes to our government. With the Lieutenant Governor gone, the Royal Court was called together on Friday and later announced that a Controlling Committee of eight men was set up, each responsible for a subcommittee. They will provide executive control of the States Department. Mr Sherwill, a former military man, has now been appointed as the new Bailiff. It's all so confusing.

There was a new rumour spreading at work on Friday; that we are going to move from the Victoria Hospital to the old Country Hospital in the Catel Parish, because it is centrally located and in a rural area. I don't want to think about what that might entail.

Suddenly my life here feels topsy-turvy and I know it is out of my control. I've decided to keep a diary because things here are changing fast.

CHAPTER FIVE
SUNDAY 23RD JUNE 1940
CAMBRIDGE

STELLA FOUND THE NUMBER OF PEOPLE IN ENGLAND intimidating. Everyone seemed to be rushing along in a preoccupied manner, totally disconnected from each other. London had been the worst, both at the railway stations and on the Underground.

Catching the train up from Weymouth had been straightforward, in contrast to the difficulty she experienced when changing trains in London. She had arrived at Waterloo, which was smoky, noisy and confusing. There were so many platforms that she felt quite lost. She sat down under the clock, out of the way of hurrying passengers, and tried without success to work out where she needed to go. It was hard not to panic.

She joined a long queue of people, and when she reached the information counter to ask about a train to Cambridge, she found it difficult to understand the Cockney railwayman. With the assistance of a kindly, middle-aged woman standing behind her, she discovered that she needed to get the tube to King's Cross Station to catch the train onwards from there.

The woman, seeing her confusion, said, 'Wait for me dearie and I'll show you the way to the Underground. I'll put you on the right line.'

Having safely navigated her way under the city Stella faced another wait for the Cambridge train, but by mid-afternoon she was on her way again. With her little money being closely guarded, she bought only a curling cheese sandwich and a lukewarm cup of tea, to renew her energy. However, on the afternoon train, sitting in the overheated carriage, she began to doze.

The next thing she knew was that someone was vigorously shaking her shoulder. 'We are coming into Cambridge. If you don't get off here, the next stop is King's Lynn.' Somewhat dazed Stella had mumbled her thanks to the guard, gathered her bags together and was ready to alight as soon as the train stopped.

There was a telephone booth on the platform and Stella knew she could delay no longer; she needed to talk to Mark. However, when she called his number a woman answered and told her that Mark was not yet home. Stella felt alarmed and quickly asked when he might be back.

'Are you Stella Ferbrache?'

'Yes.'

'Mark left a message for you. He wasn't sure if you would call today but he knew you had left Guernsey. Where are you now?'

'I'm at the railway station... in Cambridge,' Stella added.

'All right, then you had better come here right away. Mark will be back about 7 pm. It's not too far to walk.' The woman gave her an address and told her the route to follow.

Half an hour later Stella found herself outside a row of brick terrace houses. Each had iron railings around tiny gardens, with a gravel path leading to steps up to the front door. Over the doors each house had a glass fanlight which bore the name of the property. Stella entered the gate of the one named 'Redleaf' and dragged herself up the steps. She was close to tears with fatigue and hunger.

Mark's landlady, Mrs Styles, answered the door and ushered her into a sitting room, with its bay window over-looking the garden and street. 'You look all-in. I will make you some tea, while you rest, and then we can talk.' Mrs Styles was warm and sympathetic. She soon had Stella talking about her journey from Guernsey and found out that Stella had no plans beyond getting here to Cambridge.

'Well my dear, we had better get you sorted out for tonight, at least. I don't have any room here. Mark and his friend Peter have been with me since the time they were at the university. I can ask Mrs Briggs next door at the Bed and Breakfast, if she has a vacancy.'

With that Mrs Styles disappeared next door and came back to assure Stella that she had a bed for the night. 'She can't give you a meal tonight though, so I thought you and Mark might find some café and have time to catch up.'

'Well I don't really know Mark very well,' Stella flushed. 'He is a bit older than me and he has been away from Guernsey for a long time.'

'We will take your bags next door and you can find your room and then come back and wait for Mark.'

Mark had returned to his lodgings before Stella came back to 'Redleaf', having had time to wash, change her clothes and re-arrange her tousled hair into something more becoming. She didn't want to look like some scruffy schoolgirl when she met Mark. To her relief he had greeted her warmly. She felt more confident that he was willing to assist her.

Together, they had walked down to a Lyons Corner House and eaten a plate of fish and chips. Stella was surprised, though grateful, that Mark paid for her meal, but she had to give up some of her new food coupons.

Later, as they walked back to their adjacent houses, Mark said he would telegraph his father to let him know that she had arrived safely and would be staying on in Cambridge. He had already told her that, with some of the government departments moved out from London, there were many jobs available for women with her skills. She learned also that the students from the university were at home for the summer vacation, and she would readily find somewhere to live. They arranged to meet again the next day.

At mid-morning a jovial Mark came to fetch her.

'I have talked to an old friend, Alison. She's a librarian at Pembroke College and there is a vacant room in her flat. We should get over there now for you to see it.'

They walked through the maze of narrow streets, then along the busy Pembroke Road, to reach Botolph Lane. Mark stopped in front of a tall grey house, its blue front door opening on to the lane. He rang the bell for the third floor flat, telling Stella there were four flats in the building; one on each floor.

They climbed the two flights of stairs to find a young woman wearing metal-rimmed glasses, waiting at an open doorway. She welcomed Stella and introduced first herself, and then two other young women in the flat; Dawn and Michelle. The three women were approximately her age and were friendly. Alison showed Stella around the flat whilst the other girls prepared morning tea for them all.

The small, unoccupied bedroom was at the back of the flat, overlooking a tiny alleyway full of rubbish cans and bicycles. It contained a narrow bed, a small wooden wardrobe, a chair and a wicker bedside table. The flatmates shared a tiny kitchen area and a sitting-cum-dining area.

'There is a toilet and bath on the landing,' Alison explained. 'The room is ten shillings a week and we share the bills for gas and food. The bath we pay for as we use it. It has a meter for the hot water. There's also a phone in the entry hall downstairs, which all the tenants in the building share.'

'This will be ideal for me,' Stella said. 'I will take the room. When could I move in?'

'Today or tomorrow if you like.'

Stella looked at Mark, who shrugged. 'You may want to look for a job tomorrow. Also, I could bring your bags over on my bike today. I will be busy at work tomorrow.'

Once she had checked out of her Bed and Breakfast and stowed her baggage safely at the flat, Mark suggested that she get herself a bicycle from a nearby shop with second-hand cycles. He said that everyone cycled in Cambridge, as it was so flat, and many of the roads were narrow and not used by cars or buses.

Stella struggled to keep her bearings as they walked through the town but once they returned to Botolph Lane she felt confident that she would find her way to the Labour Department to look for work on Monday morning. Mark left her at the door, saying that he had a busy week ahead but that he would try to phone her during the week.

'I may have news of your parents by then,' he said.

Before she got into bed that evening Stella counted out her remaining bank notes. I need to get a job immediately she thought. I guess I am lucky that Mark has been so helpful although I don't want to impose on him. I must say he has been very thoughtful, and I rather like him.

CHAPTER SIX
MONDAY 30TH JUNE
GUERNSEY

On Friday evening Marion wandered home from work along the waterfront. There were many others dawdling along, in no hurry, preferring to enjoy the tranquillity of the summer evening, after the chaotic evacuations of the previous week.

The harbour was, as usual, bustling with activity, with people queuing on the wharf wanting to catch the evening mailboat. Nearby stood knots of family groups and friends, dotted along the pier, waiting to wave goodbye to loved ones heading off to England. Few words were spoken; their quietness a sign of contained emotions.

At the Victoria and Albert Piers, numerous vans laden with

wicker tomato baskets, were lined up to load their goods into awaiting cargo boats.

After she reached home, Marion and her mother sat on kitchen chairs in their backyard; a small fenced enclosure containing the outside privy, coal bins and a clothesline. At the rear, docks, thistle and clover grew rampant on the pocket handkerchief of land, where the late Mr Le Prevost had once maintained a lush vegetable patch. Despite their drab surroundings the pair enjoyed the last of the sunshine. Sometime after 7 pm they decided it was time to prepare their evening meal and reluctantly went inside.

Soon after they were stunned to hear planes screaming low overhead, followed by explosions that shook their house and rattled their windows. Marion grabbed her mother and pulled her into the cupboard under the stairs, where they cowered, as explosion followed explosion for what seemed like an eternity. Marion and her mother clung to each other, trembling and crying as the ground reverberated with pounding detonations.

'They said we would be safe!' Mrs Le Prevost wailed. 'The King's message last week ... after the troops all left, he was sure we would not be attacked. He said it would be a war crime since we are unarmed!'

'Well, we are definitely being bombed by the Germans,' Marion said. 'All I can think is that someone in the British Government forgot to tell the Germans that we are defenceless.'

'The bombing seems to be focussed on the harbour and town,' she went on, 'there will be casualties... there were so many people down there when I came home.'

After a long pause, with no further sounds of bombs or gunfire, Marion and her mother extricated themselves from the cupboard and went out onto the street. All around them others were emerging and huddling together in small clusters. Everyone was in a state of shock; a few were crying soundlessly, others sat on the curb as if their legs would not hold them up. They watched in silent disbelief as clouds of smoke and dust rose over the promontory above their street.

A middle-aged man in a suit hastened down the street calling out for other men to join him and go at once to give assistance at St Peter Port. They were to bring with them any first-aid materials and any sheets which could be used for bandages.

Marion ran into her home and pulled a couple of sheets from the cupboard: 'I'll come with you to help; I did some first-aid when I was a Girl Guide.'

'No!' the man said. 'You stay here and help out the immediate neighbours. Make some tea for them and then encourage them to check out their houses for damage. Everyone needs to prepare a safe place in their houses to go into or under in case those bastards come back.'

After cups of tea were handed round, and some older men shared a half bottle of whisky, Marion and another young woman set about helping their more elderly neighbours clean up the broken glass and crockery which had fallen in their homes.

They worked tirelessly to calm their neighbours and then encouraged people to determine, where, within the protection of their homes, they would be safest. At midnight she and her mother prepared themselves to sleep in the hallway with their heads and upper bodies inside the, now emptied, cupboard. Beside them was a small cache of water and dry food. They slept uneasily but the early hours of morning remained quiet.

On Saturday morning Marion went into the newsagents where she learned of the terrible destruction that had been done. Dozens of people were dead or injured. Twenty vans and many boats had been strafed by machine-guns, with some vehicles catching alight, burning their occupants. The piers themselves were blood-red with rotting tomatoes which had been scattered from their wicker baskets during the firefight.

Other Guernsey men had been gunned down in the fields as they helped farmers with harvesting. Even the Guernsey Lifeboat, out on patrol, had been attacked, killing two of the crew. The Country Hospital was under siege with patients, who had to be taken there by all sorts of improvised forms of transport since one of its ambulances had been destroyed.

By 10 am, the names of those dead or injured were listed, to cries of grief and shock. Marion was devastated to learn that her Uncle Harry, who had been delivering his tomatoes down at the Albert Pier, had been killed. She immediately hurried home and accompanied her mother on the long walk to her brother's house and vinery in St Sampson's.

They stayed that day and night with her aunt and her cousin, June, as mourners continued to arrive to support the family, and funeral planning began. Despite grieving, life must go on; June organised a group of men to pick the day's crop of tomatoes, so that they did not spoil on the vines.

Throughout the day Marion felt numb. Her Uncle Harry had been her father-figure, since her own father had died when she was ten years old. She had relied on his brusque common sense when her mother was 'nervy' and irritable. He had taught her not to let her mother's harsh words cut into her.

'Let it bounce off,' he would tell Marion, and she had followed his advice.

On Sunday morning, as the four women sat at breakfast, they had another fright. Three German planes came screaming in from the north east.

'They seem to be heading for the airport,' her aunt said. 'Do you think they will bomb it?'

'Well, they will soon find out that we have no armaments and can do nothing to resist them. They may decide to land,' said June. Only then did Marion realise that the Germans might occupy the Island as a forerunner to invading Britain.

That evening, back at their own home, Marion's foreboding proved correct. More planes passed overhead. News quickly spread around St Peter Port that German senior staff had landed at the airport. The most senior officer had commandeered a car into St Peter Port to meet the Bailiff at The Grand Hotel.

It was said that the Bailiff had immediately surrendered to the officer, with no further loss of lives, and the Germans were now in command of the Island. Marion realised that they were all now trapped until the British Army was able to rescue them.

Marion reluctantly got out of bed on Monday morning, unsure what unpleasantness the day would bring. She had no idea whether De La Mare's store would be open for customers today. She did not know if it had been damaged by the bombing and she did not know whether the Germans would allow normal business to continue.

She also didn't know whether Uncle Harry's funeral could proceed as planned. She realised there were many practical things she needed to attend to today.

She dressed and went into her mother's bedroom, saying, 'I'm going down to the shop now to see what is happening there. I will see if there are any food shops open as we should store some provisions. Then, I will try to contact June as well. You should stay here at home until I get back.'

Mrs Le Prevost was alarmed: 'Be careful and come back as soon as you can. I'll be worried sick. I don't know what we will do now that the Huns are here.'

CHAPTER SEVEN
FRIDAY 28TH JUNE 1940
CAMBRIDGE

IN A WEEK STELLA'S LIFE HAD BEEN COMPLETELY TRANSFORMED. She was living in a bustling inland city: she had a new home, new friends, a new job and a wealth of new experiences. In addition, she had concerns about her family members.

The previous Monday morning Stella's friend Michelle walked with her to the Labour Department, which was on her way to her own office. At the front desk of the department, the clerk wrote down Stella's name and put her credentials in a folder. She gave Stella a number and showed her where to sit and wait until her number was called.

Stella looked around. The room was large with mustard coloured walls and high windows letting in dirty yellow sunlight. Those waiting sat on long wooden benches arrayed in front of the clerk. Numerous cubicles opened out into the main room, and when their doors opened briefly to admit or discharge applicants, Stella saw more clerks sitting at desks in the tiny spaces. Within half an hour her number was called out and she went into the cubicle where an older man in a grey suit was seated. He indicated that she should sit down in front of the desk on which her folder lay.

'So, you are one of the refugees?'

Stella was startled. 'No. I'm an evacuee! My parents wanted me to leave. To be safe. That's different!'

He shrugged. 'Same thing really! What work were you doing in … Guernsey?' he asked, while he checked her file.

'I worked for the local government, The States of Guernsey, doing clerical and processing jobs, permits and applications… organising the census… a variety of things like that.'

'I see you have shorthand typing qualifications and are familiar with administration. Your matriculation marks were very good. We are looking for people like you. Part of the War Office has been located here in Cambridge in the Palmer Estate. They urgently need people with your skills. I will phone and arrange for you to have an interview this morning.'

As directed by the clerk, Stella caught a bus to the outskirts of Cambridge. She alighted from the bus at a pair of elegant iron gates and walked up a curving drive between a column of chestnut trees, to find Palmer House, an imposing Georgian manor house. There was a large formal garden in front of the house, a tennis court to the left of the three-storied building, and a glasshouse to the right. Behind were various outbuildings, including stables.

She went up the wide marble steps and entered a spacious hallway with a grand central staircase leading to an upper balcony reception room. Introducing herself to a secretary,

Stella was soon ushered into the office of the Director of War Records, a middle-aged man named Mr Booth, who asked her many questions about her background and work experience. He seemed satisfied by her responses and confirmed he had work available for her.

He then asked her about her understanding of the Official Secrets Act and gave her a document to read. 'Can you swear an oath not to divulge any information, written or oral, or anything relating to this place, and its staffing?' he wanted to know.

Stella agreed that she was willing to do so, and by lunch time she had a job working under a Miss Gladys Llewellyn. She would start on Tuesday and be paid two pounds and fifteen shillings a week. Her hours would be 9 am to 5.50 pm and she would be required to stay at work for air-raid duty on one night a fortnight.

Back in the centre of Cambridge, Stella headed for the bicycle shop. She spent a precious five pounds on a cycle with a rear carrier and a wicker basket in front. Triumphantly, she returned to her room eager to share her good news with her flatmates when they got back in the evening.

The next day she started work as planned. Her first working week had passed quickly and uneventfully, but Friday night brought Stella disturbing news. The four girls were at the flat, discussing their various plans for the weekend. At 9 pm they turned on the radio to hear the BBC News and, to Stella's consternation, heard that the Channel Islands had been attacked by nine German bombers.

The announcer said that there had been many casualties in Jersey and Guernsey, and that the mailboat, taking aboard passengers from Guernsey, had been hit by machine-gun fire. He said that the Islands were unable to mount any defences.

Stella was aghast and sat with her head in her hands, fearing that her parents were aboard the ship. Or, if they were at home, that they had been affected by the bombing. She felt ill with worry.

Shortly after 9.30 pm Mark telephoned her, saying he had received a telegram from his parents. It said they were unharmed, as were Stella's parents. However, he said that it seemed unlikely that Stella's parents would now be able to leave the Island. Her parents wanted Stella to try and contact her brother, at the address in Glasgow where David was billeted.

Whilst feeling some relief from her immediate fears, Stella realised that she was going to be in England on her own for longer than she had anticipated. Furthermore, she was going to have to take some responsibility for David as well as look after herself. Life was going to be more difficult than she had realised when she left Guernsey so hurriedly.

The novelty of her new life paled considering her loss of family support. She was anxious to talk to Mark in person tomorrow, not only about the likely fates of their families, but also as the only immediate link to her past life.

CHAPTER EIGHT
MONDAY 1ˢᵀ JULY 1940
GUERNSEY

*I SEE NOW THAT MY FIRST DIARY ENTRY WAS SELF-INDULGENT.
Life for everyone on the Island has been catastrophically changed in
only three days. We are numb with disbelief, grief and fear.*

*This past week I've been on day shift. On Friday morning
of the 28th I was on the 7 am shift and when I arrived, I was
told that the entire Victoria Hospital was going to be immediately
transferred out to the Country Hospital in the Catel; patients,
supplies, and of course, we staff. While this had been rumoured,
the Controlling Committee now urgently needed it done.*

*I spent the entire day packing up medicines and supplies, into
every possible receptacle I could find. Then I carried them out to
waiting vans and trucks to be ferried out to the Catel. Once there,*

I stored the medicines in the locked cabinets but left the large boxes stacked on to the floor, before returning for another load.

At the same time the two ambulances were running a shuttle service with the patients. This all went slowly, but some progress was made. I finished at 3 pm, dead tired and I was told to report at the Country Hospital for my next morning shift, to sort out the storeroom and put the stores away. When I caught the bus home after work, I thought the job would be easily completed over the weekend, when things were less busy.

Just after my family had finished supper on Friday evening, we suddenly heard planes passing above us, then flying low back towards St Peter Port. As all civilian flights into the airport had been suspended earlier in the week, we were startled and sat frozen and silent, listening intently. We then heard muffled explosions. My father realised what the noises were and said that the Germans must be bombing the harbour. He said there would be carnage, with the cargo boats being loaded at the time.

He said to me: 'You'll be needed, Rachel,' and he immediately drove me back to the Country Hospital.

It was already chaotic at the hospital. Dr Shirtcliffe, the new medical director, was worried that the Victoria Hospital might be bombed so he wanted all the injured to be treated at the Country Hospital, despite us still being in the process of moving in.

Two of us began in our new storeroom trying to sort through our supplies, to locate the splints and bandages we anticipated might be needed. Other nurses arrived and began to clear spaces for treating any wounded, while the on-duty staff continued to look after our already transferred patients.

Very soon the first wounded were brought in, in private cars. Many of them were bleeding from gunshot or shrapnel wounds, but they were able to hobble into our reception space. Soon after that the first ambulance arrived with three much more seriously injured men. Sister said we had to deal with the most serious injuries first and we left the less injured with those who brought them in, to staunch blood and reassure them, while we worked on the three who needed to go immediately into surgery.

We worked frantically all through the night and into much of Saturday. Local people brought in food for the staff, made quantities of tea, and helped where needed. At the end of that day we learned that twenty-two civilians had died as a result of the bombing raid. Tragically, one of our young ambulance drivers was killed outright at the port. He was well known to us all and always had a witty comment to make in emergency situations. He has a wife and a two-year-old child. Our professionalism failed when we heard that news, and I confess to shedding tears for him.

Sunday was hectic too. The hospital was full of the injured and we were still adjusting our processes of work to suit this building.

I understand, although I didn't hear them, that German reconnaissance planes flew over Guernsey on Sunday morning. They came back on Sunday evening and my father heard planes landing. I had, by then, collapsed into bed after my mind-numbing and exhausting forty-eight hours at the hospital.

This afternoon as I was cycling to work, on a still midsummer day, I saw soldiers on parachutes descending near the airport. It was eerily quiet after the planes flew overhead and when I looked upwards, I saw these objects, like thistledown, drifting peacefully down, swaying gently, as they descended. They were mesmerising to watch but they foretold our dire fate.

At work later I heard more news, via the hospital grapevine. Apparently, on Sunday night a German officer landed in a small plane at the airport. He was taken by car into St Peter Port where Mr Sherwill, the new Bailiff, was waiting to meet him.

I heard that without any ado, Mr Sherwill surrendered the Island, and all of us on it. It is amazing to think it was as simple as that. With just the stroke of a pen we came under German rule and are now an 'Occupied Territory', without any German assault occurring.

41

The Bailiff has now officially told us to obey German orders and not to resist. There is considerable disquiet amongst those whom I've talked to. My father is outraged. He said, 'We will never be docile Guernsey cows.'

He told me that the Germans have ordered a curfew starting at 11 pm tonight and said that no one can buy liquor, nor drive private cars. They also warned if anyone is disruptive the town will be bombed again.

I feel real pity for those here who have experienced horrible injuries and those others grieving over the death of family members.

I realise that I can't allow myself to fuss about what I can't have. I must focus on my work and my family. I must be strong and accept our new realities, rather than pining for what cannot be. I hope I can be strong enough to do so. I am in a state of disbelief. It all feels unreal.

PART TWO
OCCUPATION
1ST JULY 1939 – 8TH MAY 1945

CHAPTER NINE
JULY 1940
GUERNSEY

Marion was in the office getting the payroll ready for distribution to staff. After a week in which the staff had been mainly cleaning up fallen goods, De La Mare's was again open for business. At eleven o'clock one of the shop girls, who had been taking her break, came rushing up the stairs to the office.

'There is going to be a parade down High Street. The German soldiers are marshalling, up by Lloyds Bank, and they are going to march down past here with their band. They look ever so smart in their uniforms,' the girl laughed.

Minutes later the sound of brass instruments could be heard and soon after that the sound of boots marching down the cobble stones. Marion could not resist getting up from her desk and going to stand in the window to watch. People came out of shops all along the street. Some people, realising it was the invading army on parade, scuttled away, not wanting to dignify the show by being an onlooker. The younger people, however, were more curious, and stood around waiting for the soldiers to pass by.

Marion had to admit that the men in their green, tight-waisted jackets and long black boots looked very smart and she was surprised at how young and handsome they were. Nothing like their ugly old Führer and his sidekicks! These young men looked much like the young English soldiers that had previously been on the Island. Just like the boys who had left from here in January. The Germans had better uniforms though!

Back at work, Marion mused, 'So much has happened in the past week. Well in just over two weeks, really. There are now foreign soldiers replacing the previous English garrison which departed so suddenly. A vast number of German ships have brought troops ashore, since the surrender, keeping the harbour as busy as it was during the evacuation.

'Many houses have been commandeered, with their previous occupants unceremoniously displaced. So many ridiculous orders have been issued, by the new rulers. So many, most unwelcome, prohibitions already put into place,' she ruminated. 'Life for the Islanders is totally different. We are prisoners in our own homes and homeland.'

One thing that had annoyed her particularly, was putting the clocks back so that the Island clocks ran according to the time it was in Berlin. Now it stayed light for half the night, but it was dark in the morning. She couldn't see the sense in that.

Another thing that irked her was that the wages paid on the Island had been regulated. She used to earn two pounds five shillings a week and now was to be paid three shillings and six pence less a week, for doing the same job. Meanwhile the prices of various goods had already gone up. She knew her mother had been annoyed by that.

Her mother was already complaining that various foods were being rationed and that they wouldn't be allowed to eat meat on Tuesdays and Saturdays. Marion had joked with her that they already didn't eat meat on many days anyway, but her mother was not appeased.

'That was my choice. Not a German order!'

'Well we have been told to eat as many tomatoes as we can,' Marion had reminded her, attempting to lift her mother's mood.

When she reached home the day of the parade, she discovered that Mrs Le Prevost had had a terrifying experience. She was at home alone, when there was a commotion outside, and someone started to bang on her front door. She went to the door only to find a German soldier kicking her door, while two others stood laughing on the street. In poor English they asked how many people lived in the house? When she said 'two,' she was then asked how many bedrooms were in the house? Again, she said 'two.'

The soldier impatiently pushed past her and went upstairs. She heard him stamping around in their bedrooms. When he came back down, he was annoyed.

'You clean my boots,' he instructed.

Afraid for what might happen next Mrs Le Prevost took him to the kitchen and obeyed his order. Once his boots were polished the soldier simply walked out of the house leaving Mrs Le Prevost shaking with fear.

Her mother was still tearful and afraid when Marion arrived home.

'These men have killed my brother Harry. Now they treat me like their slave. I cannot live like this.'

47

Marion calmed her mother, but she was worried about her mother's ability to cope with what was happening. Marion felt relief that their house, so close to the town, was not one of those being requisitioned for German soldiers to live in. That would have been simply too much for Mrs Le Prevost to bear.

Marion was very happy, the following day, to comply with another instruction for all households to put up a sign in the front window saying, 'This house is occupied.'

Later in the evening, when Marion was reading the paper, she saw that local people were being asked to volunteer to help vegetable growers, over the weekend, to pick their glut of produce. She asked her mother to go with her, suggesting that her mother preserve some of the surplus produce, for them to enjoy during the winter months. Marion hoped that this would give her mother some purpose and stop her fretting. Her mother refused her proposal.

'A few weeks ago, I was dressing up to go to dances; now the highlight of my weekend is being a land-girl.' Marion hoped her mother would laugh at her jest.

CHAPTER TEN

JULY 1940

GUERNSEY

Things have been crazy at work, as well as at home. Life here is changing abruptly and it's hard to keep up with all the new edicts. People are making mistakes about what they can and can't do; sometimes with very unpleasant consequences for themselves.

We still have many patients, injured by the bombing, in the hospital. We have also had an epidemic of elderly people suffering from heart problems coming into the clinic. This has been brought about by stress, according to Dr Shirtcliffe. So, we are very busy every day. Since quite a few of the nurses and doctors left the Island during the evacuation we are very short-staffed. While I hate to admit it, my father was right. It was important that I stayed here.

The German medics moved into the Victoria Hospital, which we had almost fully vacated, before their multitude of troops arrived here. At that time, we had not been able to collect and transfer all our supplies and equipment and this had to be negotiated with the German Command for Guernsey, which took some time.

We find working in the old Country Hospital is not easy. We were used to the modern theatres and wards at the Victoria Hospital and it is a backward step being here, in what was an old persons' asylum. Because I had been responsible for moving the medical supplies, when we transferred out here, Matron has arranged that I continue in this role, as well as doing some of my regular nursing duties.

Matron called me into her office one morning a couple of weeks ago and Dr Shirtcliffe was there. They told me that they had talked to the German Superintendent at the Victoria and arranged that we should obtain the various supplies that we were unable to take at the time we transferred. I was to go with one of the orderlies in a van to collect the items they had identified. I was handed the long list of medicines, dressings and equipment we left behind.

This task meant I had to meet up with some Germans, face to face for the first time. I was nervous. The Superintendent was a curt middle-aged military man. He had a quick look at the list and sent me downstairs to the doctor in charge of medical supplies telling me, 'I'm not familiar with these things. Herr Doctor Konrad is in command of this area. You talk with him.'

Herr Doctor Konrad was more approachable and not so intimidating. For one thing he was younger. Also, he was not in a military uniform, but instead wore a familiar white coat. His English was good, without a strong accent.

'Nurse Dorey, I have identified most of these things already and you and the orderly can start to load up your van,' he said.

He then asked me about how we were managing at the old hospital with all the injured patients. I was surprised that he was interested in our plight. I told him that it was difficult, especially for treating those with burns.

The orderly and I set about moving boxes and equipment. As I was loading the last box into the van Dr Konrad appeared suddenly with another large box, which he had left unsealed. He showed me its contents.

'Here, take these Nurse Dorey. I have no doubt that these must also belong to you,' he instructed me.

As I began to say that those medicines and the burn dressings did not belong to us, he held up a hand to indicate that I should say nothing more. He shook his head. Then he gave me a long searching look and said, 'Goodbye, then Nurse Dorey. I have no doubt I will see you again.'

I was surprised by his actions. In contrast to his superior officer he responded as a medical professional should to our patients' needs.

Back at our hospital I reported to Matron Rabey that we had collected the goods and I gave her the extra box that Dr Konrad had added. I tried to explain what had occurred. She looked surprised. Then she addressed me sternly.

'I don't think I heard you correctly,' she stated, relieving me of the box.

When I started to repeat that Dr Konrad had added this extra box, she briskly cut me off. 'Nurse I choose you for this job because I value your absolute discretion. I know that you are not a gossip! Please let me maintain this view of you.'

We looked at each other and then she said, 'Thank you Nurse Dorey. You are most reliable. We need reliable nurses at this time.'

I walked away realising that suddenly I was complicit in a secret involving three people; Dr Konrad, Matron and myself. Then I thought that each of us must protect this secret and each of us must trust the other two to do the same. The consequences of the truth getting out could be difficult, if not dangerous, for all *three of us. While it's easy to rationalise my tacit agreement to this deception, I am surprised at how I readily complied.*

An advantage of the changes in my life is being able to cycle to work from our farm in the Talbot Valley. The local buses are now being drawn by horses and the service is hopeless. My father covered the bike lamp with cardboard, so that the light cannot be seen from above, and I won't break the blackout when I am out at night.

I have run into German night patrols twice already, but I have a special permit which allows me to be coming and going home during curfew hours. So far, the soldiers have been polite, but they are very abrupt, and some of them are hard to understand.

When I struggle to comprehend their commands, they become impatient and I am wary of annoying them. I try not to talk to them. I just stop, show my permit and cycle off quickly.

My parents' and brother's lives have altered too. My brother Peter is now on his summer holiday, but plans are being drawn up for the children who stayed here to all be located at one school; probably in St Peter Port. My parents think he may have to stay with some friends in the town during the week, as it is too far for him to cycle in each day.

Dad has now got responsibility to graze ten extra cattle, which were rescued from the island of Alderney when the entire community was evacuated. The cows have been given surplus tomatoes to eat; I wonder how the milk will taste? Dad has had to hand-cut the grass and our small wheat harvest, because there is limited petrol available for the farm machinery. It's hard, physical work. The Labour Department sent half a dozen men out for a day to assist.

I think it is good that Dad is busy on the farm. His attitude towards the German troops could get him, and us, into trouble. His resentment goes back to his experiences in the last war when so many Guernsey men died. There is now an ordinance making it an offence to criticise the German authorities! If he worked in town, he would find it hard to control his sarcastic tongue.

Currently, we can listen to the radio, to hear mostly German propaganda, but Dad says this is unlikely to last. He has taken to making things down in the old stables. He says we must learn to improvise. My mother rarely leaves the farm. She is preserving all our fruit and vegetables as she thinks the winter may bring shortages of food.

The Guernsey Controlling Committee has organized a census of all the crops and cattle each farmer owns and recently we handed over all our seeds for next spring, for a common seed bank. When we heard that all our chickens would be taken away to be killed and stored, Dad quickly killed one for us to eat that day. I am embarrassed to say that we did enjoy it.

I hope Dad buried the carcass properly since the authorities are making sure that farm families don't eat at the expense of other Islanders; which seems fair! There are similar limits being placed on local fishermen who must turn over all their catch to the committee.

The days are passing quickly. I haven't had a chance to see Marion since the Germans arrived. I haven't had much time to think about John either. We last talked over a month ago. Now we cannot phone or write to each other since the Germans severed the cross channel phoneline and there is no longer a mailboat service available. Surviving day to day, in a climate of uncertainty, has quickly become my priority.

CHAPTER ELEVEN
AUGUST 1940
GUERNSEY

'THINGS ARE GETTING BACK TO NORMAL AT LAST,' MARION told her mother at breakfast time. 'There is going to be a swimming gala down at the Ladies' Pool tonight and tomorrow there will be a soccer match, the Germans against an Island team, just up at Beau Sejour Park. Rachel is going to come in to stay the night with us, and we will go to the gala together. Would you like to come with us, to watch either event?'

'No. I don't want to be out in the evenings. Will Rachel be wanting to have her tea here? We are short on rations you know!'

'Rachel said she would bring us some produce from the farm, so we will be able to make do.'

Marion examined her clothes trying to decide what to wear to the gala. She settled on some wide legged linen trousers and a white cotton sweater which showed off her almond-coloured skin. Working on farms on the summer weekends had certainly given her a healthy tan. She had, of necessity, let her bobbed hair grow longer, and she swept it back behind her ears. With a dab of lipstick on, she knew she was looking her best for the evening out.

Rachel arrived on her cycle laden with fruit and vegetables from the farm. 'I thought I would change here if that's all right. I get so hot and sweaty cycling all the way here.'

'That's fine. You can use my room. Then we can have a quick bite to eat and wander down to the pools. Oh, you've brought us apples. Fantastic! Mother will be so pleased.'

Soon after, the two young women set off, joining in a growing procession of people walking in the same direction. They greeted and talked to two old school mates and some family friends, as they traipsed along.

'I haven't seen so many people about since the day the Germans arrived,' Marion said. 'It is good to have some events to go to after a weird two months with nowhere to go and nothing to do for entertainment.'

'Yes. You know this is the first time I've been into town since we three had our lunch together in June. I pretty much simply go to work and go home again. It's very quiet out at the Country Hospital and we don't see many people in the valley. What I have really missed is going down to the beach at Vazon for a swim after work. You know that we can't go to most of those western beaches now. I thought it was bad enough when the south and east coasts were placed out-of-bounds.'

'I know. I can only go to the Ladies' Pool, and since they are tidal my opportunity to swim has become very limited. Also, a lot of the young soldiers go there to the Men's Pool, so it's very crowded at the Pools now. But I enjoy seeing some young men around,' Marion joked.

'Oh Marion! They are the enemy. My John is fighting them. You can't be interested in them.'

'Well they are the only young men here. It's the new normal,' Marion retorted.

Rachel and Marion found themselves a place to sit on the bleachers surrounding the Ladies' Pool and, for the next two hours, were absorbed in watching the various races. Since no soldiers were present the crowd was light-hearted and there was a lot of good-natured banter as people cheered for local favourites to win each race. As the crowd dispersed, to get home before curfew, there was laughter to be heard all around them as the two women walked back to Paris Street.

On the following evening Marion again got dressed up; this time to go to the football match. Since Rachel had gone back home, she decided she would attend the game on her own. Again, she joined a crowd of Guernsey people, this time, walking up the hill to the park. However, on this occasion there was a large German presence, with officers and soldiers present to cheer on their team.

The Guernsey people were much more subdued than they had been on the previous night, and the local people congregated together in one end of the stand to watch the game. In the first half, which ended with two goals for each side, there was only polite applause each time someone scored a goal. There was nothing of the bonhomie of the previous evening.

In the half-time break Marion went for a walk around the grounds looking for any friends who might be at the game. A young man in uniform approached her.

'You are looking for someone special? Yes!'

Marion stopped to look at him. He was tall, with blonde hair and friendly blue eyes. She returned his smile.

'No, not really. I'm just getting some exercise in the break.'

'May I walk with you then? My name is Henrick. What is yours?'

'Marion.'

He clicked his heels 'I am pleased to meet with you Marion.'

They walked together in silence with Marion suddenly feeling self-conscious, aware that local people could be watching her behaviour. When the hooter signalled that the game would recommence Henrick suggested he meet her at the exit after the game, to escort her home. They then parted company to return to their former seats.

For the remainder of the game Marion was absorbed in her own thoughts. She could not resolve whether or not to meet up with Henrick afterwards. She knew that Rachel would be outraged if she found out. How would her mother react?

Wrestling with her ambivalent thoughts, Marion was unaware of the action on the field and was most surprised when the final whistle blew to find that there was a five-all score. When the sober crowd left the sports ground Marion kept within the stream of people heading towards St Peter Port. She had made up her mind and when she saw the soldier standing at the gate, she walked past him engaged in an earnest conversation with the person walking beside her, until she was well down the road.

'Have I done the right thing?' she equivocated, as she walked down the steep steps to Paris Street. 'He seemed nice … it might have been fun … and he was very handsome. Is there really any harm in it? I simply don't know.'

When she reached home her mother was waiting for her to return. 'How was the game?' she asked.

'It was a draw… five-all. I think the Germans engineered that! Clever thinking on their part.'

CHAPTER TWELVE
SEPTEMBER 1940
CAMBRIDGE

MARK, HAVING SMOOTHED THE WAY FOR STELLA WHEN SHE had arrived in Cambridge, was moving south as his work was relocating near Harrow, in North London. He had come to the flat early one Sunday morning in August and to Stella's pleasant surprise he asked her to come for a walk with him. They had wandered over to King's College and crossed the quadrangle to find a bench seat down in the Backs, by the somnolent river.

It was quiet, the usual flow of pedestrians and lazy flotilla of punts were not yet about, so there was only the chatter of birds and the dull buzz of bees to disturb them. After flopping down in the sunshine, Mark slowly revealed the purpose of his invitation.

'I wanted to tell you face to face that I have to move out of Cambridge next week. The group I work with is moving down south to a place called Bentley Priory, where there is another group already working on things for the Air Ministry. The chief down there, Dowding, wants us all to be based together. It will be more efficient for both groups to be working in one place.'

'Oh. Golly! That will be a big change for you. Is Peter going south as well?'

'Well, yes; it will be different. We will all live on site and the hours will be even longer than they are now. But needs must! And no. Peter is staying on here.'

'You don't need to worry about me,' Stella said quickly, to overcome his obvious embarrassment at leaving her without his support.

Stella quickly told him that she was contented with her new life. She was enjoying the experience of living with three other young women. There were interesting young people working at Palmer House with whom she played tennis on the evenings when they were on 'fire watch.' She found her work challenging and realized that Cambridge offered her great opportunities, including the chance to do part-time study at one of the colleges.

'Alison suggested it. She thought I should use the opportunity of being here to do some evening classes, and Michelle decided to do so too. We will encourage each other!'

'That's great! There are some very fine teachers in this town. You should enjoy it,' Mark said.

'You know, I was amazed when I came here five years ago, at the wealth of subjects available at the colleges. I had an open mathematics scholarship and thought I would probably end up as a schoolteacher. But I had this brilliant tutor in my first year, Professor Turing, who was teaching some most interesting applied mathematics. I found it so exciting. Most of my classmates, like me, have ended up doing special projects for the war effort. They call us the numbers guys!

'You have done well and to have built yourself a life in Cambridge so quickly, is impressive,' Mark remarked.

'You know, I was disoriented when I first arrived. I really struggled for the first two terms. Living in college was strange and it took me ages to make friends. There were two classes of students here; scholarship boys like me who were bright, and then the rich boys who were very bright and worldly-wise as well. They led a very different life on- and off-campus from the rest of us. When I made the first cricket eleven things got better for me.' He laughed. 'I'm not sure why I am telling you all this?'

'I have also come to appreciate this city; its centre is so well laid out and spacious. It's such a contrast to St Peter Port, where the town is cramped, and the streets intersect at strange angles. Then, there are the tumble of steps leading downhill to the port with houses jostled together, in a random way. This is so orderly in comparison,' Stella concluded.

Mark looked at her with surprise. 'That's so true. I haven't really thought about the contrasts before. Shall we wander on and find something to drink then?'

She nodded her assent, then both stood up, and ambled back to the roadway heading towards a local Lyons coffee shop, where they lingered in a window alcove over their tea.

'I really appreciate all the help you have given me,' Stella said as they wandered back to her flat.

'If you hadn't been here, when I arrived, I don't know what would have happened to me. I was the disoriented one then,' she laughed, 'but I've been very fortunate and while I can't say I feel optimistic – that's not possible during a war is it? – I suppose I feel confident about my ability to cope here.'

'That's good to know,' he replied, suddenly more relaxed.

'You know it's been very nice getting to know you again. I have enjoyed your company.' She blushed. 'Do you remember taking me to my school dance when I was fifteen?'

'Yes. I recall that our parents arranged it! I was not too pleased about that. I thought I was much too sophisticated to be going to a girls' school dance at the time. A bit stupid of me, in hindsight.'

'I know! I was so mortified. I guess we didn't really see each other after that. I thought you were a bit of a snob, then, so I'm so glad to have had the chance to change my mind.'

'Good! I will keep in touch when I can.' Mark promised, giving her a fraternal peck on the cheek when they parted company.

'Yes, please let me know if you get any news from Guernsey.'

While Stella had put on a brave face for Mark, she was disappointed that he was leaving so soon since there were many new difficulties for her to manage. After he left her at the flat, and whilst her flatmates were all out, she had a chance to reflect on these.

She had experienced her first air-raid in late June. On that occasion the bombs had fallen on some sugar beet fields, only a few miles further east of Palmer House, while she was on night duty. Her team had suddenly realized that their convivial evenings could become dangerous and they might have more serious obligations.

When Cambridge was attacked again in late August and the sirens went off, Stella and her flatmates made their way to the cellar of their apartment building. They had spent a very frightening and uncomfortable few hours listening to the sounds of anti-aircraft fire and the detonation of bombs. She realised the fear and despair being felt by so many people each night of the Blitz.

It wasn't only her personal circumstances which concerned her. Every day at work she was confronted by terrible statistics which she was dutybound not to discuss outside Palmer House. Stella was monitoring civilian deaths and injuries from the bombings throughout Great Britain. Each morning air-defence wardens, across the country, were required to send them information about any hostile incidents during the previous twenty-four hours. Stella and the other young women collated this information onto sheets of heavy-duty paper. After being double-checked, the tables were put into cardboard cylinders then taken by motorcycle couriers down to the War Office every evening.

Recently, Stella had been stunned to see that Swindon Airfield had experienced a night-time raid, and that two deaths and multiple injuries had occurred. She was worried that John, Rachel's fiancé, who was based there as a gunner, might be numbered amongst them. She was equally shocked when she saw that Glasgow had been bombed, leaving her concerned for her brother's wellbeing.

Civilian deaths and injuries rose, inexorably, day by day. The tempo of the war was accelerating and previous hopes of a quick rally after Dunkirk seemed in vain. The war was 'nowhere near won.'

More than once Stella had cycled home in tears; a reaction to the grim information she was forced to read. While at work, she focussed on the data she was responsible for. It was later, when she was alone, that she couldn't distance herself from the unpleasant facts she was recording. These were not just numbers, they represented real people whose lives had been suddenly disrupted, or worse, terminated. Whole families were being killed or having their lives shattered.

As these more unpleaseant thoughts ran through Stella's mind she appreciated the impact of Mark's forthcoming absence on her. She realised that his moral support had helped her at vulnerable moments. She valued that greatly.

It was a great relief for Stella when the Battle of Britain ended in mid-September, although she was shocked by the final figures released from her office, which showed that more than 23,000 people had died.

CHAPTER THIRTEEN
OCTOBER 1940
GUERNSEY

LIFE HERE GETS MORE AND MORE CONTROLLED, EITHER BY German dictate, or by the various Controlling Committee requirements. We have lost access to so much information in so few weeks. Our radios were all impounded in August, after the British soldiers were captured. The German censors makes sure that the local paper contains no news about events outside the Island, apart from German victories.

Then the Controlling Committee passed a 'Dangerous Speech Law' that prohibits us from criticising or deriding the Germans! I'm not sure why they keep such a tight rein on us? Some say it is for our protection, but I think that it gives the German's greater latitude to punish us. My Dad describes the Controlling Committee as a self-important bunch, who will not stand up to the Germans on our behalf.

The paper provides little more than lists of various decrees and obituaries. There are many of both. A lot of elderly people have died in the past three months. Local talk is that many are suffering from heartbreak and loneliness, now that their families have evacuated to England.

Our hospital is now called the Emergency Hospital and we are coping with an influx of more minor ailments because of the shortage of GPs. We are all working flat out on each shift.

I finally got word from John via the Red Cross. He wrote in early August, to send his best wishes for my 20th birthday, but I only received the letter in mid-September. I was told that I was fortunate to even get a letter, as only eleven letters got through to the Island in this first batch since June.

I had to go into St Peter Port to collect the letter and sign for it when I had a free day. It had already been opened by the German censors. In addition, John implied he was not able to tell me much as his letter was to be read by the senior officers at his camp. All I really know was that he is still at the airfield in Swindon, he was well, then, and was looking forward to a furlough in London with new friends.

It feels as though we are worlds apart. I find it hard to imagine what his life is like. He probably cannot imagine mine either.

There have been various 'incidents' in Guernsey, which have upset our foreign rulers. They have made us all pay for these events, though.

The first involved acts of resistance against the occupiers. Initially, V for Victory signs were painted on walls around the Island, which the Germans then painted out. Now they punish anyone caught making the V sign, even by gesture. Perpetrators have been severely beaten.

After the British Army bombed the airport twice in early August, injuring four Guernsey people as well as killing a few

Germans, we were forbidden to collect any bits of the bombed-out German planes as souvenirs. Any propaganda pamphlets dropped by the Allies had to be 'handed in forthwith, to the Feldkommandantur!' [Tell that to my Dad!]

The second set of events occurred a couple of weeks after the British bombings. It appears that the British Army sent some Guernsey men in the British forces to spy. They came ashore from a submarine in an inflatable boat which was lost on landing. Then because of rough seas the submarine could not return, and the men could not leave after completing their mission. Some local person betrayed them, and they were found hiding on the Island with their families. The latter have been punished and sent away to prison in France. The Guernsey men are now prisoners of war in Germany. It's said they only avoided the firing squad because they were wearing old World War One uniforms when captured.

More recently, half-a-dozen Islanders escaped from here in a small boat. We do not know how they fared, but we have been warned of 'dire consequences' if it happens again. Now fishing boats can only leave and return from St Peter Port. All the Island slipways are off limit, leaving many fishermen without work. The remaining men are closely monitored to prevent further escapes.

The reprisals the Germans more recently inflicted on us all included banning all dances and closing the cinemas. Relatively mild punishments; but annoying as recreational opportunities are few, and I don't enjoy military bands playing martial music.

People who once would overtly show their disrespect for the invaders are now being more circumspect.

There is now widespread fearfulness that local people are informing on others, as occurred for the British soldiers. It is not a nice feeling to be uncertain of the loyalty of your neighbours and fellow citizens.

Food and coal have become more difficult to obtain. Guernsey now relies on local men appointed as 'Purchasing Agents' [where do they get these titles from?] appointed by the Controlling Committee, who go to France and Belgium to get supplies for us. They have brought in fresh meat, potatoes, vegetables and some canned goods. These are, of course, strictly rationed.

After the summertime glut of tomatoes, we had an apple glut for a while, but now fresh fruit is scarce. It's a real challenge for the family cook to obtain provisions. Shops are only open for four-and-a-half hours a day so there are long queues when they are open. My poor mother is forced to cycle to the shops, and she is finding it very tiring going up all the hills.

At the hospital we have been short of soaps, bandages and other basic items. When things got desperate an agreement was reached with the German Hospital [the previous Victoria] that they would order supplies for us on a regular basis, as we cannot rely on the sporadic aid of the Purchasing Agents, whose primary task is to find food and whose medical knowledge is scant.

Once again, I have been given the task of cycling to the German Hospital with the latest list of needed items for Dr Konrad to order and have despatched from Europe. When the items have been amassed, I usually go with the orderly, in our now only ambulance, to collect them.

Dr Konrad is very polite and helpful. When he knew we were short of soap and disinfectants he was horrified and made sure that I took some with me, from his own storeroom. Fortunately, his offices and stores are near the back of the hospital and there were few people around.

That day I had to carry those packages out of the hospital wrapped up inside my blue flannel nursing cape until I could then place them in my bicycle basket, covered by my versatile piece of clothing. That made for a rather chilly cycle ride, but it lessened the risk of discovery. I got away with it and made Matron very happy. Our hospital managed to keep going until our properly requisitioned supplies arrived.

I don't have any social life, though I did have an evening out with Marion at a swimming regatta. Stella's absence was made obvious on this occasion. My life consists of work and family. The latter fills my time with lots of help on the farm needed. I don't have any free time to miss John's company.

A funny phrase just came to my mind. 'L'amour et le travail.' If I remember right, our school French mistress explained it as, 'If you don't have one, you must have double of the other.' That sounds about right for my life!

CHAPTER FOURTEEN
NOVEMBER 1940
GLASGOW

David flung open the door, immediately throwing himself into her arms.

'I am so happy you have come! I have been very homesick.'

Stella held her brother closely, then stepped back and ruffled his slicked down hair. She was very happy to see him after their six months' separation.

Stella had arrived at the central station in Glasgow early on Saturday morning having travelled up on the overnight train from London. The journey had been uncomfortable, but she had managed to get some sleep as the carriage was half-empty, allowing her to stretch out along the bench seat.

Stella had desperately saved her money for this trip north to see the eleven-year-old. David had told her that she could walk from the station to the Cowcaddens, where he was staying, and she followed the directions he had given her, rather than spend precious money on the double-decker tramcars.

She had trudged up steep Blytheswood Street, then descended the equally steep slope down to the junction at New City Road. She then searched for the entrance way to the apartments, above the department store, where David was billeted.

The five-storied tenement building was made of a sooty grey stone and curved in an arc. The building was imposing, with a turret on one end. It was ornate, with capstones over the windows. The street in front was wide, to accommodate both tramcars and road traffic. In the centre of the road were a series of large corrugated iron sheds, which, she realised, were air raid shelters.

At the eastern end of the building she found a heavy wooden door and entered a bright, white-tiled hallway with its large ornate iron staircase leading to the upper apartments. Stella, full of excitement, had climbed quickly up to the fourth floor.

After the two siblings had embraced, Mrs Mackenzie, David's carer, hurried over to shake Stella's hand. She was a lean, stringy woman in her fifties with wispy grey hair tied at the nape of her neck with a black ribbon. Her clothes were shabby, but clean. 'He has been that excited for the past week,' she told Stella. 'I will make us a brew and David can show you around.'

Stella looked around the room. It served multiple purposes; as a sitting-room, dining-room and kitchen, with a sink and small stove for cooking, in one corner. Overlooking the street were two large windows. The furniture was old and scuffed, and the room needed painting. It smelled of cooking and dust. Off this main room were two doors leading to two small bedrooms.

A communal toilet for all the fourth floor flats was outside at the back of the tenement, David informed her, when he showed her his room. His tiny room was lit by a grimy, narrow window looking over the back yard. It was even smaller than the one Stella had in Cambridge.

David's bed took up three-quarters of the space and there was no other furniture in the room. His clothes and belongings were in his suitcase and cardboard boxes under his bed. A blackout curtain hung to one side of the window and a grey army blanket covered his bed. It was a very uninviting room.

Stella was shocked. This apartment was nothing like their house on Rosaire Avenue. David was now living in far more straightened circumstances than the Ferbrache children had previously enjoyed. No wonder David was homesick.

'Where do you do your homework?' Stella asked him.

'At the table in there.' David pointed back to the main room.

'Where do you bathe and wash yourself?'

'In the sink. Sometimes we use a metal tub in the parlour, behind a screen. But it's hard to warm enough water, so I go to the public baths when I can.' Stella was horrified but tried to keep her face impassive.

'Are any of your school friends living in this building?'

'Gary Falla is just down the street and Monica Smith is next door. All the apartments are like this,' David said.

'After our cup of tea, we should go out and have a good talk,' she said.

'Yes, and I want to show you my school and the football field as well as Sauchiehall Street; it's terrific fun down there.'

Over their tea Stella tried to find out more about Mrs Mackenzie's circumstances. It seemed she had been widowed for some years. Her husband had been a tramcar conductor and she had a son now serving in the Black Watch. She had been born in Glasgow, and proudly stated that she had never been out of the city. She had offered to billet one of the Guernsey children because she had that box-room to spare and the extra money was useful. She thought David was a polite boy, but he did have a big appetite for his age.

As soon as they could Stella and David left the apartment.

'First we will go to the school. It's just through the underpass,' David said.

Stella was impressed by the school building. It was a beautifully proportioned two-storey building, with a wing on each side of a central gallery. There was an elegant clock tower above the main entrance. Unlike all the other grimy grey buildings around it, the school was painted cream and had a row of trees all along its surrounding walls.

'This looks nice. Oh! And there is a playground as well?' she noted.

'Yes, it's a good school. I still have Mr Hemmings as my teacher and all the children in my class are from Guernsey. We stick together in the playground because the local kids are a bit rough and call us 'Refos.' You know, sometimes I can't understand what people round here are saying; they have different names for things as well as funny accents.'

'I'm glad you are still in a class with your friends. Also, Mr Hemmings will see you keep up with your studies while you are here. You know Dad expects you to get into Elizabeth College when we get back home.'

They wandered on westwards to the large field at Kelvingrove.

'We play soccer here. I'm in the Standard Five Guernsey Team, and we play lots of other schools down here on Thursday afternoons. It's fun. Trouble is I've grown out of my boots and I play in my school shoes. They are useless when the ground's wet, which is most of the time. Then, I must wear them, still wet, to school and I've got chilblains. They itch a lot,' he complained.

'Can't Mrs Mackenzie buy you another pair then? Using your allowance?'

'She says there isn't enough money for that. She is always saying that, whenever I need anything for school. Or when I want to go to the pictures. Can you ask her for me? She might listen to you.'

'Is she kind to you? She doesn't hit you or do mean things, does she?'

'No, she is alright. Not like the people that the Stokes children were with. The old man beat them with a stick and, when they cried, he locked them in a cupboard. The teachers took them away to a new place and told us all that we must report anyone not being nice to us.'

'I'm glad to hear that. You know you can write to me anytime. I will buy you some envelopes and stamps before I leave.'

'I've written to Mum and Dad, but they haven't written back to me,' David's eyes filled with tears.

'Oh, David I know they would write to you if they could, but the Germans won't let them. They may not have got your letters either. You know they will be missing you so much! I miss you too; even though you used to be cheeky to my friends!'

David gave her a wan smile.

'Does Mr Hemmings know I am visiting you?' Stella asked.

'Yes. But he told me not to talk too much about it to the other kids who don't have any family in England. I guess I am lucky about that, but I do miss Mum and Dad.'

'I know. I miss them too.'

Stella chose not to tell David how worried she was about their parents. David has enough to cope with already, she reasoned. 'Okay, where next? Lead on McDuff!'

They headed back eastwards so that David could show her the church that the Guernsey children and their teachers attended, as well as the local bath house. From there they climbed back up Blytheswood Street to reach the busy town street.

'There are movie houses along here and lots of shops. I like the second-hand shops. There are heaps of model cars and old comics. I sometimes spend my pocket money in them,' David told Stella.

'Looks as if there are lots of pubs here too,' Stella said, as a group of men spilled noisily out of a tavern, onto the footpath.

'Oh yes there are lots of them. Mrs Mackenzie sometimes comes to one of them.'

'She doesn't leave you alone at night, does she?' Stella worried.

'No. Just on Saturday afternoon, when I usually meet one of my friends. She's okay, Stella.'

They wandered through the centre of the city with David showing Stella some of the fine buildings around George Street. Footsore at four o'clock Stella took David to the tramcar terminus and sent him off back to his new home.

'I will write to Mr Hemmings to see if you can come down to Cambridge for Christmas. It's cheaper for you to come down on the train, than it is for me to come here, and since one of my flatmates will be away, you can have my bed. I will ask her if I can stay in her room.'

'That would be smashing!' David's eyes shone. 'That's only a few weeks away. I won't tell anyone else,' he promised.

With a quick hug Stella and David parted and Stella returned to the station to begin her long trip home. She sat in the carriage pondering on the information she had gleaned from David.

'He looks clean and tidy. He has grown, and he seems reasonably happy. He obviously thinks Mrs Mackenzie is all right, even if she is a little mean with HIS money! But what can I do about it? Just keep in touch with him and Mr Hemmings. It's not ideal for anyone either here or in Guernsey,' she concluded.

On Sunday afternoon, soon after she had got back to Cambridge, Mark made his fortnightly telephone call to hear her news.

'So, you survived the train and the underground alright.' he began.

Stella laughed and answered. 'I had some coaching from my friends.'

'Well, how was young David? Do you realise he was only a little boy when I last saw him?'

'I've asked David to come down for the Christmas break. I think he will be able to manage the train, if I meet him in London. Perhaps you will have a chance to see him then.'

'It's too soon for me to know about any leave over that time, but I might be able to get into London for a day. Let me see what I can arrange. It will be good for David to see some of the sights. Also, I would be glad to show them to you!'

Stella told Mark about her visit and shared her concerns about her brother's spartan situation.

'It sounds to me as if he is one of the luckier kids. He has a reasonable billet. Not perfect; but he won't come to too much harm. More importantly he has you. I think you should write to your parents again as I've heard that the Red Cross is accepting mail for the Islands. Your parents will be very relieved that you have seen David. I'm sure that will give them some comfort.'

'I am sure that they will be reassured, too, that you are keeping an eye on me. And so am I,' she said fervently.

CHAPTER FIFTEEN
DECEMBER 1940
GUERNSEY

'THINGS ARE LOOKING UP,' MARION TOLD HER MOTHER.

'Well I don't think they could be much worse,' was the grumbling reply.

'They could be! I have just heard that we will be getting some extra rations for Christmas. We can have a feast. I think we should get Aunt Ethel and June to join us. It will be strange for them without Uncle Harry. They have had a tough six months keeping the vinery going. The glasshouses flooding in November, after that big gale broke so much glass, has made things even more difficult for them both. It's been a great struggle to get any repairs made and to get labour for the heavy work. They need something to look forward to.'

'We will need them to give us some of their food ration coupons then. And I don't know about any presents.'

'It's okay Mum. I will sort out the food. We need to enjoy Christmas; if only to spite the Germans. It's important not to let things get us down. Do you know, there is going to be a special Sunday matinee at the Regal on Christmas Eve? You should go. You used to enjoy going to the pictures.'

'Not if they are showing some German rubbish with subtitles.'

'No, I think it is an old English film. I will check it out and maybe get tickets for you and Aunt Ethel. My Christmas present for you both!' Marion insisted.

'I don't want to sit there with the Germans.'

'You won't have to. If they do go to an English film, which is unlikely, they always sit upstairs in the gallery, while you will be down in the stalls with the Guernsey folk. It will be good for you to go. So, no more arguments.'

Marion was happy to be busy making plans for the holiday. She and her mother would go to Matins at St John's Church, as usual. Hopefully, no German soldiers would be there at that time, to upset her mother. Then she would come home and cook a roast dinner for the four of them. There were plenty of potatoes around, with a shipment just brought over from Jersey. There was tinned fruit available and they would finish with coffee and sweets.

'Not quite like the old days, but we have to make the most of what we have,' Marion continued to cajole her mother.

Marion found the well-used Christmas decorations in a box under the stairs and put them up around their front parlour, despite her mother's complaints. She found the old wreath, dusted it off and hung it over the front door. There would be no Christmas tree, since the few trees on the Island had already been chopped up for firewood, so she placed the somewhat tatty Christmas angel on the mantelpiece instead. She placed a row of candles in jars on the windowsill and stood back to see how it looked. 'Only so-so!' she confessed.

On Christmas Eve, the Germans agreed that the Islanders' radios, impounded for two months, could be returned, and Marion collected theirs from the repository on Smith Street. During the evening she and her mother enjoyed listening to the Christmas songs and a dramatization of *The Christmas Carol*.

'It feels like old times,' she told her mother, who sniffed loudly in response. Marion tried not to be disappointed. All her efforts to please her quarrelsome mother seemed to bring only a grudging response.

Boxing Day was crisp with ghostly sunlight barely penetrating grey clouds. Marion had made plans to go roller-skating with some of the girls from work and after a quick lunch she set off to meet them at St George's Hall, only minutes from her house. Hazel and Miriam were waiting for her in front of the roller-rink, where they joined a queue of eager skaters.

With bags, coats and shoes left in the Women's locker room, the three women donned their skates and joined the crowd surging clockwise around the rink. The music blared out as they sped around, sometimes singly and at other times joining up in a long conga line.

Marion was adept at skating and at Hazel's insistence she showed them some fancy steps she had mastered. She was surprised to see that other skaters stopped to watch her and when she finished a few people clapped. Hot and short of breath she went over to the rails to rest.

'Well, Miss Marion we meet again.' She looked up to see Henrick and a group of German soldiers standing on the boardwalk around the rink.

'Perhaps you and your friends might like to have some lemonade with us?' he asked.

Marion was about to decline, when Hazel, who had joined Marion at the rail, immediately said 'Yes please!' and signalled to Miriam to join them.

The three young women led Henrick and two of the soldiers over to a table in the back of the hall. Introductions were made and two of the men went off to purchase their drinks. Hazel, a vivacious and lively young woman took command of the conversation, telling the soldiers about herself and eliciting information about them in return. Hazel and Miriam laughed loudly and flirted with the men, whilst Marion sat quietly, avoiding eye contact with the soldiers at the table. She felt uncomfortable, as Rachel's previous admonishment still ran through her mind.

Because of the noise erupting from their table, other skaters and spectators turned to look at them, openly showing their disapproval of the three women drinking with the soldiers. Marion disliked the attention focussed on them, so she put down her empty glass. She got up quickly, said 'Thank you.' and returned to the rink. Soon after she saw Hazel and Miriam leave the hall, followed closely by two of the soldiers.

Marion skated alone for a while but realised that her pleasure at being out with other young people had now ended, so she might as well go home. She collected her outdoor clothes, handed in her skates and left the hall. Feeling dejected, and not eager to spend too much time with her mother, she decided to walk along the esplanade to a small park beside the harbour.

She sat, hunched up in her coat, its collar up around her ears, hands buried in her pockets, wondering if she had been silly to walk off from the table when she did. She knew Hazel would tell everyone in the shop about it. She knew those two girls wouldn't go out with her again, either.

'I'm lonely. What sort of life am I going to be able to make for myself here?' she wondered.

She stayed watching the wan colour leach out of the expanse of sea and sky before her, turning dreary and slowly blackening. Thoroughly chilled, and with a mood that matched the sky, she made her way home. Her mother was in one of her irascible moods.

'I hope you enjoyed yourself, at least. It was not much fun for me being all alone on a holiday afternoon.'

'I've got a headache. I think I will lie down for a bit.' Marion escaped to her room.

The following day, when Marion was back at the shop, the manager requested a meeting with her. The news was bad. He told her, 'I am going to have to let some of the staff go. We are very soon going to have barely any stock left to sell and the Purchasing Agents cannot give clothing or domestic chattels, a high priority.'

He continued, 'The people here can no longer afford to buy things, either, even if we could get them. The Germans bring in all they need so the business is in financial difficulties. I am very sorry Marion, but I am going to have to cut your hours back. I will want you here from 10 am to 4 pm on four days and only 10 am until 2 pm Thursdays. You have always been a reliable worker. I know you and your mother need the money, but that's the best I can do.'

'When will this take effect?'

'At the end of the week but I will pay you your current wage until the 5th January.'

Marion felt panic. The cut to her income would cause a problem for them. Her mother would be even more embittered, and Marion would be forced to spend her increased free time at home. 'I will have to find something else to occupy myself,' she thought.

CHAPTER SIXTEEN
MARCH 1941
GUERNSEY

SECRETS. THEY ARE MULTIPLYING LIKE RABBITS, IN THE *community. We are all keeping them; secrets from colleagues, secrets from friends, secrets from neighbours and secrets within the family.*

I must have been a bit dense or too self-absorbed not to notice before. I've only recently realised that my father must have got access to another radio. No wonder my mother has been so anxious over the past months.

It was only after the Germans impounded all the radios back in the autumn that I became surprised at the things my Dad was telling us. He seemed to know things about the progress of the war that were at odds with what we were hearing locally. One day he said something about an air attack on English airfields including

Swindon, where John was based. I was upset and didn't think to question him then, about how he got that news.

Around early December, when he told us something else about the bombings in England, I began to wonder 'how does he know that?' After an amnesty at Christmas, when our radio came back briefly, it was clear that he was listening illegally to the BBC. I dared not ask him because I don't need to be burdened with more than my own secrets

I know he has been adapting his farm tools to cope with having no fuel for farm machinery, but that could be a cover. He is clever with his hands and he could easily have made a radio receiver. I hope it is well hidden because the penalties are high if anyone is caught listening to one.

My mother is a bag of nerves. She is fretting for my brother who only comes home from the Occupation School infrequently. However, I think it is better that Peter is away from here, where he may pick up Dad's attitude and say something that gets us into trouble. Only a week or two ago a Guernsey woman was sent to prison in France for saying 'Heil Churchill' in a coffee shop in town. Someone reported it and retribution was swift. She was sent to prison in France.

I must say I have learned to be very careful about what I say to anyone and I try not to express opinions. It is strange to feel so wary of former friends and colleagues. I feel very isolated.

It is now fourteen months since John enlisted and left for England. It seems much longer. I know I have changed in that time. I'm much less spontaneous; more serious. I'm also sceptical about anything I hear. I wonder how John has changed after a year of action in the artillery.

I've had a lot of time to think about our relationship. Too much maybe? I've tried to put it into perspective. I've come to think it was a good thing that we didn't get married before he left. I was too young, and we had only been going out for six months. Getting *engaged helped us to cope with the impending separation, and the uncertainty about our future, but it was a bit precipitate. At the time it felt important to make a commitment to each other, but it was unwise.*

I care about him and worry about his welfare, but I feel very disconnected from him. I am afraid we have becoming estranged as we each learn, separately, to cope with our different experiences.

There is no way this war is going to be over quickly. The Germans are acting as if they will be here for a long time and there is now little local resistance, apart from the local phone lines being cut. We have heard that there is resistance in France. Why have we capitulated so easily?

Is it because we are such a small island and we are under close surveillance from the many German observation posts? So many young men have left, who, if still here, might have harassed the Germans with sabotage. Clearly the Germans are dealing with resistance more harshly and we don't want friends and neighbours to be punished for individual misdeeds.

If there is still civil disobedience, it is well-hidden.

I must say that I was going to keep this journal as a record of what was happening here. More and more, though, it's become a place where I am recording my thoughts. There really is no-one I can share them with.

Well there is Marion, but I am not sure that would be wise as she is such a chatterbox. She came out to see me and had to stay a few nights because of flooding in the valley. She expressed some interest in one young soldier she had met at the football match. I was a bit shocked by this.

She was, also, very despondent and does not know what to do with herself. I made some suggestions about her finding voluntary work, but I don't think she will. I know her mother is difficult, so she needs to have something to occupy her, away from their home.

I have missed Stella. We could always talk about the serious stuff. I haven't had time or transport to visit her parents during the past months.

What's happened here in the past few weeks? It seems we slip along from having enough food briefly, to a protracted shortage. Some weeks we can do things and the next week they are 'Verboten.' The primary industry of our occupational forces seems to be issuing orders or doing surveys. I find myself laughing at the officious language they use, but at the same time I know they will mete out revenge on us, for any infringements.

I find myself deeply suspicious of the intent behind their edicts. They are calling for people not born in the Island to register. I ask myself, 'Why?'

The Salvation Army are not allowed to preach, 'Why?'

Local clubs can only meet if they are approved. 'Why? Is the Great War Machine really scared of what the Women's Institute is up to?'

The local committee are also constantly making new decisions, some of which seem ridiculous. Here's one that made me laugh out loud! "Corsets can be sold without clothing coupons!" Why? The wealthy matrons of St Peter Port, obviously cannot be caught slumping?

On the positive side, though, the Red Cross has set up an office at Elizabeth College. Some mail is coming in, and going out, to the UK. We can now send mail directly to Jersey and to France. Because we are running out of local stamps the ones available must be cut in half.

I probably should say something about our medical services. We are always finding ourselves short of things. We are constantly asking the citizens for items that we can use in the hospital. In the past two months this has included rubber inner tubes to be cut up for tourniquets. Belts and buckles are needed for use during surgery. Our equipment now looks like something from a Heath Robinson cartoon!

I continue my monthly trips to the German Hospital with our list of needed supplies. I keep telling Dr Konrad of the things that are needed urgently, and usually he will help us, before our order is formally processed.

The shortage of GPs has been very apparent over the winter months. Many people came to the hospital with rampant chest infections. Mortality rates for the elderly are worsening.

I've just re-read my rambling notes. They sound a little subversive.

I have now found a good hiding place for this journal.

CHAPTER SEVENTEEN

APRIL 1941

GUERNSEY

MARION WAS RUSHING AROUND THE HOUSE IN HIGH excitement. She was due at the opening night for a play at the Repertory Theatre, in which she was playing a small part. She had enjoyed drama at school and liked the opportunity to play extroverted roles.

A chance meeting, with a former fellow pupil, Sarah, in early January, had landed her a place in the production of *Three Half Crowns* by an amateur troupe, formed after the occupation began. The opportunity had come when she had been depressed at losing hours at work, and it provided her with a chance to meet new people. Marion was hungry for the lively conversation and laughter whenever the group were together.

The play would run for six nights at the Repertory in the town centre, then would go out to church halls in two of the central parishes for two nights each, and then return for a finale in the town.

There were only a dozen people in the troupe, and they had to fulfil many roles; helping with the sets and costumes, doing the make-up, taking turns as prompt, as well as learning their parts.

The play was based on a murder committed in a 1700's gaming house in London. The civilian victim was killed by an army major; in a vigorous duel. The play was selected because it gave great scope for the leading male actors and provided numerous smaller roles for the women. But, as one of the players intimated slyly, it also reflected some of the current vindictiveness in Guernsey, which the German censor had not realised when he approved the play's production. A large audience was anticipated at all the venues.

Marion's primary role was that of a serving wench at a tavern where the duel took place. With her good looks and trim figure, she hoped she would be noticed, albeit briefly, as she provided some of the more comic aspects of the play.

'Are you sure you don't want to come?' she asked her mother again.

'No. I don't go in for all this make-believe and nonsense. Tarting yourself up and speaking like a Cockney! Your father would not have liked it.'

'I think he would have been proud of me. He would have wanted me to be successful.'

'Successful!' her mother snorted. 'There will only be a few local people watching, and some of the Germans. Hardly the West End of London!'

'That's true. But I have enjoyed myself and I've made some new friends!' Marion was defiant.

Marion left early to go to the theatre and once there helped set up the props before donning her costume and applying her stage make-up. She was excited rather than nervous. When her time on stage came about, she played her bawdy part with gusto, to maximise the laughs.

The first night audience comprised many of the members of the Controlling Committee and included senior members of the community. They sat on the left of the theatre. Also, in attendance was a group of senior German officers, who were relegated to seats on the right-hand side.

The audience applauded enthusiastically as the curtain came down, and again when each of the cast came forward to take their bow. When Marion's turn to step forward came about, there were hooting voices and stamping feet. Marion beamed at the attention.

Whilst the Guernsey people trooped off home to beat the curfew, a few of the heavily be-medalled officers remained in the foyer, waiting to speak to the cast. The players were invited to go for a drink at a house in St. Martin's, where an officer was billeted. Assured that they would not be in breach of the curfew, the cast agreed, and all found themselves herded to cars parked nearby, which took them to a house named 'Woodleigh'.

The house, hidden behind high trees had a half-circle, gravel driveway. The two-storied stone building was large and rambling, with a wide glass entry porch leading into a marble hallway. The reception room on the left side of the hall was wood panelled and lavishly furnished with antiques. There were many paintings on the walls, in embellished frames. Elaborate decorative rugs were strewn upon the carpet. It was spacious and brightly lit by chandeliers, easily accommodating the thirty or so at the party.

There were platters of food on sideboards and junior staff plied the guests with wine and spirits. For the first time in her life Marion was offered a glass of white wine in a long crystal flute. She heard that it was champagne.

'So, you were the serving maid?' An older officer, with a slight limp stood beside her. 'An enchanting performance, I think.'

Marion, affected by excitement and alcohol, could only nod in response.

'You no doubt have acted many times. A professional perhaps?' he continued.

'No. No! I've only been in school plays before this,' she admitted.

'Such beauty and such talent should certainly be on the stage.'

He took her elbow in his right hand. 'I saw you looking at those paintings. I live here. I will show you the most famous ones, if you like.'

Marion allowed herself to be walked around the downstairs rooms to see the paintings. Some of the artists' names were known to her from school, but there were many she was unfamiliar with. The officer was knowledgeable about the artists, so she listened attentively to his words.

As more wine and food kept appearing the party became increasingly lively. Marion lost all sense of the time as she circled the room, talking with many of the officers. They were all very polite and full of praise for her performance.

She was surprised when James, Major Oneby in the play, came up to her to tell her that transport home was being organised. She was to go in a car with him and his wife, Sarah, to be taken home by a young officer, who lived near to their homes in St Peter Port.

Marion, very lightheaded, was pleased to be taken right to her front door and as she struggled to put her key in the lock, was glad of the help offered by Tobias, the driver. She crept into the house but knocked tipsily into the hall stand, making a loud noise. As she climbed the stairs, trying to avoid the creaking tread, she heard her mother.

'Is that you Marion? You are very late!'

'Yes. Go back to sleep. I'll tell you about it in the morning.'

Marion woke with a headache, feeling nauseous. Her watch indicated it was already nine o'clock. She dressed slowly, preparing herself reluctantly for her mother's inevitable inquisition.

The later showings of the play were equally well received, especially those for the local people in the outer parishes. Marion was pleased to see Rachel's parents in the audience at one of these events, and to learn how Rachel was faring.

Some of the same officers, who had been at the play's first night, returned for its finale. Again, a party was held for the cast; this time in a manor house in the Vale. Once more fine food and wine were plentiful. Conversation was loud, and gallant comments were soon replaced by openly flirtatious ones. Marion felt more confident on this occasion and engaged in teasing chatter with two of the younger officers.

Some of the actors, because of this initial success, wanted to put on another play in mid-summer, but James and Sarah demurred, indicating that they were unhappy about their attendance at parties held by the Germans. They explained that they did not wish to be identified as collaborators.

Another actor, Simon, asked if others wanted to form a new group, and with some people assenting, undertook to call the remainder of the troupe together to form a new dramatic society, in a few weeks. Marion was keen to join a continuing group and hoped to take a larger role in the next play.

On a spring-like Sunday, Marion set off to the Brothers' Cemetery to put crocuses on her father's grave. She cleared away the remains of the lily of the valley that she had placed there at Christmas and tidied the edges of his plot by pulling up some weeds. It was becoming obvious that there was no longer a verger to attend to this overgrown cemetery near the centre of town.

Reluctant to return home to her mother's sharp tongue Marion crossed the road to enter Candie Gardens through the bottom gate. She walked uphill and went to sit in a sunny spot below Queen Victoria's statue. From here she had a good view of the offshore islands. She began to watch the various people in the park.

She became aware that there was a group of young soldiers congregated on the stone flagged terrace above her. Then she watched as a collection of giggling young women wandered up the path to the terrace, to gather in front of a glass rotunda. Marion realised that a military band was due to perform at noon and decided to sit and listen to the music, from her wooden bench.

After the concert ended a young soldier dropped down on to the seat beside her.

'Good afternoon Marion. It is a lovely day,' he said.

She startled, then realised that the soldier was the officer Tobias, who had been her chauffeur after the two parties held for the cast.

'Good afternoon to you,' she replied.

Tobias stretched out his legs and turned to Marion.

'Why are you here all alone on a fine afternoon?'

Marion told him of her task that morning and her reluctance to go home so soon, saying that she had wanted to enjoy the sunshine and the view. Tobias, curious, asked her about her plans as an actress. In her turn Marion expressed her hope that she would get bigger roles in the future. She said that as the theatre was the only entertainment on the Island that the new troupe aimed to provide more plays. Tobias told her that their troops were due to see a German actress perform on the Island very soon, for their own entertainment.

Tobias said he was pleased to have been posted to the Channel Islands after the difficult times he had experienced in Belgium and France. He found people in Guernsey mostly friendly, and he enjoyed the beautiful coastline and quaint lanes. He produced a worn photograph of his family to show Marion.

When the onshore breeze got up and the air became much colder Tobias asked, 'Would you like to have a cup of coffee? My billet is just on the other side of the park. We have real coffee you know, not the stuff made of chicory!'

Marion, eager for an alternative to going home, agreed. The two then walked across the park into the narrow lane and entered the gateway of a cream-coloured house. It was three-storied and called 'The Palms' to celebrate the two tall trees in a central garden bed. They walked across the gravel forecourt and climbed the marble steps, to enter the double front doors with their large brass handles and decorative locks.

Tobias took Marion into a pleasant sitting-room running the length of the house, with huge multi-paned windows showing views over the front and back gardens. The latter was a very formal topiary with sculpted plants.

There were five or six young soldiers sprawled around the clusters of leather chairs and embroidered couches in the long room, which had three marble fireplaces, where fires burned strongly. Marion was amazed and resented their profligate consumption of scarce firewood.

The men were variously occupied playing cards or chess. Marion was briefly introduced to them, but because they were preoccupied, she went to sit alone, feeling awkward, on a window seat whilst Tobias went to organise some coffee.

The smell and taste of the coffee was unlike any she had drunk before.

'Mm!' she said to Tobias, 'this is different. It has an unusual taste.'

'Yes, the beans come from North Africa. I think you might get to like it. We don't drink tea as you do. Just coffee.'

Marion, still feeling uncomfortable in this grand house full of young men, drank the coffee quickly, burning her tongue as she did so. She hastily said her goodbyes to the men and hurried home. She only told her mother that she had been to visit her father's grave and, afterwards, listened to music in the park.

CHAPTER EIGHTEEN

JUNE 1941

CAMBRIDGE

STELLA WAS GLAD THAT THE WEATHER HAD FINALLY improved. She had found the winter in Cambridge to be very cold and damp. She was tired of the perpetually lead-coloured sky and the bleak flat landscape which merged into the grey mass of cloud, obliterating any horizon.

In January, after David had returned to Glasgow, there had been a huge snowfall in the town. The streets were blocked by piled-up snow and as it thawed the streets were running with water which then turned to ice in the evenings. This made walking treacherous and she had been unable to cycle around, instead having to rely on an irregular local bus service.

After months of respite there had been an air-raid in the middle of January and, with the fire hydrants covered in snow and the pipes frozen, it had proved difficult to put out the many fires caused by incendiaries. The cellar they used for a shelter was unheated and the girls in the flat had wrapped themselves in eiderdowns while they waited out the series of raids which had continued until May.

That last raid had been the worst one, with many houses destroyed and others damaged by bombs or fires. But at last the Blitz had ended. Hitler had turned his bombers to the east in his battle against the Russians, leaving the English and Scottish cities and towns to clear up the damage wrought by a nine-month air campaign.

Stella was once again cycling to her work within the Palmer Estate and her duties no longer included the unpleasant task of reporting civilian deaths. As the days had lengthened the staff had arranged for regular tennis matches to be played and Stella was involved in playing in a mixed doubles team with a friend and colleague, Michael. They were placed quite well on the tournament ladder and used their lunch times to practice whenever possible.

Final examinations for her university courses were held in June and Stella was hopeful of getting good marks as she intended to do further study in September, to get her diploma. On the first anniversary of her flight from Guernsey she reflected on how much she had experienced in just one year.

She sat in the flat confiding in Alison, 'I must have been very gauche and unsophisticated when I arrived here. We led such a simple life in Guernsey really; sports and outdoor activities only. This past year I have discovered a much richer world.'

'Yes, it's certainly different living in a university town. Where I grew up, in Chelmsford, there wasn't much to do either and when I was offered the library job here, at Pembroke, I jumped at the chance to get away.'

'Mark must have thought I was a mere child!' Stella reflected. 'He was so kind in helping me out when he had lots to do and his own life to lead.'

'Maybe! Perhaps it helped him too,' Alison said. 'He had broken up with his girlfriend the previous Christmas and was downhearted for ages. So, looking after you was probably a good diversion for him.'

'Oh! I didn't know that. He never said anything to me.'

'Well, I shouldn't tell tales out of school, but Kate went home at Christmas break and suddenly got engaged to the oldest son of a very rich family in Dorset; old family friends, I believe… I don't think she and Mark were a good match. She had social pretensions and he wouldn't have been rich enough to meet them.'

'That must have been hard for him. He did tell me once that he had found it hard to fit in when he first came here. Perhaps that was what he meant?'

'Well, I think he has got over that romantic setback at last. He seems to enjoy talking to you on Sunday nights.' Alison laughed. 'Changing the topic. You should be due some summer leave. Have you thought of what you might do? I am going away with my hiking group, to walk in Wales.'

'No not yet. I did think I might go up to see David again, and then visit Edinburgh. I'm told it is a lovely city and very different to Glasgow. I could stay in a university dormitory, which would be cheap and convenient.'

Later that week, Stella received one of her regular phone calls from Mark, He told her the news he had gathered in a much-delayed letter from his parents and relayed a message from hers. They both expressed their concerns about the effect of the food shortages in the Island.

'I know we have rationing but it's worse than just rationing there. Everyone is finding it tough with inadequate food and heat,' Stella said.

'Yes, Dad said there was no electricity available from 11 pm to 7 am. I don't know how people manage. My grandparents were poorly all through the winter.'

Mark continued, 'I have a furlough coming up. Now that the Blitz appears to be finished, we are going to be given some leave. Have you any holiday plans?'

'You know I was just talking to Alison about that the other day. She is going off with her hiking group and Michelle and Dawn are visiting family. I was thinking of visiting David and then going on to Edinburgh for a few days. I haven't much money, so I thought of staying in a university hostel.'

'I've never been to Edinburgh. What would you think about meeting up with me there? We enjoyed our time in London with David. I would like to see Edinburgh with you.'

'Really! Well yes, that could be fun. Do you think we can arrange that?'

'Find out the dates for your leave. And sort out the Glasgow trip and I'll then organise my leave to coincide. I will ring you again next week.'

Stella hung up the phone and lingered in the hallway. 'Does Mark really want to spend his leave with me, or does he still feel he needs to look after me?' she wondered, shrugging her shoulders.

'I guess I will find out. And one way or another it will be nice to explore the city with someone I like a lot.'

A week later the arrangements were made. Stella would leave for Glasgow on the first Friday in July and spend three full days with David in Glasgow. She would then go to Edinburgh on Monday evening, meet Mark at Waverley Station and stay at Edinburgh University for four nights before she returned to Cambridge and Mark to London. Her girlfriends all shared her excited anticipation of this holiday. Her tennis partner, Michael, was less enthusiastic.

CHAPTER NINETEEN
JULY 1941
SCOTLAND

STELLA'S TRAIN PULLED INTO GLASGOW'S CENTRAL STATION early on Saturday morning. The overcrowded night train offered no comfort, so Stella arrived stiff and bleary-eyed. She went into the restroom at the station to have a wash and tidy herself, before having a cup of tea and a scone at the station buffet. The walk from there over the steep hill to Cowcaddens allowed her to stretch her cramped legs and she relished the warm sunny morning.

David threw open the door of the apartment and ran to greet her at the top of the stairs. He was suntanned, had grown taller and was broader in the shoulders than when she had last seen him at Christmas.

Mrs Mackenzie greeted her warmly. 'He has got big. I keep having to buy bigger shoes. And you should see his appetite! I find it hard to fill him up on our rations.'

David interrupted: 'I have so many things to show you. I have it all planned out. I know where to take you.'

Mrs Mackenzie laughed. 'He goes all over the city to see things and he spends a lot of time in the library. That teacher of his – Mr Hemmings – he gives him lots of homework. Keeps him out of mischief, I reckon.'

'No. No!' David jumped in. 'He knows I am interested in architecture and he is helping me with my maths and drawing. I have a project to do over these holidays, on a local architect, and I want you to help me with it. Please Stella?'

'Golly, you are asking me about something I know nothing about,' she responded.

'That's okay. I want us to go and see some of his buildings, the Mackintosh buildings, there are lots of them quite near to here. Also, we need to go to the museum. I will tell you all about him.'

Mrs Mackenzie threw up her hands. 'It's all a mystery to me. I've never been to half the places he's been to. But he is a smart lad and doing well at school. He is no bother and we rub along together quite well.'

David confirmed this with a grin and nagged Stella to leave her suitcase in his room and immediately depart on their expedition.

They headed westwards into Kelvingrove, a very different part of the city, on a rise affording long views down to the Clyde River. Its roads were wide and tree-lined, the houses large and elegant, and there were many parks.

'The university is up here,' David explained. 'It has a great museum. You can see a dinosaur's egg there.

'There's also an art gallery with lots of paintings of Scotland. The country is very rugged and deserted. It is quite different to Guernsey! But what I want you to see is Charles Rennie Mackintosh's house. You will never have seen anything like it. It's smashing! It's not big, and it's very simple. You know, he even made his own furniture and lights to go in it. Mr Hemmings says he was very talented. But not popular.'

Stella was amazed at her brother's enthusiasm and knowledge. He had found a way to cope with his estrangement from family and home by immersing himself in learning new things.

'I plan to go to university,' he told her. 'Mr Hemmings is helping me to get there.'

'Mum and Dad will be very pleased. They didn't want your education to suffer through this dratted war.'

Over her remaining days in Glasgow, Stella and David walked miles together to see the range of buildings that David had identified as being important to see, finishing up at one of the Willow Tearooms. Here they spent an eye-watering amount of money on the tea, sandwiches and cakes on offer.

Stella found herself becoming interested in this type of architecture, and the siblings had long conversations about the deceptively simple arts and crafts style. 'I now understand why you like it so much,' she told him.

For the first time Stella felt that the age gap between her brother and herself was beginning to close. He was no longer the young schoolboy and was becoming a thoughtful and informed companion. 'I will have a lot to tell Mum and Dad about,' she said as they parted at the station.

The train journey to Edinburgh took only two hours and as Stella went through the platform turnstile, she found Mark waiting, as he had promised. He gave her a big hug and seized her case.

'We will leave this in the left luggage for a while and go and get a meal. Are you hungry?' he asked.

'Yes. I am a bit and I have so much to tell you about Glasgow and David.'

They climbed up the stairs from the deep cutting where Waverley Station was located onto Princes Street where crowds of people were ambling along enjoying the summer evening. Stella stopped to look around whilst Mark pointed out the landmarks.

'To your left, up there is the castle. Up there on the right is Carlton Hill. See the hill with what looks like a Greek temple! Look! Further round! That's Arthur's seat. Apparently, it's worth the climb as the view over the Firth is outstanding. We can start exploring them all tomorrow.'

Stella looked around her, amazed at all the unusual buildings he had shown her as well as the extensive parks surrounding them. 'It's so green in this city!' she exclaimed.

'Where we are now, is Princes Gardens,' Mark explained, 'and there is a monument to Sir Walter Scott.' He pointed to an imposing Gothic tower containing a tall statue. 'Hundreds of steps lead to a lookout at the top,' he told her.

'Now we are going to go across North Bridge to the old city where I have found a great old pub. It's only a short distance and we can catch up over a drink and a meal.'

Mark ordered a gin and tonic for Stella and a Guinness for himself and they settled for cod and chips with mushy peas for their meal. 'I promise you something better tomorrow night,' he said.

'This is fine. I have just had to endure Mrs Mackenzie's cooking, remember,' she laughed.

They found a booth where the pub noise levels were slightly lower and were soon absorbed in conversation. Mark was very relaxed and told many funny stories. In turn she talked a lot and there was much laughter and good humour between them.

Stella felt giddy. Mark was different. He sat leaning towards her, watching her face intently, his hands fiddling with the condiments in front of her. The air between them felt charged. She thought, 'I don't just like him. I'm very attracted to him! I think he is wooing me?'

Mark looked at his watch. 'Very reluctantly, I think we need to go. We must fetch your case and I need to get you to your hostel because they have a curfew at 10pm. I know it's a bit crazy but them's the rules. I am in the men's hostel; down the road; we don't have such draconian constraints.'

He put his arm around her shoulders, hugging her close, as they returned to collect her bag and then they walked hand in hand back across the bridge, heading south, in the dusky light, to the university. Outside her hostel Mark kissed her in a manner that was certainly not brotherly, and which she willingly returned.

'Maybe tomorrow we should look for somewhere else to stay. What do you think?' Stella asked, aghast that their pleasant evening was to be prematurely terminated. 'Somewhere without a curfew.'

'Good idea! I was reluctant to make that decision for tonight without talking to you, but I will check out some places for tomorrow.'

'Our first real kisses,' she thought as regretfully they parted for the night. Stella slept fitfully. She was excited and restless. Her relationship with Mark had changed notably and unexpectedly. She had confirmed for herself that he was more than just her friend and that it appeared he felt similarly.

They met early in the morning and with their combined luggage took a taxi down to the very pretty St Andrew's Square where a grand hotel, in Georgian style, stood on one side of the central park. It provided a stark contrast to their spartan accommodations of the previous night.

'This must be very expensive!' Stella exclaimed as they got out of the cab.

'It's my treat. What you need to decide is if you want a single room or are willing to share a twin room with me.'

Used to odd sleeping arrangements in Palmer House and unwilling to incur further expenses for Mark, she said without any hesitation. 'I'll share.'

'We can't check into a room yet. Why don't you sit there,' he pointed to some leather chairs in the lobby, 'while I do the paperwork. They will put our bags in the room when it's ready and in the meantime, we can get out and explore. I hope you've got some comfortable shoes on. There is a lot to see.'

They spent the day, cooler with dark cloud looming up from the Firth, walking for miles around the old city. Mark had brought his camera and insisted on taking her photograph at every historic monument they came upon. They hiked up the myriad steps and steep paths to the castle, enjoying the views as they paused for breath. They wandered in and out of the various buildings within the castle walls. 'It makes Guernsey's Castle Cornet seem very small in comparison,' she said. He laughed.

In the afternoon they explored the labyrinth of alleyways between the tenement houses and laughed at the crazy jutting floors and leaning walls on some of the ancient buildings. They walked the Royal Mile to see Holyrood Palace, but, were more impressed by the nearby Bath House built for Queen Mary. In the late afternoon, when the long impending rain began to fall, they returned, somewhat footsore, to their 'posh' hotel.

That evening they went to a small cafe that a friend had recommended to Mark. They sat at a table facing into an internal courtyard, where the rich smell of geraniums perfumed the air. They ate well, drank wine and talked over the high points of their day and their plans for tomorrow. As they waited for the bill, Mark took her hand: 'I'm really glad we are having this holiday together Stella. It's good to discover this lovely city with you.'

'I agree. It's been perfect.'

The following day they decided, recklessly, to climb up to Arthur's Seat. As they neared the top Stella decided to run up the steep, grassy track. 'I'll beat you to the top.'

'You reckon?'

She heard his footsteps pounding up behind her and with a sudden burst of energy she accelerated her pace. Both, puffing with exertion, made the top together and threw themselves down in the long grass to recover. They lay beside each other quiet and content until he pulled her onto her side to face him.

'You are very fit. I struggled to catch you.'

'I know. It's all the cycling and tennis.'

'You know I am in love with you?' he said.

She smiled at him and touched his face with her fingertips. 'And I with you,' she replied.

'Mark, I need to ask you. You don't think we feel at ease with each other just because we have a shared history and I needed your help when I arrived. Do you?'

'I asked myself that after we were in London with David. No! You are not the little girl next door any longer. Nor are you the waif who washed up on my doorstep a year ago.'

He kissed her. 'You are a strong, independent and interesting woman and I very much fancy you, as you might have noticed last night.'

He kissed her again. 'Seriously, we've both come a long way since Rosaire Avenue, to get to this point today and I am very happy about it. What about you? What do you think? Am I still the big brother?'

'Definitely not. I started to see you differently last year, as we got to know each other again. I just didn't dare hope that our relationship would develop. I wasn't confident that you would be interested in me.'

'Let me show you how interested I am then.' He pulled her close and she responded to his embrace with a passion that surprised and satisfied them both.

Two days later they returned to London together, each to return to their different homes and war work. Mark was adamant: 'I will get up to Cambridge when I can get a lift, and otherwise we can meet up in London. I don't want us to be apart for long. I will phone you when I can.'

CHAPTER TWENTY
JULY 1941
GUERNSEY

So much for good intentions; I haven't had time to write in this diary for months, but a lot has happened in the interim. Some of it unexpected.

At Easter, John wrote to tell me he was in love with a girl in Swindon and wants to end our engagement. His letter has taken over three months to get here.

I'm not entirely surprised by his news. He must have felt that I put my life [such as it is!] in Guernsey, before my commitment to him. I can understand that. I also recognise his need to live his life fully now, because of its own uncertainties.

After a brief cry, I removed my ring and put it away. Do I wish him well in his new relationship? Not sure that I do, but I do hope he gets through this war. We were young and carefree in the summer of 1939, when we spent our time sailing in his dinghy or going to dances with other couples. It was another world then, and we are no doubt different people.

My mother felt the broken engagement more keenly than I did. I know she was concerned about my being hurt but I think she was worried about what others might think. Perhaps she believes I 'will be left on the shelf,' because I had a previous love? At this moment, that doesn't worry me.

I am more worried about things at home. Mum has become more and more depressed. On some days she cannot even get out of bed. Other days she cries a lot and is absent-minded and disorganised. Keeping the house going has become impossible for her and I must fit housework in around my shifts.

Over the summer Peter has been home to help Dad with the farm, because they are working long hours trying to grow more crops as well as looking after more cows. I try to attend to the washing and making meals, as well as preserving food. Anything else [like cleaning the house], barely gets a look-in. Domestic labour takes up all my free time.

We have had a good summer with many days in the 80s during June. The fruit trees are again laden, and we have been well off for vegetables too. We put in sweet corn for the first time. We have been told to eat it whole or to grind it into some sort of meal, for making bread.

I know we are doing better than the townspeople in getting home-grown fruit and vegetables. Nearly everyone is short of meat. People living near the coast are foraging for bird's eggs and gathering limpets and crabs to compensate for the absence of fresh meat.

Dad got into trouble for not supplying all his milk to the Controlling Committee. He was giving a few pints to the neighbours, where the wife is pregnant, and they have three youngsters. He was warned and fined two pounds. He will have to be more careful.

While the Committee has since announced a free milk scheme for those who are pregnant or are invalids, they are now looking more regularly at Dad's records, to ensure we provide our estimated quotas.

We are now all required to get identity cards. The German authorities want to know details of our place of birth. The Committee and the police are assisting the Germans to get this information from all the people living on the Island.

Many people are afraid of what this might mean. They fear that those who are foreign-born, which includes those born in England, might be sent away to camps or discriminated against in some way. Their worst fear is that the Germans might treat them as they did the Jewish people in Germany and Austria, by taking away their homes and businesses.

I have not seen or heard anything of Marion now that Guernsey's local telephones are no longer in operation. I did hear, though, that she was in a drama group which has performed in the town theatre. I know she will be enjoying that. I think she only has a part-time job now. I don't have any news about Stella. I do feel very cut off from friends.

Things at the hospital don't change very much. The food shortages are impacting on our in-patient care and we try to get people home quickly where they can rely on their own food rations. We are making 'tea' out of roasted carrots or parsnips, and 'coffee' out of roasted acorns, for our patients.

We had to ask the community to return empty medicine bottles because we have run out at the dispensary. We are getting regular bulk supplies of medicines from the Germans but need to dispense these in small amounts to the patients.

I had to cycle to the German Hospital on a very hot day in June [it reached 99 degrees] and arrived red-faced and exhausted.

Dr Konrad said something to me in German. When I asked him what he had said he laughed and looked a bit embarrassed. I asked again, and he said, 'It's the beautiful girl on the bicycle.' I was the one who was doubly red-faced then!

He made me sit down in his office for a while to recover and brought me some real tea and biscuits. We talked informally, and he asked me about my family's circumstances. Somehow, I found myself telling him about my mother's depression. He told me he had just begun to specialise in diseases of the mind at medical school in Hamburg, before the war started. He said depression was not surprising in our situation.

He asked me if my mother was getting any treatment and I told him, 'No. Because my father believes she should just snap out of it.' He said that she probably needed some help and he gave me a container of herbal medicine, which is commonly used in Germany, to see if it would help her. He didn't know the English name for it.

I have been giving it to her for three months now but there is no significant change yet. I know she suffered from depression for some months after Peter was born. I didn't tell Matron about these pills. I know I should have. I do feel guilty about my omission.

It seems to me that serious ethical breaches come from a series of minor, small steps; small decisions, which set one on a path which is difficult to step off. I know sometimes people do take a very calculated big step, to advantage themselves, but most of us err in incremental steps, unwittingly, and then it is too late.

My Dad doesn't know about the medicine and he would be angry with me and with Mum. He is resolutely opposed to local people who collaborate with the Germans. He says that to do this is to undermine Great Britain's war effort and it is 'treachery of the worst kind.' Would he see my professional and now my personal actions as collaboration?

For him it is morally simple. To me it is more complex. I had no choice but to undertake my professional task of getting the hospital supplies. I did, however, have a choice about taking that cup of tea which I took as a friendly gesture. I also had a choice about taking the medicine offered for my mother. I could have refused both, I realise in retrospect.

I am genuinely confused about how we should react to each other in our professional relationship. Are we fellow human beings, or only mortal foes?

I am troubled at the thought we cannot treat each other with respect and humanity, simply because of nationality. I believe that I responded to both kindnesses shown to me instinctively and in good faith. Am I deceiving myself? Am I just trying to make excuses for myself?

What I have done can't now be undone. I must be careful but, at the same time, not allow blind patriotism to negate other essential human qualities.

CHAPTER TWENTY-ONE
AUGUST 1941
GUERNSEY

MARION LAID HER BEST CLOTHES OUT ON THE BED. SHE had set her hair in curlers overnight and she now proceeded to brush it into shape, with large waves at the sides and at her forehead, so that it formed a dark frame for her face. She was pleased with the effect it created.

She then put on a beige linen shift which showed off her slender figure. She tied a long tangerine scarf around her neck and put on her only pair of high heels. She glanced at her face in the mirror, applied the little lipstick that she still had and pencilled her eyebrows. Once that was done, she stood on a chair to check her hemline and dress. 'Not too bad,' she muttered.

When she entered the kitchen for breakfast her mother snorted: 'You are all dressed up with nowhere to go young lady!'

'I'm having my identity card photo taken this morning. Then I'm auditioning for another acting role. I want to look good.'

Her mother laughed. 'The picture will be tiny; just your face, you silly thing.'

Marion temporised: 'Well, I may be able to get a copy of the photo for the theatre. They can use it for publicity for our next play.'

'I don't think that's likely.'

'Anyway, I like to dress up when I can. I like to look nice!'

Marion, fuming, ate her breakfast in silence and left for work without a word, banging the front door behind her. She was weary of her mother's constant griping, but knew she had no way of getting away from the home she had come to loath and in which she was now trapped.

She walked down to the old States Building on the quay, remembering all the times she had waited outside this building in previous summers to have lunch with Stella.

She mused, 'I really must go to see her parents to find out how Stella is. I've no idea what has happened to her since she left. I'm sure it can't be worse than it is here.'

After a short wait in the office Marion was asked to fill in a form stating her name, address, date and place of birth and religion and then she was ushered into a cubicle where a photograph of her head and shoulders was taken.

As she left the cubicle the German soldier ordered, 'You must return in three days, to collect your card, which you will be required to always carry on your person. Not to have it, when required to show it, could result in imprisonment,' he said abruptly.

Marion, surprised by his officiousness, left the office, and continued walking towards the narrow stone steps going up to

High Street. She looked up to see a car drawing up along-side of her and paused to see who was in the vehicle. A German officer climbed awkwardly from the back seat and joined her on the footpath. It was the senior officer whom she had met in April, at the party after her first night.

'Miss Marion, I missed your last show, I believe. I heard it was very funny and that you were very good in your role. I hope you will be performing again soon and that I might be there to see it.'

Marion shifted her weight from foot to foot, wondering why the officer had stopped her. She looked around to see if anyone had noticed their conversation.

'Oh! *Full House*. It was fun to be in. It was a good comedy. I am auditioning for another play due to commence in August, which will also be on at the Repertory. It's called *Stray Lady*, a detective story.'

'Well I hope you are not about to stray! I am sure with your beauty and talent you will have an important role. I will be sure to attend. Now can I take you somewhere in my car?'

'No thank you. My audition is to be held nearby. Just up the slope opposite the town church.'

'Then I shall see you another time. Goodbye Miss Marion.'

Marion watched the car drive off. 'I'm glad I dressed up today! Maybe we will be invited to some of those officers' parties again. That could be fun!'

The first night for *Stray Lady* had a full house. Once again, the German Officer Corps made up a large part of the audience along with the members of the Guernsey Controlling Committee. It was said that the Bailiff was attending. Marion was playing the role of a housemaid and had many comic lines to deliver. Her timings and gestures on stage had both improved, as she gained more confidence as an actress.

After the show the cast were invited for supper at the home of the German Commandant, Major Katz. Here they were treated to fine French wine and a table full of meats, cheeses and other delicacies which the cast members ate and drank with relish. They had no idea such good food was still available on the island.

Marion was soon approached by Major Katz who formally introduced her to Sonderführer Fredrich von Stein, the officer that Marion already knew by sight, but not by name. He took her hand and bowed to her, telling her how much he had enjoyed the play. Marion, nervously, told him her surname, and tried to match his courtesy by using his title but found herself stumbling over it.

Major Katz laughed at her efforts and when the major moved off to make other introductions, von Stein laughed.

'Please just call me Fredrich. My title is a bit of a difficult word to say. I intend to come again to the final night of the play on Friday,' he continued. 'I will see you then?'

On the final night of the show Marion put on her best performance ever, enjoying the times that the spotlight fell on her. As the curtain lowered after the last performance, she scanned the audience, seeking out Fredrich, and, when she caught his eye, gave him her best smile. He approached her in the foyer after the show, and with two other girls engaged with the play, and with two other officers, the group of six went off to a private house for another supper party.

This party was much less formal and there was music and dancing that continued late into the evening. Marion was tired but exhilarated when the driver took her home. Fredrich had invited her to dinner at his house on the Fort Road, on the following Saturday. His driver, Tobias, would fetch her at 7 pm if she was agreeable.

She sat in her room thinking about Fredrich and the forthcoming dinner. He was at least twenty years older than her. His blonde hair was greying at the sides and temples and his skin was pale. Whilst taller than her, he was slightly built, and he walked with a limp. He had piercing blue eyes, and while he was not unattractive, she was not smitten with his looks. However, she liked his charming manners.

He clearly had a much better education than hers. She could learn a lot from him about a more sophisticated society than she was familiar with. He was also a senior officer and had access to fine food.

If he was interested in spending time with her, she felt as though she could help herself, and her mother, by making the most of this unexpected opportunity. The dinner party would not be a public event so posed little risk to her of suffering public opprobrium. It was not going to hurt her reputation.

She did not perceive Fredrich as a romantic interest. Rather he was an interesting conversationalist. It would be more fun than her moping around at home, avoiding her crotchety mother.

With the help of one of her friends from the theatre, the wardrobe mistress, Marion acquired a stunning dress to wear on Saturday night. It was an emerald-coloured cocktail frock, which, when tied with a scarlet sash, fitted her well enough.

When she came downstairs on Saturday evening her mother asked, angrily: 'Where are you going dressed like that? I hope you didn't waste your clothing coupons on that outfit!'

Marion told her mother, 'No, I've borrowed it from the theatre. I am going to a dinner party at the home of a German officer.'

Her mother scowled. 'You are a foolish girl. No good will come of this.'

They continued to argue until the driver arrived for Marion. Once more she entered the grand house, 'Woodleigh', but this time she was shown into the library, on the right of the hallway, by the houseman. When Fredrich joined her there, drinks and appetisers were served.

'You look sensational my dear. I should mention, there are no other guests tonight. I have you all to myself. I wanted the opportunity to talk to you without interruption.'

Marion showed some surprise. She had hoped for a wider audience for her social conquest.

As they sat at a small window table in the long dining room, eating an elaborate dinner, he proceeded to ask her lots of questions about her family, her life in Guernsey and her aspirations. Although surprised at the tenor of the evening, Marion was happy to talk about herself.

She talked of the loss of her father and the effect that had in limiting her opportunities. The fact that her mother had only a small pension and relied on Marion for financial help, had meant she took the first job on offer. She revealed that her ambitions had been constrained on the Island and she said that she had hoped to leave to see more of the world, but that would have meant leaving her mother all alone.

He listened carefully, drawing her out further so that she realised that, during the meal, she had disclosed her entire life story to him. As well, he seemed interested in her opinions about life on the Island since his fellow troops had arrived there.

After the meal, they moved to a small sitting room, where coffee was served with chocolates and tiny cakes. Fredrich then leaned back in the leather winged-back chair and gazed at Marion.

'You have been very open with me. Now it is my turn to be frank with you Marion. I like you, and I find you attractive and entertaining. I like your ambition and that you are direct and honest about it. I have a proposal for you to consider. As you know I have a senior position in the army and am likely to be here for some time because of this injury,' he said, gesturing at his left leg. 'It's a souvenir that keeps me out of the front-line of soldiering.

'So! I need a female companion in Guernsey. Someone to converse with when I am off duty. I would like you to be that person!'

He continued, 'I should be quite clear that I am married and have two children, eighteen and sixteen, back in Cologne. My father was a professional soldier and as the eldest son I joined the army when I was twenty. In 1921. I specialised in engineering; designing bridges, buildings and fortifications and such like. My family is wealthy, and my wife comes from a similar military background. She knows the realities of being married to a soldier. We are well-suited, and I have no intention of leaving my wife.'

'While I am here, I must entertain various important people. I need an outgoing and pretty hostess and I know you would be good in this role. Also, I am much attracted to you and your youthful exuberance.'

Marion was astounded at his request. She got up from her chair and walked to the window, gazing out into the garden.

'I don't think I was expecting a conversation like this.'

'Did you think that our flirtation was an end in itself?' he asked quietly.

'I enjoyed your attention. I guess I was being a bit frivolous and didn't think beyond that.'

'Yes. Probably. However, you will still have my attention. I can promise you that. There are other things that I can offer you in return for your being my companion. Your life will be busy and interesting. I do have access to things you cannot obtain here, as you already know. I assure you that I am kind and fair-minded. I will look after you. What do you say? Can we have a mutually beneficial arrangement?'

Marion paused, trying to think through the implications of his request. Should she agree to his proposal or not? He waited patiently, watching her as she tried to identify the pros and cons of his proposal for herself.

'Can I have more time to think it through?' she finally asked, turning to face him.

'Of course. I am happy you will consider my offer. Perhaps tomorrow, no Thursday maybe, you can confirm? I know you have a job but that with the reduced shop hours you are free on Thursday evenings and in the weekends. I propose you spend those days here with me. There will also be evenings when I have social obligations, which I would expect you to attend, and which we can arrange so that they fit with your theatre work. However, it would not be appropriate for you to spend time with other German soldiers,' he warned.

Fredrich rose from his chair and approached Marion at the window. He leaned forward and kissed her cheek. 'I have enjoyed our evening. Now I will get the driver to take you home and on Thursday he will come for you at 7 pm. If you agree to my offer, then you should come here with him, for dinner with me. If you don't want to take it up, you should tell him that you are not able to come. Goodnight dear Marion.' He took her hand and kissed it.

Marion vacillated about a decision for days, but her mother's continuing disapproval and snide comments culminated in a bitter row between them on Thursday morning, when Mrs Le Prevost was alerted to Marion's plans for the evening.

That evening Marion waited, with a small suitcase, outside her mother's house for the driver to arrive. She was flushed and agitated. Her mother had asked her to leave home! As far as she was concerned, Marion was another 'Nazi lover' and was not welcome in her house.

CHAPTER TWENTY-TWO
FEBRUARY 1942
CAMBRIDGE

WINTER HAD ARRIVED EARLY IN NOVEMBER, WITH ICY mornings extending their chill until midday. This unseasonably long cold weather continued through December and into late February, making it impossible for Stella to cycle to work. Instead, a special bus service had been established to run the staff to and from Palmer Estate. A chilled group of talkative young people met each morning at 8 am for their short trip to work. A much more sombre group returned after dark at 6 pm.

Stella was now leading a group of six staff monitoring Merchant Navy casualties. Each day, a grim toll told of the difficulties encountered by the men and boys trying to keep the shipping lanes to the USA open. The price of getting food supplies and raw materials to maintain the war effort was being paid in the deaths and injuries of these men. The team in Palmer House often found their collation tasks a depressing daily reminder of the real price of the war.

Stella, as team leader, had set up a process at the end of the day's work, where her staff could debrief about the data they had been recording. She found that this was proving helpful for them, and soon all other units at the house followed suit. Her supervisor was most pleased with her initiative.

There had been a few bombings in Cambridge in the early autumn which meant that the night patrols at the Estate had been continued. Now on bitter winter nights those on watch spent riotous hours playing cards to pass the time. Stella enjoyed these duty nights, despite the cold and general discomfort, and the group she was with had formed close friendships. Some of the women knew that she had a 'serious boyfriend' but she had, so far, not talked about Mark to her colleagues.

One night one of the young women, in a teasing attempt to get Stella to share her secrets, announced to the assembled group that Stella's boyfriend was really the Dutch spy, recently revealed to be found living in Cambridge. He was said to be posing as a journalist for the Free Dutch newspaper, but rumour had it that he was really working undercover for a German spy-ring.

The young woman continued to embellish her story. 'He came over with the evacuees from Dunkirk,' she said. 'It can't be a coincidence that he came to Cambridge only days before Stella did. And he lived just down the road from where she lives in Botolph Lane.'

Another young woman joined in. 'Where did you meet him Stella? What is he really like?'

Stella laughed. 'What rubbish Jennifer. None of it's true,' she said, turning to the others for support.

'Ah so that's why you are so secretive,' one other woman claimed. 'Did he tell you he was a spy? Did you tell him about our work then?' she asked.

'Come on. You all know this isn't true.' Stella started to blush and feel uncomfortable.

'Well, if your boyfriend isn't the spy, who is he then?' Jennifer asked. 'There are so many foreigners living here now.'

'Perhaps he is one of the American pilots based around here,' said another.

'No!' said one of the men coming to Stella's defence. 'Stella doesn't look like a good-time girl! Have any of you seen her chewing gum or wearing nylons?'

They all laughed.

'No, I think Stella is too serious-minded for that. He must be one of the soldiers doing the war degree at Kings. You know Stella is studying there, don't you?' said her friend Michael.

'Oh! Please stop teasing me,' begged Stella. 'You are all being so mean. But maybe I should have been more forthcoming.

'Yes. I do have a special boyfriend,' she confirmed, 'and he comes from Guernsey, too. He is working just outside London for the Air Force. That's all. When I have something else to tell you I will. I promise.'

'You had better!' they chorused, delighted to have got some scrap of information from the reluctant Stella.

The following Wednesday Mark called to say he was coming up to Cambridge for the next weekend and had organised a small hotel for them.

'Will you meet me off the 6 pm from London?' he asked.

Stella waited impatiently at the station on Friday night. Mark arrived and walked slowly down the platform looking serious. He pulled her close but held her stiffly, in a brief hug.

'What's wrong?' she asked.

'Your mother asked my Dad to write to me,' he began.

'Why? Why would she do that? Is something wrong at home?'

'Yes, I'm afraid so.' He held her tightly. 'Darling I'm so sorry to tell you that your father has had a stroke. It happened in early December. He was in hospital, but he was still very ill, when Dad wrote. Dad said the doctors were not sure what the outcome might be.'

He steered Stella over to a bench seat by the waiting room. 'It's a terrible shock, I know. Would you like me to get you a tea?'

'I don't know. I can't really take it in. What are you telling me? Do you think he will have recovered by now or are you telling me he may be seriously damaged? But we don't know. It's terrible knowing it happened more than two months ago.'

'Yes. When I got Dad's letter on Wednesday, I got hold of the Red Cross to see if they could help us find out his current situation, but they could only promise to get a letter to Guernsey with the scheduled shipment next week. They said there should be another shipment from Guernsey in the next two weeks. Essentially, we will have to wait for that, and hope there is better news. We should write to your Mum tonight.'

'So, we are in limbo? Poor, poor Mum. She is all alone really because my grandparents are so old. And Dad, do you think he is suffering?'

'My love, it is awful not knowing. I know my folks will help your mother all they can. As for your Dad I am sure the stroke happened quickly. The hospital will do their best.'

'David! What am I to tell David? Should I tell David? He will be frightened by the news and heartbroken if Dad has died. God! I don't know what to do! Or what to think!' She turned to Mark as the tears finally welled up. 'It's so bloody unfair.'

'Yes, it's rotten to be so far away, when your family is suffering. But we will get through this together. I promise to help to the best of my abilities. I love you.'

Over the next two days they prepared letters to Stella's mother and Mark's parents. After much discussion Stella decided that she would only contact David when they had more certain news. She thought it would be too unkind to leave him in the state of upheaval that she was experiencing. It was with a heavy heart that she saw Mark off to London again on Sunday evening.

When she got back to the flat Alison saw her distress.

'Are you okay?' she asked seeing Stella's drawn face.

Stella quickly told her of the news from Guernsey. The girls all gathered around her to give her a hug.

'We know this war is so much more difficult for you with your family living under occupation,' said Alison. 'It's another burden you have to carry that we don't. I hope you get more news very soon. And I hope it is good news – that your Dad is getting better.'

'I've asked Mum to write to me here, but we may hear from Mark's Dad first,' Stella said.

Three weeks later she returned from work to find Alison waiting for her with a letter stamped by the Red Cross. The writing on it showed it was not from her mother and she opened it with trepidation. It was from Mr Webb.

He revealed that her father had never regained consciousness and had died four days after his stroke, on 10th December. He said that his funeral was held two days later and that her mother was upset but was staying with family for the next few days. Mr Webb said that he was writing to Mark at the same time as he was writing to her.

Stella sat quietly. 'How can it be that you are going around thinking of someone as being alive when in fact they have been dead for some weeks? You know I never thought about not seeing my Dad again when I left Guernsey. Everybody thought we would only be gone for a matter of months and that we would be home by 1941.'

'Now I can never say the things I should have to my Dad. He was a good man and a loving father. He always wanted the best for David and me. Letting us come to England and Scotland was for us to be safe, whilst he had tasks in Guernsey that he had a duty to complete.'

She wept soundlessly, whilst Alison stroked her back. Mark phoned her after he finished his shift and discovered his own letter.

'I will ask for compassionate leave in the morning and you must do the same. I will go to Glasgow with you to see David as soon as my furlough is granted. We can phone the school when our travel details are sorted out. Darling, I am so sorry I am not with you tonight. I love you so much and I know you are very sad. I am sure, though, that Alison and the others will look after you and I will talk to you tomorrow. I will be thinking of you. Just hold on till we are together.'

CHAPTER TWENTY-THREE
JANUARY 1942
GUERNSEY

THE PAST MONTHS HAVE BEEN DIFFICULT. WE NEVER IMAGINED *the war would go on so long and that there would be no help from Great Britain or the Allies available for us. We really are going to be in this situation for a long time.*

We spent Christmas Day at home, with Mum well enough to join in the decorating of the house with the tiny branch we used for a tree. She was able to cook the meal for all of us, as well, which was great progress.

We invited a widowed family friend, Mrs Perelle from the Catel, and one of the valley families to join us on Christmas Day. There were presents only for the youngest children, who were happy just to unwrap their gifts, although they were all second-hand. For the older members of the group we each offered a gift of our time and company, to do something enjoyable. We had such fun coming up with suitable ideas for everyone. It was altogether a success and cheered us up no end.

We made the most of the special food rations for Christmas and the allocation of oranges last week was most welcome. Our vegetable garden and preserved fruit from last summer is keeping us healthy. We are better placed than some others. Unlike many people we are still managing to keep our coal range lit during the day, using hedge cuttings from around the farm for fuel. These little things make a big difference for us.

Some of the different parishes around the Island have opened communal kitchens because their residents are short of fuel for cooking. Many people bring up their dinner dishes to be cooked, overnight, in hayboxes. Life for those housewives has become very difficult. They spend hours queuing for food and then after preparing their dinner at home must also traipse to the church and back, twice a day so that the family can eat a cooked meal once a day.

I have heard that the number of occupation forces on the island is still growing, so there are thousands more mouths to feed. Because of petrol and oil shortages the Germans have brought over large numbers of horses for transport, and they too, compete for food with our own stock.

The Germans make sure their own men are looked after first and the local civilians struggle with what's left to adequately feed their families. Several men, including some policeman, have been in court for stealing food. Others are in trouble for selling food on the black market.

It is difficult for people in these circumstances to always be honest.

We grew up with the Ten Commandments, but no-one really told us how difficult it is to adhere to them in times of turmoil.

Can we be deceitful, or lie, to save other people? Can we steal, to feed a hungry child or a sick relative?

I digress! I meant to be positive.

Peter has left school and is working with Dad on the farm permanently. He is only just fifteen, and hasn't yet done his matriculation exams, but Dad did not want him to continue at school. Dad was frustrated that the school hours were constantly being cut back and at the same time the children were expected to use much of the school day learning German. That was too much for him to tolerate.

We had a couple of unemployed men working on the farm through the harvesting season, but one was moved on to chop wood for fuel and the other to collect seaweed for fertilising the ground. Once they left Dad really needed more help.

Dad believes that by working on the farm and managing the farm accounts Peter will keep learning in a practical way. He says it will be safer for Peter as well. He may be right.

Selfishly, I am glad to have Peter back home full time. It helps Mum's morale and energy. This then gives me a bit more freedom from the weight of home responsibilities in addition to my hospital duties.

It might also keep a rein on Dad, whose trenchant dissatisfaction with the numerous edicts from the Food Production Committee, or the 'Flaming Prohibition Committee' [as he calls them] could lead to trouble for us. He is under pressure to grow more on our land, as well as keep up the amount of milk he supplies. That isn't easy to achieve.

Dad has been inventive in growing herbs and different things for our own use. He has made small gardens in old barrels, which he placed out of sight around the farm. He fenced off patches of fennel in the fields, as well as letting the cress grow rampant, in parts of the stream going through our property.

Like other farmers he set traps around the cliffs to catch wild rabbits which he brought home. He is now breeding rabbits for us to eat. He has built hutches out of odd bits of timber, lying around our farm. He says it was, good after all, that he had been a hoarder.

I know other farmers are also being inventive. One of them has built a hand-powered threshing machine and another made a musical windmill to scare the birds from his crops.

Lots of changes have happened at the hospital. In October the Superintendent at the German Hospital required us to do an audit of all our equipment, stores and medicines. Then he asked to see our patient records for the past year. After this he suggested we needed a more formal approach to ordering supplies and for them to be 'strictly consistent' with our immediate needs. That means no more stockpiling! I helped with gathering the information.

We fear this is a signal for more cutbacks. I hope this doesn't mean Dr Konrad is under scrutiny. Matron and the Hospital Committee were so worried about what this might lead to, they invited the local GPs to work with the Chief Surgeon to write a submission about the current health conditions affecting the Islanders.

They wrote a report which identified the current mortality rates and compared them with our pre-war figures. They also showed that people are now dying of different causes – malnutrition, skin diseases and serious injuries [from mine explosions] are prevalent. Neonatal and infant diseases have decreased, but cases of rickets have increased as well as scabies and headlice. This means we need different equipment and medicines.

The committee then put together a case that there were serious deficiencies in the health services, such that we were unable to provide for acceptable 'in- and out-patient care' on the Island. They argued that this was a breach of the Geneva Convention.

I was intrigued by the way these reports were written. The language seemed very bureaucratic. But then the Germans are so formal with everything done in writing and in triplicate. I learned a lot, seeing how our committee produced the information to persuade the Germans to give us more aid. We will now have to see how far the Germans will be willing to address the problems identified.

As for a more formal approach to managing supplies; that is to start in February. It will no longer rely on a girl [me] on a bike, with a haphazard list from our hospital. Instead, there will be a new joint Health Planning Committee, comprising Matron, Dr Shirtcliffe, two of the GPs, and a community nurse, plus two medicos from the German Hospital. One of those being Dr Konrad, who is already well informed about our plight.

I am to give administrative assistance to the new committee; but my main job will be to co-ordinate in-patient and out-patient care. Our hospital will manage daily appointments for all the GPs, as well as do the lab. tests and distribute medicines outside the hospital. I am excited by the prospect. It's a new opportunity for me to learn more about health administration.

I will be so pleased not to have shift work as it will give me a bit more time for myself. I hope to meet up with some of my old friends. I am contemplating boarding closer to work as well, because bicycles are being requisitioned by the Germans, for their own use, and I could lose my transport. I also want to be a bit more independent now things are better at home.

During the autumn the British launched a Commando raid in Guernsey against an important offshore lighthouse. They took German soldiers based there as prisoners and stole their naval code books during their attack. We suffered a new reprisal from the Germans when the popular theatre performances were discontinued for some time.

We then had another raid from a British plane on the harbour in January, which killed some local men. It's a bit hard for us to stomach these deaths. The British took all their troops off the Island, leaving us high and dry and exposed to German bombing in June 1940. Now they are endangering us all too often. Altogether Mr Churchill isn't popular with everyone here!

Our fears about the identity cards were not misplaced. My nursing friend Therese, who has been working here for three years, has had a large red J [for Jew] stamped on her card. She is well-liked for her enthusiastic personality as well as her nursing skills. The patients also love her because she plays our old piano for them in the evenings. We are all worried for her safety.

Another concern is that each house must have a list of its occupants pinned up inside the front door, ready for random inspections. We can't be sure how this will be used in the future, but there are lots of rumours about people being evicted if their houses have empty rooms.

My father became furious about this and when I tried to calm him, he turned his anger onto me. He pulled me out of my chair and marched me out the front door. I was afraid of what he meant to do. He shook me roughly and pointed at the date stone above the door.

He said. 'My family have owned and lived in this house since 1720. No German will throw us out of here, except over my dead body.'

I was very shaken by this incident. As was my mother. My relationship with my father has changed for the worse.

Which reminds me that I met Stella's mother up at the Catel last week. I was very sad to hear that Stella's father has died. I remember him as a kind man. His stroke was apparently brought on by stress in his job at the newspaper.

Stella's Mum said that he was struggling with meeting all the censorship requirements made by both the Germans and the Controlling Committee. She said he hated having to print German propaganda about its military victories. The last straw was having to print a weekly German paper for their local troops, at the expense of the local newspaper.

She said Stella and David would be devastated by the news of his death. She hadn't yet got a letter back from Stella. That is obviously adding to her distress.

CHAPTER TWENTY-FOUR
FEBRUARY 1942
GUERNSEY

ONE GLOOMY MORNING IN NOVEMBER, FREDRICH SAID TO Marion over breakfast, 'We have an important man coming to the Island and we will need to entertain him for dinner. Could you talk to Joseph, please, about a dinner for twelve, on Saturday next?'

Marion was quick to agree to the task, as she had come to enjoy planning menus for a regular routine of dinner parties at their house with subordinate officers and their local girlfriends. Joseph was a good cook and had access to a wide range of foods. Luckily the house had a collection of European cookery books with suitable dishes for such occasions. While the dishes were new to Marion, she had come to enjoy their subtle flavours and formal presentation.

'Who is this man?'

'His name is Dr Fritz Todt. He was an engineer originally. Now he is the Minister of Armaments and Munitions. He is responsible for building the Atlantic Wall. He is here to look at our fortifications as Hitler is worried that since we are now fighting on the Russian front, the British might try to recapture these islands, and he wants them to be impregnable.'

'Do you really think that recapture is possible?' she asked hopefully.

'No not really! We have built up the number of our troops here and we have good aircraft cover to repulse any attack. We could be overcome if the Allies decide to divert forces from other frontiers. But I also think that is very unlikely.'

He elaborated: 'We will do what we are ordered to do. I will be shepherding Todt around the coastal batteries and then going out to Sark and Alderney with him. After that, we will see what additional facilities he thinks we should have. He reports direct to Hitler.'

'I'm interested that your superiors think the British might believe we are important enough to recapture! They weren't so interested in us in 1940.'

'Well, in my view, the Islands are not as strategically important as the other fronts the British are fighting on. But perhaps they are politically or psychologically important to the British, once more. Anyway, we need to hear from Dr Todt. We also need to be totally discreet about our own thoughts!' he cautioned.

'Yes, I know. Be charming and give nothing away. I've learned a lot in the past few months.' She laughed. 'I used to say the first thing that came into my head. Not any longer though.'

Fredrich and Marion had established a comfortable domestic life together during her time at 'Woodleigh'. Marion had a bedroom, dressing room and bathroom upstairs at the rear of the house. It was spacious, luxuriously furnished and sunny.

Fredrich's suite was at the front of the house and included a small office, where on occasion, he worked in the evenings. The house was warm and well lit, with its own generator for when power cuts occurred. They had converted the glass conservatory into a relaxing sunroom where Marion liked to curl up in an overstuffed chair to learn her scripts. Marion had access to Fredrich's car and driver, when necessary, for her to continue her theatre commitments.

Fredrich, as he had intimated was polite, generous and kind towards her. She, in turn, was undemanding and tolerant of his requests of her. It seemed that she had made a good decision in coming to live with him. Marion's only difficulty was in her relationship with her mother.

Initially, Marion visited her mother but had been angrily repulsed on each occasion. On her last attempt to make peace, some months ago, her mother had insisted that she take the last of her belongings back to her 'love-nest' and never return to her childhood home. Her mother had been voluble in her contempt for Marion.

'Look at you in your fancy clothes. I know all about the foreign food and partying whilst we go without. But you've sold your soul to the devil. You are no longer my daughter.'

'Don't you realise I want to help you too?' Marion had countered.

'I would rather starve first,' her mother replied. 'Go back to your German and don't come here again.'

Marion had then left the house on Paris Street, realising that reconciliation with her mother was not going to occur for some time. She asked the driver to collect her boxes, and then to drive her back to the Fort Road. She saw the curtains twitching in the adjoining house as her mother's neighbour eavesdropped on their noisy row.

The dinner with Dr Todt at the end of November was successful but Fredrich had expressed concern about Todt's plans for the Island.

'Todt intends to bring in a workforce of displaced people to build massive new gun emplacements and bunkers around the coast. He also wants to build a hospital underground. We will have to bring in massive shipments of steel and concrete.'

'Where will these people live? The troops have already taken over most of the spare houses! What about the food they will need?' Marion asked.

'Some will be billeted but he plans to build a number of camps around the Island.'

'Well. That might help with housing but what about food? It's difficult for the local people to get enough food already!' she said.

'I know. We raised all these things with Todt. He seems to think these things can be easily fixed. He has grand ideas. He even wants to put in a railway system, to get materials around the Island. I am trying to work out the logistics for his plans. This may prove impossible.'

For many weeks Fredrich worked long hours on the plan and held a series of private meetings with staff in his office at home. When the planning phase was completed, he seemed tired and dispirited. On the week before Christmas he came home looking desolate.

'Todt's plans have been supported by Hitler and are to go ahead immediately. All the workers will be supervised by Todt's men, not the Army. My job will be limited to getting the camps set up to receive the workers. I must also arrange the supplies to build all these things. After that I don't know what will happen! They have already got standard building designs which will only be modified in minor ways to fit local conditions. My engineering work will be very limited.'

'What does all this mean?'

'I don't know. I've been ordered to go back to Germany at the end of this week and to report to Army HQ in Berlin for talks. I should have a better picture after that. I've been told to take some home leave as well,' he added.

Marion was startled. 'Will you be here for Christmas?' she asked.

'I'm sorry, but no I won't be here.'

Marion sat down. 'Okay. I understand! What does it mean for you in the longer term then?'

'I'm not sure. I will do my best to see that you are looked after whilst I'm away. I should be back by early January.'

During the next few days each kept their anxieties about the current uncertainties to themselves. Before he left Fredrich asked Marion to prepare a list of items he could bring back from Germany for her.

'I am sure there are clothes and cosmetics you would like me to get for you,' he offered.

When he returned, after an absence of ten days, he greeted her with great affection. He had brought back new clothes for her. 'You will be as fashionable as the ladies in Berlin now.'

Marion in turn was happy to see him. She had been lonely but had found some comfort in reading some of the many books in the library at 'Woodleigh'.

Marion decided not to ask Fredrich about his time with his family and he told her nothing of his visit to Cologne. He was a little more forthcoming about his time at Army HQ.

He muttered, 'HQ are not happy with all the expenditure on fortifications in the Island. But I have been told to do all I can to make it happen. It's going to be extremely busy for me in the next few months. It might be a little dull for you though.'

'I will keep busy. I've started working my way through the books in the library here. I'd never heard of some of the authors, but I have found some that I have enjoyed.'

'That's good. It's an impressive collection. The man who lived here previously, was obviously quite a collector of French and English books as well as art. I think he must have been a Jew.'

'Jews. I didn't know there were any in Guernsey. Why do you think that?'

'Well, all the art and furnishings, as well as the library, indicate wealth and a classical education. The family probably came as refugees from Europe. Perhaps from Russia, via France, in the early 1900s. Now they have fled once again; leaving all this behind. That's my guess.

'You must tell me what you have read and enjoyed so far. I may well have read the same authors. It's a good chance for you to extend your reading.'

Although Marion had been discreet about her relationship with Fredrich, it was inevitable that an expanding group of people knew of it. While at work some of the girls were still friendly, many of the older women ignored her. Her boss had become distant and when, in the New Year, it was apparent that the store would now be closing on Mondays as well as all day on Thursdays, the manager told Marion that he could no longer afford to keep her on the payroll.

He seemed relieved when a day later Marion decided that she would immediately finish her job without working out her notice. The growing tension at work was becoming too difficult for her to face.

When Marion appeared in another play after New Year, she had a very minor role and she became aware that other cast members did not want to include her in their conversations. The friendly chatter, that they had previously all engaged in, stopped when she arrived.

She began to feel self-conscious and isolated. Consequently, her performances on the stage were flat. After the final night she was not invited to the end of show party. Instead she returned home immediately to Fredrich, who was, as usual, working late.

'You seem to be so busy,' she had complained when he told her he was unable to attend the theatre that night.

'Yes. I have more duties. Todt has been killed in a plane crash and I must prepare full briefing reports for his successor by the end of the month. The new man is another one of Hitler's protégés called Speer. There are rumours amongst the generals that Todt might have been assassinated.'

'That sounds a bit scary. Are you worried?'

'These are difficult times,' he replied.

'I think that will be the last time I get a part in a local play,' she confided to him next morning.

Fredrich was sympathetic about her loss of both her job and her source of company but, as he had predicted, he was so absorbed in his work that they rarely entertained at home and seldom went out with others. Marion found she had few diversions available to her. She spent much of her time alone; either reading or on long walks, along country lanes.

It quickly became apparent to her that her world, whilst still materially comfortable, had shrunk in ways she had not been able to anticipate last August, when novelty and excitement had beckoned. She craved that again.

'I've lost my friends and family! Have I burned my boats in spectacular fashion?' she wondered.

CHAPTER TWENTY-FIVE
JUNE 1942
CAMBRIDGE

Stella woke early, full of excitement. David was arriving from London along with Mark in the early afternoon and both would stay with Mrs Styles at 'Redleaf', Mark's old boarding-house. Mark's Cambridge friend Peter was organising a stag party for this evening whilst Stella and the girls had a celebration arranged at the flat, with some of her friends from work.

Tomorrow at 11 am she and Mark would go to the Cambridge Registry Office for their wedding. A dozen friends and David would be their witnesses and then they would all have lunch at 'The Bull's Roar', a 17th century pub beside the Cam.

Alison and the other girls at the flat had each helped her by giving her one of their clothing coupons, so that Stella had enough coupons to buy a new dress and shoes for her wedding. Hopeful that the weather in June would be warm, she had bought herself a copper-coloured, faux-silk dress; one she could wear again for cocktail parties and formal social events. It had a deep V neckline, and a close-fitting top which flared out below her hips. The colour highlighted her auburn hair which she now had grown to shoulder-length. Michelle had offered to tame Stella's halo of rampant curls into the latest sleek look for her wedding day.

This morning she needed to finish her packing and run some errands before going to the station to meet David and Mark. Tomorrow, in the evening, she and Mark would be borrowing Peter's car and having a brief honeymoon in Norfolk before she moved south to Bentley Priory, where they would live in the married quarters, with David in their care at weekends.

So much had changed since Stella and Mark had gone up to Glasgow the previous January to tell David about his father's death. That had been a harrowing trip for Stella, knowing that she was bringing devastating news for her brother, and that she could not stay long with him, to help him cope, afterwards. David's old schoolmaster had been helpful in arranging for them to meet in a private office at the school, after they had arrived. He brought them tea and sandwiches, then fetched David from his classroom to join Stella and Mark, before tactfully disappearing.

David had been forewarned that they were here to see him and approached Stella cautiously. 'Why are you both here?' he asked.

'We've had some news from Guernsey that we need to talk to you about,' Stella started.

'If its bad news I don't want to know.' David got angry: 'I've tried not to think about Guernsey for the past two years. I've tried to get on with living here with strangers. If I think about home, I just want to cry; and we are not allowed to cry. They tell us we must be brave and not give in to homesickness. I just want to do that, till it's all over and I can go home again.'

Mark interceded: 'It's tough for you I know, and you have been very brave for so long, but we do need to talk, even though its painful for you, and for us. We are here to support you now. Let Stella tell you what we have heard.'

Stella struggled to hold back her tears as she hugged David's rigid frame, he broke free of her embrace and sat impassively on his chair staring intently at Stella. He let Mark put a hand on his shoulder and David nodded at Stella. 'I'm ready.' He listened blank-faced, fists clenched, as she told him of their father's death.

David said nothing and gave no reaction. He sat like a coiled spring but kept his face tightly controlled. After a long silence Mark suggested that he and David go out to the playground to kick a few goals with a football, while Stella went to see Mrs Mackenzie, then they could all walk into town for lunch.

Mark later confided that David had unleashed his grief on the soccer ball, repeatedly blasting the ball the length of the pitch. After tiring himself out he threw himself forward onto the ground and sobbed into his arms while Mark sat quietly beside him, patting the boy's shoulder.

When Mark and David reunited with Stella, David was quiet and composed and he put his arm through hers as they walked to Sauchiehall Street to find a teashop.

The following afternoon they took David back to school. He had been worried about what he would say to his friends and was relieved to know that Mr Hemmings had already told his classmates.

Whilst David was back in class Stella and Mark met with Mr Hemmings, who said he would be looking out for David during the next few weeks. He said, 'I wanted to talk to you about David's schooling. He is a very bright boy. Very motivated. University material. But I don't think we can offer him enough here. He is ahead of his peers and marking time as the rest of the class struggle along. I think we should be trying to get him into a grammar school where he will have a wider range of subjects available, as well as some competition.'

'Do you think he could come and live with you, Stella, and go to a school in Cambridge? I think it would be good for him academically, but I also think he is going to need your emotional support now. He could finish the term here while we sort something out. I think he will manage if he has something good to look forward to.'

'Yes, it's possible. I don't earn a lot and I share digs with other girls. I don't get home till about 6 pm but he is old enough to be on his own for a couple of hours. Would I get some financial help?'

'Yes, we could give you the same as we give Mrs Mackenzie and I would look for a scholarship for David's education. We will get permission for him to transfer on compassionate grounds. If you agree, we could tell David before you leave. I think that would help him enormously.'

On the train that evening Mark said, 'There's a very good school at Harrow you know. That might be the place for Mark, if he meets their standards. Otherwise I'm sure we will find a suitable grammar school for him close to the Priory.'

Mark continued: 'This is not the time nor place for a proposal, I know, but I've been thinking about it for some months. Let's get married in the summer and together we can make a home for David. Will you marry me my darling Stella?'

Stella reacted with surprise. Through laughter and tears she said 'Yes'.

Tomorrow, on the 29th June, the second anniversary of her arrival in Cambridge, she was going to marry the boy from next door. The boy she had once dismissed. The decision her parents had taken, in organising for her to leave Guernsey had led to this most unexpected outcome.

She had come to love Mark and they had a companionable relationship. She knew she had so much to look forward to, in her future life with him. But she also had regrets to be leaving Cambridge and the English people who had rallied around her after she arrived as an evacuee.

CHAPTER TWENTY-SIX
SEPTEMBER 1942
GUERNSEY

THE YEAR IS PASSING QUICKLY AND THERE HAVE BEEN SOME *positive changes in my life.*

At the beginning of March, I moved from the farm into a cottage in the Catel parish, opposite the church, to board with an elderly friend of my mother's. I have two nice attic rooms which look across the fields down to the west coast beaches. I can walk to the hospital from there in ten minutes.

The only disadvantage is that because we are at the central high point of the island, we have a German Observation Tower at the top of the road. But maybe being overlooked by the enemy somehow makes us less visible to them!

I eat my dinner at work, so I must make my breakfast and

tea here during the week. Most weekends I visit the farm and eat Sunday dinner with the family. Mrs Perelle is quiet, very private and occupies the ground floor, leaving me to the awkwardly shaped upstairs rooms which I use as a bedroom and a sitting area. I am enjoying my independence enormously.

I am enthusiastic about my new job. It keeps me in contact with lots of medical people from around the Island. While there is a large administrative component to the job, it still calls on my nursing knowledge. I also like being the secretary for the Medical Planning Committee.

This committee is facing some new and challenging situations which have broadened my knowledge of public health. We have had a big increase in the rat population on the Island, because there are fewer cats about. The rats are threatening public health and we need to educate people about the possibility of typhus. Doctors are now authorised to enter private houses if they think they might be harbouring the source of this disease.

Another big problem has been a decline in children's health. The youngsters are very thin and somewhat listless. Puberty is being delayed for the girls. The committee had to lobby the Controlling Committee to increase the milk and fruit allowances for children under ten years who are showing serious dietary deficiencies.

I like to be party to the committee discussions and to participate if asked. It helps me to feel informed about what is happening for the health of our community during the various crises that have arisen. My confidence has grown. It feels good to be recognised, when I am asked to contribute to the debate about possible solutions.

Best of all though, I've had a great summer; the advantage of not being on shift work. For the first time in two seasons I have been able to go swimming. Because it was unseasonably warm, some of the mine-free beaches were opened for bathing from late May.

That turned out to be fortuitous as we have had water shortages since the early spring. The beaches proved very popular and not just to cool down. Lots of sweaty bodies got clean at the beaches!

I began going down to Cobo Bay on my weekends; generally alone but occasionally with someone I knew. I must say that I enjoyed the solitude of my two-mile walk to reach the beach. I could listen to the birds, watch the hovering hawks and enjoy the scent of the wildflowers. As the narrow road is sheltered by high granite walls and shady trees, the uphill return is not arduous either.

My fitness improved, I got very tanned and my hair bleached to a white blonde. On the beach I felt truly relaxed. I enjoyed the warmth of the sun on my skin, the pungent smell of seaweed, the crunch of sand under my bare feet and the thrum of the tide. All combined to make me happy. I felt buoyant and at peace with the world on those days out. It rekindled happy childhood memories.

One Sunday in July, Dr Konrad almost fell over me. I was lying on a towel reading, on top of the cobbled slipway, after a luxuriously warm swim in the incoming tide. There was a group of soldiers playing soccer on the hard sand further up the beach by the gun battery. Suddenly the football landed beside me and he did too, having tripped in pursuit of the runaway ball. I'm not sure who was the most surprised.

He apologised and sprinted off with the football but returned after some minutes and asked if he could sit down on the warm slipway. I said, 'Yes, Dr Konrad', and he said, 'I think we could be less formal Nurse Dorey?' We both laughed and said, 'It's Dieter and Rachel then!' It's hard to be formal when all you are wearing is a baggy old bathing suit!

We ended up chatting there for over an hour. I found out quite a lot about him, and he in his turn, about me. He is only twenty-seven but looks older because of his round glasses and his serious gaze. He has an athletic build and seems very fit. He has a sense of irony and constantly made me laugh.

He said he had a wonderful childhood. He grew up on a farm north of Hamburg where his father had a herd of Holsteins. The farm was on an isthmus of land, near the rough Atlantic sea, which was very windy with frequent storms blowing in from the west. In the summer his mother used to take him and his two younger brothers to a cabin on the Baltic Sea, not very far north from their home.

He told me how the foursome would all sit on the milk wagon behind an aged tractor, amongst the metal cans, and bounce along the lanes to the railhead where they would catch the train north. He said it was not unlike living on this Island, and that the Baltic coast had long sandy beaches topped by grassy dunes where the boys would play. He said the similarities, both in environment and lifestyle, made him feel instantly at home here.

After he finished his medical degree in Hamburg he worked in a special clinic for the poor people of the city. It had a variety of educational and social services as well as medical, and the different staff worked as a team to deal with all the multiple problems besetting the patients. He was planning to go on to specialise in psychiatry, but he was conscripted into the army instead.

In my turn, I confessed to soon being twenty-three and told him about my life in Guernsey. We swapped a lot of information about our early lives and were amused over their similarities.

When I got up to leave, so that I would be home before the curfew, he reached for my left hand and asked me why I no longer wore my ring. I was startled. He was equally surprised when I told him that the engagement ended more than a year ago.

He hesitated and then said that the war had changed the hopes and opportunities for people in our age group. I simply agreed and we spoke no more about it.

Two weeks later Dieter was sitting at a table on the grass verge beside the beach kiosk, having a drink, when I walked past and waved to him. I crossed the road to the seawall and saw that the sea was rough, with a squadron of waves assaulting the foot of the wall. A stiff north-wester was blowing up the spume and my face was quickly covered in salty spray. It was not a day for swimming.

Dieter came over to the wall. He told me that the kiosk shouldn't call his drink 'coffee.' It had been awful! I laughed and said that we had never drunk proper coffee, even before the war. I said it used to be chicory essence, but we drank it to feel sophisticated, not for the taste. He laughed and promised he would buy me a real cup of coffee one day. It was my turn to laugh then!

I asked him if he had seen the dolmen, the ancient, stone burial chamber on the rocky promontory at the north end of the bay. He said he would like to see it, so we walked along the coast for another mile, to the granite reef where the dolmen was concealed. It was sheltered from the prevailing wind amongst scrubby gorse and broom bushes, all in fragrant flower. By then I was tired, so we sat down to rest.

We talked companionably for the remainder of the afternoon. It's been so long since I was able to talk informally to a man. I walked home feeling elated. I felt young again. While I always respected Dieter as a compassionate doctor I now knew that, in different circumstances, he could be a friend.

Before we parted, Dieter asked me if I had ever been up to Lion Rock, a tall granite pillar which jutted tooth-like from a ridge at the other end of the bay. I told him there was an old track leading through the pine plantation which led up to the rock. I agreed to show him the path, on another occasion.

Unfortunately, we never visited the Lion Rock. In late July the Germans closed all the beaches off again. It was a punishment for the Islanders, because the British Navy had sunk many German ships in the Channel.

I had to accept that our pleasant conversations were over. It had been only a brief interlude of personal friendship. In the last months I've only seen Dieter at fortnightly meetings in the hospital.

We are back to the professional basis of Dr Konrad and Nurse Dorey.

This month we have seen all British and Irish people on the island rounded up and evacuated to Germany at very short notice. Hundreds of people went to St Peter Port to see them leave, and everyone sang 'Rule Britannia', which made the German Commandant very angry.

We are all very worried about what might happen to these evacuees. All their property has been handed in to a depository as all they could take with them was one small case, for each person. Some leading figures on the Island have now gone, along with their wives and children. We simply cannot imagine what will happen next. Life here is totally unpredictable.

CHAPTER TWENTY-SEVEN
NOVEMBER 1942
GUERNSEY

Now, after my 'glorious summer', I am facing up to my 'winter of discontent.' From my good spirits during the summer, I hit a low after my birthday, in late August. Then I came down with a cold and 'strep' throat and was physically miserable as well. For weeks I had no energy and struggled to work.

The reason for my gloom was complicated. I felt so happy last summer and one of the reasons for that was my getting to know Dieter. I enjoyed his company. We had a lot in common through the similarities in our upbringing as well as our mutual interests. These things attracted me to him, intellectually. But I also felt an emotional response, as well as [I must confess] physical attraction. I realised, belatedly, that I wanted more than friendship from him.

After those brief social encounters ended, I began pining for a soulmate, and a lover. Those two short afternoons reminded me of what I have lost and reawakened my longing for love. I feel very lonely and I want someone who cares for me. I yearn for the warmth and comfort of a body responding to mine. I've begun to feel that my youth is wasting away.

The realist in me knows that it was only a brief friendship, much as I might like the relationship to be otherwise. Life really is bitter-sweet.

I know that Dieter and I must keep our relationship solely on a professional basis, and, since those stolen hours, that has been the case. But there is a constant battle going on between my head and heart which proves not easy for me to manage when we work together.

I'm not very experienced when it comes to men. Before this there was only John; but that was somehow different to this. For some months John and I were part of a mixed group of teens playing tennis, and then hockey, at weekends. I am not sure why that changed during the following summer, when many of our group started going out as couples, including John and me.

Looking back, I think it was almost the expected thing for young adults to do. Without the threat of war would we have even contemplated marrying? Perhaps we would have moved on to other relationships with new people, given a bit more time? It's hard to know now.

Another source of my blues was that since August, the German grip on us has tightened another notch.

Because of an outbreak of venereal diseases over the summer months, the governing bodies combined to issue an English/German notice, forbidding any relationships between German soldiers and Guernsey civilians. It stated that penalties would be harsh for anyone who breaches that order. It doesn't appear to apply to officers and worthy local citizens, however.

A lady from the Salvation Army, who is very ill, has recently been admitted to hospital after being in prison for some months. Her terrible crime was to preach on the street and draw attention to the appalling conditions that the Todt workers live under. No one dares to visit her in case they will also be in trouble!

I have heard that many Todt workers on the Island have suffered serious injuries working in the quarries and on the railway, though they do not come to our hospital. Apparently, they are even more poorly nourished and clothed than we are. Their camps are unsanitary and totally unheated. Deaths amongst them are rising.

It's hard to imagine how much worse things could be. Life here is mean and uncertain. We have nothing to look forward to.

CHAPTER TWENTY-EIGHT
DECEMBER 1942
GUERNSEY

MARION STOOD IN THE HALLWAY AT 'WOODLEIGH', TEARS pouring down her cheeks. Beside her stood her worn suitcase and a collection of cardboard boxes. She awaited the arrival of Fredrich's driver, Tobias, who was coming to collect her and her baggage and take her on her last journey by chauffeured car. She was destined for sanctuary in her aunt's vinery.

Over the previous spring and summer Fredrich had worked hard, overseeing the massive building projects around the coast. Huge anti-tank walls had been built around the low-lying beaches on the west coast. Large concrete gun emplacements were erected between and beside the huge granite rocks on the coastal promontories, all bristling with enormous guns.

Fredrich told her that the largest, high on a southern clifftop, was guaranteed to send its shells thirty kilometres, to deter any possible Allied landings.

Fredrich was responsible for the munition dumps and underground barracks at crucial spots around the Island. All of these were facilitated by a purpose-built railway and the energy of slave labour. Whenever Marion went out for her daily walks around the water-lanes she could hear the thrum of jack hammers and heavy equipment, signalling that yet another defensive military emplacement was being built.

One autumn day, when the work was close to completion, Fredrich ordered the car to drive her around the Island to see all the completed fortifications. She was surprised at the scale of work. They had transformed the whole Island. The line of tall Martello Towers around the coastline, built to repulse Napoleon, were now interspersed with squat, well camouflaged German defences.

That night she asked Fredrich about an encampment of rough huts that she had seen. It was on some peat swamp, in a bleak windswept area on the northernmost tip of the Island. She saw that the camp was surrounded by a barbed-wire fence with a steep ditch beyond it.

'What is that camp I saw? Out between Fort Doyle and Fort Le Marchant?' she asked. 'It's a terrible place to live.'

'It houses some of the prisoners from the Eastern Front. The Slavs mostly. They comprise part of the Organisation Todt workforce. There are two other camps around L'Ancresse Common.

'The lagers are basic, yes. But remember these people came from very poor backgrounds. They are not used to much. These Poles and Ukrainians are just illiterate peasant farmers. They are used to surviving in a harsh environment.'

'Well it's an awfully cold and windy place and the huts don't look very well built. There are no trees, only sedge grass and rushes. Nothing to provide shelter or fuel. I thought most of the workers were going to be billeted like the troops are?'

'There are too many of them for that to happen. Nearly 7000 extra people have come here this past year. The skilled workers are in billets. Those in the camps are just the rock crushers and manual labourers. They are used to physical work. You should stop worrying about them,' he finished tersely.

At this point Marion decided to pursue her questions no further since Fredrich appeared annoyed with her inquisition.

Fredrich continued to finish off the many building projects and by late November he informed her that his big task was completed. The entire Guernsey section of Hitler's Atlantic Wall was now in place.

He was pleased to have met his deadlines, but it had taken a toll on him. Marion thought that he had aged perceptibly over the past twelve months, with more lines etched into his face. His hair was now totally grey, and he seemed perpetually tired. She knew that matters political, as well as military, were consuming his energy and former good humour.

Marion knew that he was looking forward to some respite from the demands made of him. Maybe he could have some leave and they could organise a big Christmas celebration at their house.

Unexpectedly, two days ago, Fredrich had come home early, looking more haggard than usual. With breaking voice, he told her, 'I've been recalled. I'm to go to the Eastern Front. To Stalingrad. It's effective from tomorrow.'

'No surely not. You are so tired. You need a break! We need it!' Marion was appalled.

'Everything here is done. They don't need my skills anymore. And besides, things on the Eastern Front are not going well. Seems I might be useful there.'

'You know, the East is a repeat of 1914-18. You would think we could have learned from that military disaster. It's ironic that I'm now being asked to do what my father did in the first war! To go to Russia! I'm not convinced that we will do any better in this war either. I am also sure my gimpy leg will make me a liability, not an asset, on the frontline.'

'We have so little time. Couldn't they delay this for a while? It's too abrupt. We're unprepared.' Her voice quavered and her tears began to flow.

'Time and Hitler wait for no man,' Fredrich gave a weak smile. 'It won't take me long to pack. But first, we need to work out things for you. I am so sorry I am letting you down. This house will be requisitioned but I've arranged that you can stay here for a couple of days, before Tobias will take you wherever you want to go.'

Marion sat down, head in hands. 'I never anticipated this. I have no home and no job now! How will I survive?' Her hands were shaking.

Fredrich poured them both a drink and came to sit beside her on the couch. He put his arm around her shoulders and kissed her cheek.

'We have done well together over this last year and a half, haven't we? I am very fond of you and I am going to miss you. I have an address to give you so that you can contact me. Anytime. It's with an old friend; a discreet old friend in Cologne. He's a lawyer. It is likely that I will have some difficulties in writing regularly, but I will do my best.'

'I can't think straight. What should I do?'

'Well we need to think about where you can live. Could you go back to your mother's house?'

'No never! She is too angry with me and she now has a soldier billeted there. My Aunt Ethel may possibly have me to stay. She is a kind woman and I get on well with her and my cousin June.'

'Right, I will get Tobias to take her a letter from you immediately. I need to know tonight that you will have somewhere to live.'

With Fredrich's help Marion wrote a brief note and Tobias was despatched with it, under instruction to wait for a written reply.

'Come, let us enjoy our last dinner,' Fredrich pulled her up from the leather seat and took her arm as he led her to the dining room. 'We must be thankful for all the good things we have enjoyed.'

'I know. But it's hard to realise it is over. I was lucky to have met you and I have learned so much from you. I really was a very unsophisticated girl, living a very simple life before I met you. I care for you a lot. You have been kind and patient with me.'

'I care for you too. You have supported me through difficult times,' he said.

That night, he held her close as she wept.

Yesterday, in the cold overcast morning, as he kissed her goodbye, she said, 'Till the next time, then.' She stood in the doorway, determined not to cry, as Fredrich was driven off.

The day passed quickly as Marion prepared to leave the house. She tried not to think where Fredrich might now be; it was too painful. She packed her clothes and her few treasured belongings. She found that Fredrich had left his monogramed cufflinks in her room and she placed them in an envelope along with some Deutschmarks and a few photos taken of them during the past year. She tucked them all into her handbag, along with the address Frederick had given her.

She looked longingly at all the books in the library, still so many unread, wishing she could take some with her. In the end she chose one book, which she and Fredrich had discussed at length, and slipped *Candide* into her suitcase, leaving a note in the desk drawer to say she was borrowing it.

Today, Tobias arrived as planned and she was driven down the hill, towards the town and around the coastal flats to her aunt's house. He eyed her in the mirror, noticing her puffy eyes. 'What are you going to do?'

"I don't know. Help my aunt with her vegetable crop. Lie low for a while, I think.'

'A pretty girl like you. You can have another boyfriend, I think. Yes?'

Marion lifted her head and looked straight back at him. 'No Tobias. I'm not going to do that again. No more boyfriends for me.'

'We will see! Perhaps someone younger. Yes?'

'No!' Feeling irritated by his persistence, she turned her head to stare out of the window, willing the conversation to end.

'Leave my boxes at the door please,' she instructed Tobias when they arrived at her aunt's house. Marion followed him to the door, clutching her handbag and suitcase. She put the case down and turned to Tobias to shake his hand. 'Thank you for your help and all the driving you have done for us, for me. Goodbye.'

'I will see you again no doubt?'

'No Tobias. I'm returning to my real world now. The fantasy life is over.'

Marion rang the doorbell and heard a key turning in the heavy oak door. She was drawn into the comforting embrace of her aunt.

CHAPTER TWENTY-NINE
DECEMBER 1942
BENTLEY PRIORY

Stella and Mark were dressing for a formal dinner at the Priory. They rarely got much time together, so Stella was excited that they could go somewhere as a couple. It was the first time that they had been invited for such a grand dinner in the Officers' Mess, at the invitation of the Air Marshall.

Mark observed that 'while they really were amongst the lesser mortals at the Priory' the invitation had come because of Mark being on a very 'hush-hush project' with another two mathematicians. The dinner was a token to reward them for the very long hours they were working, and because Churchill was coming up to see the 'top brass' for a briefing.

This project had started soon after Stella and Mark had

come to live in one of the apartments at the Priory, after their honeymoon in July. The apartment had one bedroom, a tiny bathroom and a larger living area, with a fold-down bed for David when he returned from Harrow for the weekends and holidays. Its furnishings were modest, but enough for their needs. It was on the third floor of the east wing and had been created from the loft space, well away from the officers' much grander suites.

The Priory was set in lush park-like grounds. The exterior of the main building, including its central clock tower, was covered in brown and green camouflage paint, with all its mullion windows blacked out.

Stella had found work at High Command immediately after she arrived. She was based in one of the local houses on the site and worked from late at night to late morning. With a group of WACs, who were plotting the flight paths of the bombing raids over Europe, Stella and three other women listened for the pilots' words to break radio silence.

The terse comment 'Log that' to their navigators signalled that a plane from Bomber Command was about to 'go down', along the route out or on the homerun. Stella's responsibility was to keep a record of the number and locations of the downed aircrafts. If a plane came down in the Channel or in some rural part of England, or Scotland, Stella's team co-ordinated rescue missions immediately. The work demanded close attention and cool nerves.

If the plane had gone down over 'Occupied' Europe, then the returning pilots surrendered their nightly logbooks when they reached their bases, and the cost of the previous night's missions in lives and planes was tallied up.

Stella had missed her friends in Cambridge but soon got to know a group of young women amongst the plotters and recorders with whom she socialised. It was much easier to be with people who weren't going to ask questions about her work, and who understood the daily pressures of the job.

Mark too mixed mostly with his workmates at Kestrel Grove, just a quarter of a mile away, and on the few occasions when he and Stella had free time together, they usually escaped to London to see a show.

David had settled well at his new school and enjoyed living, during the week, in a dormitory with the other students. He was learning Latin as well as French, and enjoying Advanced Mathematics, Physics and Design. His architectural ambitions were known to his house tutor who made sure that he undertook projects to advance his knowledge.

His tutor had commented on David's adaptability and the ease with which he related to all the boys. 'It can't have been easy coming here from two years in working-class Glasgow,' he had said to Stella.

At Mark's suggestion, Stella had joined the Channel Island Refugee Committee based in London. They were doing a lot of welfare work with the women and children who had been evacuated, giving grants of food, clothing and money to help these fatherless families to survive in the UK.

It was also their objective to lobby government on behalf of the people left in the Islands. They had set their goal for this Christmas to have the Channel Islanders mentioned in the King's Christmas speech to the nation. It was known that this would give great cheer to those at home.

Stella, along with many others, was writing to MPs asking them to support their cause. The committee was also gathering information about the worsening situation back in the Islands to pass on to the local papers. They felt it was important that word about the plight of the Islands was widely known.

Both Mark and Stella were worried by the infrequent and heavily censored news they received from Guernsey. They knew that Mark's parents were still living in Rosaire Avenue. They found it difficult to accept that German soldiers were billeted next door in Stella's former home while Stella's mother was now living with her parents. They were worried that Stella's grandfather had caught a chill after collecting shellfish, and that this had turned to pleurisy.

'I can't fix this dammed tie!' Mark called. 'I need my beautiful wife to help me.'

'Okay I think the tie is done right, this time.' She smiled at him, walked to the wardrobe, and pulled her wedding dress off the hanger. 'Will this dress be all right?' She stepped into it and smoothed it down over her hips.

Mark turned to look at her. 'You look lovely in it. Do you want me to button you up?'

'Yes, could you do them up for me. They are so hard to reach.' With this task completed he spun her around.

'You look as stunning as you did at our wedding,' he said, looking at her reflection in the wardrobe mirror. 'I do love you so much.' Stella curved her body into his and sighed as he lifted her hair and nuzzled the back of her neck. 'If you kiss me like that I might not want to go to dinner.'

'Just one more kiss then,' he said, repeating the gesture. 'And then we will go.'

'I think we will be sitting with Baz and Julie tonight. They tend to keep us civilians at arm's length at these dos. But I'll point out the 'big-wigs' from there. Anyway, the grub should be good, not to mention the wine. A far cry from what we get in the canteen.'

'I'll enjoy it. Baz and his wife are good company. And it's good to get dressed up and to do something different.'

Some hours later as they got ready for bed Stella said, 'You didn't tell me you would be introduced to the Prime Minister.'

'I didn't know. It had to do with the project. Churchill

clearly wants to keep abreast of what we are doing. You know, he acted a bit strangely when I told him I was from Guernsey. He snorted, muttered something and moved on to talk to Baz very quickly. Not too enamoured with the Channel Islanders I think.'

'That's what my committee thinks too.'

CHAPTER THIRTY

FEBRUARY 1943

GUERNSEY

MARION EASED HERSELF OUT OF BED GENTLY, AWAITING the light-headedness and nausea that had made her days, since New Year, unbearable. As she lowered her feet to the wooden floor and slowly stood erect, she felt well. 'My goodness! Is it over at last?' she wondered.

Marion found living in her aunt's house to be far removed from her life with Fredrich. She had to re-acquaint herself with small, dark rooms and the frequent absence of heating and light. Meals were spartan and the choices limited to what could be gathered or purchased locally. While the three of them had enjoyed the special items that Joseph had kindly given her from the 'Woodleigh' larder, they had only been able to eke them out over a few weeks. She now had to live like the rest of the local people, and she had found that difficult.

During the coldest nights of the winter the three of them slept in the kitchen on daybeds as it was the warmest place in the house. Heating water for baths had become an infrequent chore. Instead they made do with a kettle-full of water each, for a sponge bath in front of the coal range. They all avoided the freezing outhouse in the evenings, using a commode instead.

Some of Marion's evening clothes were sent to the clothes exchange so that she could, in return, get clothing suitable for her work in the glasshouses. June, who was the same size as Marion, replaced a few of her once 'tidy' Sunday clothes, which were now getting ragged, for some of the smart clothes in Marion's extensive wardrobe.

Aunt Ethel, who was of solid build, had to take down the heavy, tapestry curtains from a tiny attic bedroom and fashion a huge shawl, which she belted round her waist to wear in the house. At night it provided an extra cover for her bed. June and Marion described her as looking like a blue ball.

After an initial wariness towards each other they had settled into a comfortable life together. The glasshouses, no longer able to be heated for early tomatoes, now grew potatoes and winter vegetables. The Food Production Committee had decided what was to be planted and provided the seeds.

June and Marion worked in the glasshouses each day alongside two elderly Guernsey men provided by the Labour Department. While the family received only their allocated vegetable ration, they were able to take advantage of plant thinnings and any damaged crop. A large pot of soup was kept perpetually on the range and topped up with whatever became available. They were luckier than those living in the town without gardens to supplement their food supplies.

Marion's mother refused to come to Aunt Ethel's house once she knew that Marion was living there. She was angry with her sister-in-law and niece for housing Marion. At Christmas time the three women at Bordeaux had joined up with a neighbouring family to celebrate, as best they could, sharing their special Christmas rations.

Early in the New Year, Marion had realised she was pregnant. It took only a few days before Aunt Ethel and June also became aware, when she was wracked with a morning sickness which, in fact, lasted most of the day. Marion felt too ill to eat.

In the end her aunt said she must see a doctor as she was barely eating enough for herself, let alone a baby. At that stage Marion didn't know if she wanted this baby. She knew that there were local women who could help her, as they had helped many other local girls, in a similar situation.

When she told her aunt this, Aunt Ethel reacted angrily. 'You can't do that! Don't you know that a girl died just last month, having an abortion. It's too dangerous. Besides, some of those so-called midwives will stop their practice, now that one of them has been charged with murder.'

Her aunt was pragmatic. 'You're not the first and you won't be the last to be pregnant like this. Half the people on this Island were born on the wrong side of the blanket, including you! So, don't you listen to the gossips. They've all got skeletons in their cupboards. It's going to be a summer baby which will give it a good start. You and I will have to get out that old sewing machine and make a layette out of whatever we can find. Cheer up girl, it will be all right. And we will help you.'

Marion's first thought was to write to Fredrich at the address in Cologne he had given her. She had received a brief note from him in mid-December telling her that he was to be airlifted to Stalingrad on a provisioning plane the next morning. She knew it was unlikely that any letter would get to him easily, and any response was unlikely to be in time to help her make any decision about their child.

It was bad enough that she was already regarded by some people as a German's whore; what would it be like if she bore a German's bastard child? More questions beleaguered her. Could she raise a child on her own? Would Fredrich even want her to have his child? Would he stand by her once this war was over? It was all overwhelming and, because she felt so ill, she could not make rational decisions.

After eight miserable weeks, she was coaxed by her aunt into getting an appointment with a local doctor through the clinic at the Emergency Hospital. There she was put onto special food rations and given pills to reduce the sickness.

As she began to feel better Marion grew more optimistic and decided to continue with her pregnancy. 'I can't deceive Fredrich,' she finally decided. 'He needs to know and make his own decisions about me and the child, when he is free to do so.'

Another of the benefits of going to the clinic was that she had met up with Rachel again. Marion thought that Rachel would be angry to know that she was pregnant. Instead her friend had been understanding of her situation.

Rachel had been practical, saying it was important that Marion get good ante-natal care and that she needed to start on the special rations immediately to help the baby's development. Rachel had even offered to see if there were any baby things in their attic at the farm, that Marion could use.

'I know I didn't accept your meeting up with those German boys initially. I was annoyed because John had left here to join the Army. I think I was a bit jealous that your life was much more interesting than mine. You know John found a new girlfriend, don't you? Our engagement has been over for almost two years.'

'No. I didn't. How awful for you,' Marion said.

'Well I was a bit surprised, but I wasn't terribly hurt. Probably I only had wounded pride. We would have grown apart. Partly because of this war but also, I know I have grown up since he left here. We were so naive and inexperienced in 1939.'

'Weren't we just. Do you know anything about Stella? You know I resented her going, but it can't have been easy for her either. I heard that her father died suddenly.'

'Yes. I saw Stella's mother, just recently,' Rachel said. 'She has moved up to live with her parents at Bailiffs Cross, which isn't far from where I now live. They are quite old. Mrs Ferbrache was forced out of her house after her husband died, when the Germans requisitioned it. It was very difficult for her losing her husband after already losing Stella and David. Then to lose her home. She looked very tired and worn down. Anyway, she did give me news about Stella. You would never believe it!'

'Tell me.'

'She got married last June to Mark Webb! Apparently, when she was evacuated, she went to Cambridge and he helped her out. He later moved to somewhere near to London for his work, but about eighteen months ago, romance blossomed.'

'I can't believe it. Remember how Stella described him as snobbish?'

'I know. Do you remember when her parents asked him to take her to our senior dance and it was a real fizzer for her! I don't think either of them enjoyed it at all.'

'Well it's good now obviously! What is Stella doing?' Marion asked.

'She was doing some work to do with the war, just out of Cambridge, as well as studying part time. Now she is doing the same sort of work near to where Mark is based. David was up in Glasgow with his school but got a scholarship to a grammar school, near where Stella lives, so now he is staying with them. Mrs Ferbrache is very happy that David and Stella can be together. She says she has less to worry about now.'

Marion was able to talk freely to Rachel about Fredrich. She sketched out their months together and told her about his departure at short notice, and the fact that he didn't yet know she was pregnant.

'That must be dreadful for you. How are you managing?'

'Well my aunt and cousin at Bordeaux have been marvellous. They took me in as my mother has disowned me. The three of us get on well and I work in the glasshouses with June. It's a far cry from my life with Fredrich though. But it's okay.

'Fredrich was a generous man and very thoughtful. I miss our conversations. He was very knowledgeable and sophisticated in his tastes.' Marion added quickly, 'He was no Nazi either. In fact, that was why he was transferred. Because he disapproved of the Nazis' use of Todt workers. He also thought that building all these fortifications was a waste of resources and weakening the war efforts of the Germans. He made that apparent to his superiors and it was held against him.'

'Yes, not all the Germans here are Nazis. Some were forced into uniform,' Rachel responded. 'I've had some dealings at work with a doctor at the German Hospital. He was conscripted and had to give up his specialist training. He's a very good person. A doctor first, a German second.'

'It's a pity we drifted apart, but I would like to spend time with you again,' Marion said.

'Yes, me too. I work better hours in my current job, and you will have to come to the clinic regularly. We can get together more easily.'

Marion returned home from the clinic feeling much happier than she had been in the months since Fredrich departed. She knew that she could rely on her aunt and cousin, as well as her friendship with Rachel, to support her. With them on her side she could face up to the other people who would condemn her.

CHAPTER THIRTY-ONE
MARCH 1943
BENTLEY PRIORY

Stella woke to a beautiful spring morning. Sun streamed into the apartment and she could hear birds trilling in the adjacent parkland. On the previous evening, she and her fellow workers had celebrated the forthcoming Easter break with a small party in the cafeteria, after work. It had been a happy event with much laughter and good humour.

Since Christmas, Mark had been away for some four weeks with his project team and Stella had missed his company. Baz was also away, but he and Julie had a baby boy, who kept Julie busy. Mark's team had all been removed to an unidentified Air Force base in the north of England to complete their project.

All Stella knew was that they were having some mathematical difficulties and working long hours to 'sort things out.'

This afternoon though, Stella was going into Harrow to fetch David home for the holidays. They were planning to go to a movie and catch the late bus back to the Priory. Stella had saved her food coupons to ensure that David had his share of chocolates for Easter. They would celebrate with a special dinner in the canteen on Sunday night, with other families. It would be easier to eat there than try to cook in her skimpy kitchen where she was reliant on one-pot meals.

'We are comfortably off,' thought Stella.

A Red Cross message from her mother implied that things were much more difficult in Guernsey. Her mother's note had been redacted in places, but she had revealed that she was now working at a communal parish kitchen. She said Stella's grandparents were very frail and had each been ill during the winter.

A letter had come from Mark's father recently as well, but Mr Webb had devised a coded way to pass on information and only Mark could work out his cryptic clues. Stella found it impenetrable and needed Mark to decode it for her. It would have to wait till Mark came home.

From her contacts in the Channel Islands Society, Stella heard many stories of privation and illnesses which led her committee to be increasingly concerned for the families left behind. Their efforts last Christmas to get the Channel Islanders a radio message had failed. The committee was now focussing on writing to all Members of Parliament to keep them informed of the plight of the Islanders. However, it appeared as if the establishment didn't really want British people to know what was happening in the Islands.

Stella was now on a subcommittee which made speakers available to various community groups in the Home Counties, to pass on the news about the Islanders. The committee was very frustrated that they could get little publicity and that only a few church groups had expressed any interest in having them as speakers. Everyone in England seemed to be dealing with their own wartime concerns, with little energy for other, more distant, peoples' plight.

Stella met David at his hostel in the early afternoon. He was packed and ready to leave but wanted Stella to meet his chum, Richard. Richard's family lived in Bristol and he was going to spend his holiday with his grandmother in London. Stella was introduced to a tall, dark-haired boy with glasses and a west-counties accent. 'He's a "scholi", too,' explained David, which Stella understood to mean that he was also on a scholarship.

'Richard is a year above me, but he is keen on art and we would like to go to some galleries in London during Easter break. Stella, can I go up to London to meet Richard next week?'

'I need to think about that David.'

'Please, please,' David persisted. 'Just say yes.'

'I'm not saying no, I need to think it through and work out a convenient time. Why don't you get Richard's grandmother's address and I will try to arrange a time convenient for us both?'

'I'm okay going up on the train if you are worried about that!'

'Yes, I know. Let's just say "probably" and work out the details when we get home.'

'We should take that as a "yes" then, Richard,' David said. 'I'll be seeing you then, somewhere, sometime,' he sang. Both boys started to laugh and Stella, with eyebrows raised, shook her head. 'I can see you are growing up fast and that you are going to be a handful in future!'

Over afternoon tea in a local shop David talked about school, about the boys in his form and his meeting Richard at Sunday high tea with his tutor.

'Mr Comrey-Jones thought we would have things in

common. And we do. So, we knock around a bit after school. His father is a minister and his mother died, so that's why he is a "scholi" and why it's hard for him to go home.'

'I understand why he might be a good friend for you. Do you get on all right with your form-mates, though?'

'Oh yes. I don't get bullied or anything like that. I learned how to stand up to bullies in Glasgow. No-one tries it on more than once. Mr Hemmings taught me how to deal with them. With words.

'He told me, "You can choose to either sink or swim", and I'm a swimmer.'

Stella laughed. 'Dad would be so proud of you. Tell me about the friends in your form?'

'I get on well with a couple of them. Really well! Angus and Tom. They don't come from rich families. More like ours. We three play soccer and cricket and are doing well in class. Some of the boys are not very interesting, especially some of those who went to prep school together. They stick together at school and in the holidays, and they aren't interested in us.'

He elaborated: 'They think they are sophisticated because they like fancy parties and shooting animals. You don't need to worry. I'm finding my own way and following my own interests.'

'Well, I'm pleased to hear that. You do sound very mature. Some adults find snobbery a bit hard to take, but you seem to have not let it affect you.'

'No point!' he said.

At David's prompting they attended Charlie Chaplin's first talking film, *The Great Dictator*, which was slowly doing the rounds of county theatres. David particularly enjoyed the parody of Hitler, and left the theatre copying the speech and mannerisms of Adenoid Yankel, the dictator.

Stella found the caricatures funny but was disconcerted by

the film's close approximation of what had happened to Jewish people in Germany and Austria in the 1930s. She was quiet on the bus home whilst David, unaware, enjoyed reliving the amusing parts of the film.

Midway through the holiday, Stella took a day's leave and she and David caught an early train to London. They met Richard in Trafalgar Square and the boys left Stella so that they could spend time in the National Gallery, arranging to meet up with Stella again at 4 pm for tea.

Stella made her way down Regent Street to Oxford Street. She needed to buy some clothes for herself and for David, who had grown a few inches since he started at Harrow, nine months ago. She enjoyed looking into the large shop windows as she walked past the lavish stores. She was surprised to see the range of luxury items still available for those with money. She made her purchases quickly at Marks and Spencer's before walking on to Marble Arch, heading towards the Serpentine, where she bought a dry paste sandwich for her lunch. It was the only sandwich on offer at the little kiosk in the park.

A chill breeze was blowing but, wrapped in the woollen coat she had brought from Guernsey, Stella was warm enough to sit on a park bench to eat. She enjoyed watching the wide variety of people wandering through the park and speculated about their lives.

There were servicemen, in many different coloured uniforms, probably on furlough from Allied armies. Most had their arms wrapped around a young woman, she noticed. There were young nannies shepherding toddlers attached by walking reins to large-wheeled perambulators. Also, many elderly couples were getting their daily outing. It looked like a peaceful, normal spring day in Hyde Park.

'If the Germans had got here in 1941 it would, no doubt,

look very different,' she mused. 'Much like the Islands must now look! It must be so awful seeing German flags flying; with German soldiers wherever you look.'

Stella and the boys had tea and cake at a Lyons Corner House whilst they enthusiastically told her of their exploration of the gallery. Both boys were delighted with their discoveries. Richard was most knowledgeable about painting styles and his face lit up as he described various paintings for Stella. He seemed to be a nice boy, though clearly a lonely one. 'You and David should do this some other holidays,' Stella offered. Richard nodded enthusiastically: 'I'd like that.'

CHAPTER THIRTY-TWO
APRIL 1943
GUERNSEY

WELL WE HAVE HAD ANOTHER HARSH WINTER. THERE WERE BIG gales in October and January, with many fishing boats and glasshouses wrecked. This greatly worsened our food supplies. Our gas supply was cut from 2 pm to 5 pm each day thus limiting time available for lighting and water-heating.

We are working longer hours at the hospital and are all very tired. The hospital is desperately short of non-medical items, like linen, crockery and cutlery. We have had to appeal to local people to help us with any surplus items that they haven't yet bartered away.

Because of petrol shortages, doctors can only visit each parish once a day. So, if people need help after the doctor has finished his rounds in that parish, they must wait till the next day to see him.

I have heard, unofficially, that Dr Konrad has been known to help in some emergencies, of which there have been a few.

One was when a group of men were trying to cross the minefields to get to the beach, to pick shellfish and get seaweed to eat. One died, and three had serious injuries, including one with his foot blown off. We had to find blood donors very quickly, but the records had not been kept up to date. One of the initial survivors did not get help soon enough and died. So, two more families are without breadwinners. We felt so helpless.

Our joint Medical Planning Committee's lobbying has had some successes. A children's allowance has been agreed to by the Controlling Committee. This gives five shillings per week for each child under fifteen years, to help parents pay for increasingly expensive food and clothing. The local paper also set up a Help the Children Fund which so far has brought in four thousand pounds for about 500 destitute families.

We have had many illegitimate births since Christmas, the result of last year's lovely summer. All pregnant women are admitted to the hospital at thirty-eight weeks, so that they don't go into labour at home, unattended. The hospital is asking for people who can board out some of the unwanted babies of either soldiers or Todt workers. I am so glad that Marion has decided to keep her baby as I don't think that these other babies will thrive without a mother's love.

The Medical Planning Committee has arranged to feed people if Guernsey is cut off from food supplies from France. The communal cooking facilities will be transformed into proper feeding stations. Ninety first-aid posts are established around the Island where a network of volunteers can do basic first aid, since the ambulance won't be able to run without petrol.

Stealing has been rife from farms and shops. Sometimes when the culprits have been the Todt workers, for whom life is so horrific, that is excusable. At the same time, some of the farmers and traders have been charged with black-market offences. One of Dad's neighbours was illegally selling meat at exorbitant prices, which seemed inexcusable. It feels as though our social morality is breaking down as our physical plight worsens. 'Survival of the fittest,' I suppose, but it is not Christian behaviour.

I had a terrible row with Dad in February. He still had included me on the housing occupation list, inside our front door. He is supposed to make any unused bedrooms available for billets. I was afraid that he, and I, could get caught out since I was on Mrs Perelle's house list, as well. He raged at me again and told me to mind my own business, in future. I will keep my distance from him, as our constant differences upset my mother.

I haven't much free time now, and what time I have off, I usually need to catch up on sleep. Perhaps I will feel more energetic now that we are coming up to summer again. Cobo beach has just been opened again, so I plan to go there on Sunday. Too cold yet to swim, but a chance to relax and have a day out.

There will be lots of people there, no doubt, as all the parks have been closed for months, because the troops' horses need to be fed on that grassland. Everyone needs the chance to be outdoors, in the sunlight, to boost their health.

CHAPTER THIRTY-THREE
JULY 1943
GUERNSEY

On the third Monday in July Marion checked into the maternity ward. Her baby was due within the week and she was glad to have some bed rest, as her ankles and legs had swollen in the summer heat. The baby's head was engaged, and Marion found that climbing the narrow twisting stairs at Aunt Ethel's cottage had become an awkward task.

Besides that, she was looking forward to catching up with Rachel when she came off duty each day. Rachel had been a true friend to her over the past few months. The two of them had rediscovered the basis of their teenage rapport and begun to confide in each other once again.

In May, at long last, a letter from Germany had arrived for

Marion. A German soldier on a bicycle arrived at the house in the early afternoon and knocked on the door. Marion, who had been resting on her bed in the heat of the day, lumbered down the stairs in response to Aunt Ethel's call that there was a letter for her.

She was excited and thankful that a letter had arrived after such a long wait, and was surprised that the envelope had been typed, expecting to see Fredrich's elegant script instead. She returned to her room to enjoy the letter in private.

'I wonder what he thinks about this baby?' she thought as she pulled the letter from its envelope.

She unfolded the paper realising immediately that it was not from Fredrich. Seeing only the name at the foot of the page she screamed loudly 'No!' which brought her cousin June running up to her room.

'What's wrong? Mum said you had a letter from Fredrich.'

Marion handed her the letter. 'It's from the lawyer. I know it is bad news. I can't read it. Tell me what he says.'

June silently read the letter then looked at her cousin sitting anxiously on the bed. She sat down beside Marion and put her arm around her waist. 'It's not good news, I'm afraid. Fredrich is missing in action, somewhere in Russia.'

Marion sat silent and pale-faced. After a minute or two she asked, 'What else did he say? Did Fredrich know about the baby?'

'No. Herr Drukner says he sent your letter to the Army Headquarters, but it was never dispatched from there. It was returned to him much later with the information about Fredrich being missing. He has written to you as soon as he could find out some details. He has kept your letter in case he hears something positive.'

'Does he say what happened and why Fredrich is missing? When did it happen?'

'Well, this Justice Drukner said he has made some enquiries of army friends and of some of Fredrich's family, but not much information is available. He said that Fredrich flew into Stalingrad in a transport plane taking supplies to the troops on 19th December. Fredrich was supposed to be in Stalingrad only briefly, gathering military intelligence to assist the army. Whatever that means! Then there was a big battle and he was trapped in the city with most of the German Army, trying to hold on to the city.

'He says the Russians took thousands of prisoners when they regained the city at the beginning of February, but also many German soldiers died in the fighting. That is why they can't be sure what happened to Fredrich.'

She continued, 'He says that Hitler said the army was heroic.'

'So, he may be a prisoner of the Russians then?' Marion asked.

'He said he would contact you when anything more is known.'

'I thought he was going to say Fredrich is dead. But he may have got away; or been taken prisoner, then. I will have to be hopeful.'

'Yes, it's all uncertain. You must not distress yourself. It's not good for your baby.'

'So Fredrich doesn't know about this baby either,' Marion realised.

'No! Your letter is still undelivered.'

'Well I hope Fredrich's friend keeps it safe. I wouldn't want his family to know, before he did.'

Marion kept herself busy preparing for the baby's arrival, convincing herself that Fredrich was probably out of danger, in a camp somewhere. She knew now, from gossip on the Island, that the major defeat of the Germans in Stalingrad had finally turned the war in the Allies' favour. She felt hopeful that it could not last too much longer. In the meantime, she must focus on keeping herself well.

She had continued to help in the glasshouses until a few weeks ago when her bulky body began to make it hard to bend forward. Most days, though, she was able to help in the packing shed, where their vegetables were prepared to go to the local market.

Since the weather had become warm, she had begun to see some of the Todt workers out and about looking for food from the hedgerows. A couple of men, in their blue striped pyjamas, passed regularly down their U-shaped lane. At first Marion had smiled at them as they passed by. She had been struck by their youth and their thin bodies in their tattered clothes.

She asked her aunt if there were any of her uncle's clothes still upstairs and, on learning that there were some in the loft, asked her aunt if some could be given to the workers. Her aunt had seemed doubtful.

'We might get into trouble. The Germans have asked us to give up unused clothing before, but I couldn't give Uncle's clothes to the Germans. Harry would turn in his grave if I did that.'

'I think we could arrange it, so they wouldn't know who had given them any clothes. Their pyjama things are so worn and thin. They are barely decent and certainly give no warmth.'

'If you think we wouldn't be found out, I could find something or other.'

Aunt Ethel and June brought a box from the loft down onto the landing and the three of them riffled through the clothes. They found an old gabardine raincoat and a woollen jacket which Marion said would at least provide some protection in the blustery weather.

A few days later, when Marion was in the garden, she saw the two men at the top of the lane. She called out to

June, who ran into the house and collected the clothes and the two young women had then hastened up the lane, in the opposite direction, until they reached the corner where the lane reconnected with the main road.

They looked back towards their house and could just see the men still ambling along, looking for any plants they might be able to eat. Ensuring that there was no-one else around, June placed the clothes at the foot of the signpost, then they continued to walk home the long way, thus avoiding meeting the men. Later that day, when June went to collect their milk ration, she noted that the clothes were no longer where they had left them.

When Marion was outside, hanging out clothes with her aunt, a couple of days later, the same two men walked past the glasshouse. Each sported a new item of clothing over their pyjamas. Aunt Ethel laughed. 'It's good to see those old things put into use again. I think your uncle would approve.'

That evening June commented that the two men came at roughly the same time of day, on Sundays and Wednesdays. Their pattern of foraging along their lane seemed regular. She wondered if they could continue to leave some things for the men; maybe some of the vegetables or some other food, on a regular basis. Her mother had agreed so long as they were very careful not to alert either the Germans, or the local Controlling Committee. 'We need to make sure the neighbours aren't aware either. Some of them would very likely report us.'

From then on, June had begun to leave a couple of potatoes or carrots or some early beans in the bushes at the corner of the little-used lane. She was careful to place them there just before the men usually arrived so that no one else might find them. Some old socks and shirts were also left out, over the next few weeks. After that the two men would call out 'Hello!' to them if they were in the garden. The women knew that their gifts were appreciated.

Once admitted to the hospital Marion was placed in a ward with three other pregnant women who were ready to give birth. One woman was older and about to have her third child. She had frightened the others with stories of her past experiences. One other young woman was married but this would be her first child. Marion and the other young woman were single and neither of them chose to reveal their baby's parentages. Nor did they discuss their futures.

Marion talked to Rachel about the childbirth stories she had heard. Rachel laughed: 'Look, it's different for everyone. Some people feel pain more acutely than others. Some have a quick delivery; others take a long time. You have kept fit, you are young, and your baby is not too big. I will try to be with you when your labour begins and tell you what to do.'

'That would be good as Mrs Sidwell has got us all a bit scared.'

On the 31st July Marion awoke in the early hours to find her bed wet and realised that her waters had broken. She got up to find the night nurse who confirmed her suspicion that the birth process would soon begin.

'Go back to sleep if you can, you need to be well-rested,' she instructed Marion.

Contractions awoke Marion at 6 am and her labour was short and intense. With Rachel encouraging her, Marion's baby girl was delivered by midmorning. Marion lay back on her bed, with her swaddled baby beside her, whilst Rachel ensured that a message was delivered to Ethel and June, to tell of the six-pound arrival.

When she left the hospital a week later, the baby was suckling, and Marion had become confident in handling her little girl, who was not yet named. Marion was unsure if she should put Fredrich's name on the child's birth registration, but she was certain that her daughter would have her surname.

After discussions over a few days with her aunt and cousin, Candice Rachel Le Prevost was registered as the daughter of Marion Elizabeth Le Prevost with the father said to be 'Unknown.' As Rachel suggested, Marion wrote immediately to advise Fredrich's friend about the baby's birth.

CHAPTER THIRTY-FOUR
AUGUST 1943
GUERNSEY

I'M A GODMOTHER! MARION HAD HER BABY GIRL ON 1ST AUGUST, and I was able to be there for Candice's birth. The baby is lovely, with Marion's dark hair and olive skin. Marion says that her dark blue eyes come from Fredrich. She seems to be a placid baby and Marion is a very natural mother.

It is such a privilege for me to have a formal role to play in Candice's life, which, given Marion's situation, will be important. Her baptism was a quiet occasion, held privately, with just Marion's aunt, cousin and I there, to support them. It was, though, a happy event, in our increasingly miserable circumstances. It has given a real lift to my mood.

I was low in spirits again over the last winter. A whole lot of different things seemed to get on top of me. Physically things have got tougher with ever smaller food rations, as well as restrictions on using gas, electricity and water.

Add to that, difficulty in obtaining basic hygienic items. For example, we are now reduced to using chalk dust combined with soot as a substitute for toothpaste. We use ashes mixed with sand for our version of soap. It's impossible to feel clean, let alone pampered. How I long for a big hot bath, with Pears' soap and soft towels; something I used to take for granted!

While recently we were able to get some fabric for new clothes, the choice was limited to either a coarse blue or grey cotton. Nothing to make me feel young or feminine. The dresses, all made by a contingent of local seamstresses, are made from the same pattern and with only three sizes available. All told, we all look like and feel like elderly nuns in our ill-fitting uniformity. Getting replacement underwear is a problem. Luckily, I can get away without wearing a bra, but as there is no elastic available as replacements when it perishes, I must tie up my knickers with twine. So ugly!

As for shoes, all have been re-soled in wood, rather than leather or rubber. They are heavy to wear and make a loud clatter on the hospital's wooden floors.

Another threat to my femininity is my body. I am very thin, my face gaunt, my clavicle protruding, and all my joints knobbly. I haven't had a period for many months and my breasts have all but disappeared. I hate to catch a glance of myself in a mirror. I am aghast at the skinny stranger I see there.

I have experienced a gulf growing between me and my father and brother this year. They see everything as very black and white. Dad's hatred of the Germans is too consuming. He is also voicing very harsh judgements about many of the local people. It has turned him into a constantly angry man. I find it upsets me and I am 'on edge' when I am at home.

My father was not well disposed to my rekindling my relationship with Marion. He demanded to know why I would *condone her having a relationship with a German and for her having a child! He said he knew her mother had disowned her, and he would do the same to me if I behaved like Marion. He said that some men on Guernsey would get even with Marion and the other 'Jerry bags', when the time came.*

I am horrified by his attitude and lack of understanding. Peter is copying Dad, with all the same prejudices. While Mum keeps wanting me to come home for visits, I am avoiding it.

Everyone on the Island [Germans, Islanders and the slave workers] is having to find their own way to survive. While there is generosity there is also pettiness and malice. This occupation is bringing out our best and our worst characters.

The reason for my winter gloom, though, was additionally complicated, I confess. I find myself still longing for an ongoing personal relationship with Dieter. I know he is a good man. I desperately want to have him as a friend. I didn't know the physical wrench of loneliness before.

We've only seen each other at planning meetings, but after one meeting he helped me put on my coat. I had to fight the almost overwhelming impulse to let myself sink into his outstretched arms. I think he might have felt a similar whim; but that could be wishful thinking! I cannot stop thinking about him and wishing...

In retrospect, I didn't experience these physical pangs for John!

It was good to be able to talk to Marion about my confused feelings. She understood my self-torment. She simply said I needed to do what was right for me. It's just that often I don't know what that is! My wants versus my obligations. Sadly, I know it must be the latter. It is bitter-sweet.

Marion, in return, has confided in me. She admits she was seeking adventure when she became involved with Fredrich. She wanted a more glamorous life. She says, though, she came to care for him and as time went by and appreciated his kindness. It will be important for Candice to hear good things about her father as she grows up. She will encounter too many people who will dismiss him simply as a 'German.'

Marion says that motherhood has changed her. She is enraptured with her baby and determined to give her the best life she can. She says she is trying not to think ahead and to enjoy each day with whatever it brings.

She told me that Fredrich had introduced her to Voltaire's writings which she found helpful. Essentially, he said life was just a journey and you must make your own way through whatever territory you encounter. The measure of a person is how well they face up to that journey.

She has now lent me Candide, *the book that she and Fredrich read together, and which she has celebrated, with Candice's name.*

One way or another she has helping me to cope! Hopefully I am doing the same for her.

CHAPTER THIRTY-FIVE
DECEMBER 1943
BENTLEY PRIORY

MARK AND STELLA WERE IN THE MIDDLE OF PACKING UP their rooms at the Priory and preparing to move back to Cambridge. They were both in high spirits as the local GP had just confirmed that Stella was pregnant, with their baby due in late June. Last night they had announced their news to friends at the Priory, during their farewell dinner. Baz and Julie, who were also leaving, had been thrilled for them, and Julie had promised that they could have Christopher's outgrown baby clothes.

Mark had returned home from Lincolnshire in late May, with his team, in great excitement, finally able to talk about their successful project.

'We managed to work out a trajectory to drop Wallis's bouncing bomb onto the lake and have it slam into the dam wall to breach it, so that it flooded industries down the River Ruhr, and put them out of commission,' he told Stella. 'We were able to hit two dams.

'It was mathematically complex. It all depended on the weather and the lake's surface conditions on the day. But we built up a series of scenarios, each with their specific angles and hoped we could predict the right model to use, on the day selected for the raid. One out of the dozens available proved right for the day.'

'It must have been extremely dangerous for the pilots, flying so low over the dams?'

'Yes, it was. But they also had to avoid being spotted flying into Germany, which meant flying very low all the way there, to first, avoid radar and then, the search lights and gun batteries. Some of the pilots had been on an earlier flying raid, at very low levels, a few weeks before. They knew what to expect this time. On the first mission, their target was Berlin. You know, the flight where four Mosquitoes dropped bombs on a radio station where Goering was making a speech to celebrate Hitler's 10th anniversary.'

'I didn't know that involved low flying.'

'No, it wasn't announced at the time because we didn't want the Germans to suspect we had some new tricks to call on. Those planes flew across the North Sea just above wave height and when they got over land, they tree-hopped all the way to their drop site. Our raid did the same thing.' He elaborated: 'They had to modify a number of the Lancaster bombers, to lighten them so that they could carry Wallis's bombs. It was a pretty complex mission in all.'

'Amazing!' Stella responded. 'Guy Gibson and his crews have done such an outstanding job for us all. But your team had a pretty important job as well. You must be thrilled at the mission's success?'

'Yes, it was both exciting and nerve-wracking. We are all satisfied with the outcome. But we lost seven crews along the way. It was a high price those boys paid.'

Mark described the success of both the bombing raids as a turning point for both Britain and Germany. 'For us it feels as though the tide has really turned in our favour. For the Germans, they know that fighting on two fronts has weakened them disastrously.'

'I've got some leave due in June, so we should get off-base for a few days. Where would you like to go?'

'That would be lovely. We need some time together. What about North Wales? Alison told me that it was a beautiful place to visit.'

'Well we might have a whale of a time then,' Mark laughed. 'Seriously though, we need to make some plans for our future. I think my secondment here could end fairly soon.'

Mark's leave didn't eventuate till early September. On a drizzly, cool day they caught the train from London through Chester and along the north coast of Wales to Bangor, where they had rented a cottage overlooking the sea for a couple of weeks.

They marvelled at the views from the train as it steamed slowly along the coast, past picturesque holiday towns where rows of caravans sat in large parks alongside the railway line. On the north side were the flat grey sands stretching out into the bay for miles. To the south the vivid green fields dotted with sheep led up to the steep, treeless, mountain sides, where the skeletal forms of pitheads and the black slash of slag heaps were to be seen.

'I'm so glad we chose to come here. I love this countryside. It's so mountainous and wild,' Stella announced. 'We seem very tiny in this huge landscape.'

In Bangor they found a taxi which took them to their destination. Stella exclaimed with delight when she saw the cottage. It was a low, grey, stone building with a steeply gabled, slate roof and mullioned windows.

She was surprised to see how closely it resembled cottages on the west coast of Guernsey. It had two rooms downstairs with flagstone floors and two small bedrooms in the attic space. The living room had a glass door opening onto a terrace, which provided sweeping views of the Anglesey Straits, including the lofty sculptural bridge joining the mainland to the Island.

They felt like a couple of children rushing around uncovering the secret spaces of the house and garden. It was to be their first long holiday together as well as their first time living in a house, entirely on their own. They stood on the terrace watching the sunset, arms entwined. 'This feels like a second honeymoon,' she whispered.

'I think it will be,' he replied.

Their first few days at the cottage were delightfully lazy. They got up late, ate breakfast in a sunny corner of the garden, read and took long walks through the wooded Roman camp, up the lane from the cottage. On other days they strolled down the steep hill into the town to buy provisions. Towards the end of the week they started travelling further afield on local buses, taking in the many historic and scenic places close at hand.

One of their highlights was a trip across the barren tops of Anglesey to the western lighthouse, where they perched on the cliff top, surrounded by screaming seabirds, allowing themselves to be pummelled by the tumultuous winds coming in from the sombre Irish Sea. Like children they stretched out their arms, leaning forward so the wind would hold their weight, laughing as they teetered when the wind speed dropped away. They scrambled down the rocky path to the foot of the lighthouse and sat on its stone platform to eat a picnic lunch.

Another trip saw them climbing along the narrow castle walls at Caernarvon, under the beady eyes of the resident ravens. And yet another journey gave them access to the slopes of Snowdonia where they clambered, in bleak weather, through bracken and bogs, identifying the myriads of plants on the treeless slopes. Various field birds flew upwards with raucous cries as they scrambled past. They felt like the only people in a vast landscape.

At the end of their holiday they returned to the Priory and began to make necessary arrangements for moving back to Cambridge.

Mark was soon offered a place in an applied mathematics research unit, attached to the university. The Americans had given a large financial grant to enable the unit to develop a machine which could manipulate huge amounts of information. Mark was again working with colleagues he had studied with before the war commenced. Baz was also to join the team.

'It's a bit of an intellectual hot-house,' Mark said. 'Maths is certainly getting more and more interesting. When I started at Cambridge, I thought I would, at worst be a schoolteacher, at best a don. Now the field is expanding so fast that I can enjoy applying my knowledge, more than I would have teaching reluctant students.'

Finding somewhere to live was more difficult because of a housing shortage. However, in November, Mrs Styles had phoned them to say that she was planning to move to Kent to live with her daughter. She asked if Mark and Stella would like to buy 'Redleaf' from her.

They immediately agreed to do so and moved into the now tired property where Mark had spent most of his student days. It needed repairs and painting, but afforded them a roomy home, within cycling distance of the town centre. With David's help, during the Christmas vacation, they started on the major job of renovation.

They very quickly re-established their connections with old friends. Stella wanted to continue working for a few more months but discovered the Civil Service was unwilling to give work to married women. She asked her old friend Alison who oversaw the archives section of the city library, and who had recently married Mark's old flatmate Peter, about finding employment there. In February, a part-time position became available, which Stella accepted with enthusiasm.

CHAPTER THIRTY-SIX
MAY 1944
GUERNSEY

MARION TOOK CANDICE OUT INTO THE GARDEN FOR A sunbathe. The little girl was now crawling and pulling herself up onto her feet using any obliging support. She had a mop of dark hair and a wide toothy smile. Candice had remained a happy child enjoying the care and attention of three doting women. There was always someone available to cuddle her or play. While there were no toys, Candice was content with pots, pans and utensils. She loved to be sung to and for stories to be told to her.

During the winter months Marion's milk had dried up, which had upset her greatly. But Candice had adapted quickly to cows' milk and her rations had been just adequate. Now

Candice was happily chewing on whatever was available, including the rusks she was eligible to receive.

Marion had to insist that her aunt and cousin didn't give Candice any of their rations as it was important that they all stayed as well-nourished as possible. The death rate for people had gone up markedly over the winter months for both Islanders and Todt workers.

Keeping Candice clothed was more of a challenge. Old cardigans were unravelled and reknitted up as leggings and sweaters for the baby. None were in the traditional baby colours, nor textures, but Candice was kept warm. She still slept in a large drawer laid on the floor, but a bigger bed was soon going to be necessary.

Marion, June and Aunt Ethel were kept busy growing potatoes and vegetables in the glasshouses over the winter months. Sometimes they had assistance, but their preference was to meet their production quotas independently. Aunt Ethel had realised that the fewer people who knew about Marion and the baby, the better for all of them. After one disastrous visit by Marion to the St Sampson's shops in August, where she was verbally abused, Marion had stayed at the vinery throughout the entire winter, not venturing far from the local lanes. Visits from Rachel helped break the monotony of her daily routine.

June was able to move around the community and she brought back the news and gossip to tell the other two. A daily underground newspaper called GUNZ [Guernsey Underground News] passed on by a trusted friend in St Sampson's, had kept them up to date with some of the Allied advances until February. The Islanders had all become aware of British aircraft regularly flying over. After four long years they again heard bombing in Normandy. They saw this as a sign of hope; that finally the Allies would regain a toe hold in France, and then come to the Islanders' rescue. Aunt Ethel said, 'This ordeal will soon end. We must keep hope alive just a bit longer.'

June had formed a bond with one of the two Todt workers who roamed their lane regularly over the winter, when food was hard to get. Unlike Marion, June was able to speak the Guernsey patois, and with this had been able to converse regularly, albeit briefly, with one of the men, Jacques, who came from Normandy.

He had been rounded up in Granville in early 1943, in a raid looking for able-bodied men to work on the Island. His ration card was confiscated, and he was forced onto a boat going to Guernsey, to help build the German Industrial Railway. Jacques had no chance to advise his family of his plight, before his forced migration, because they lived on a farm, some ten miles inland from the town.

Jacques spent up to 14 hours a day toiling out-doors, but unlike most of the other Todt workers, had some freedom to move around the Island. Whilst it was forbidden for Islanders to feed the workers, June continued to provide him with whatever they could spare, helping him to survive. Suddenly, in late April, their developing friendship ended abruptly when he was urgently repatriated, with other French Todt workers

Marion had developed great affection for her aunt. Whilst her uncle had been alive Aunt Ethel had been an unassuming background figure in Marion's life. Since her uncle's death Marion had witnessed the growing strength of her aunt. Her compassion and wisdom filled the gap left by Marion's mother, in the same way that her uncle had replaced her father.

Marion knew how fortunate she was to have had such support. Without it she would probably not have been able to care for her child. The thought of having had to leave Candice with strangers, or worse, in the new home for illegitimate children, was blood-chilling. Instead, Candice was snugly placed with love and attention, despite their straightened circumstances.

CHAPTER THIRTY-SEVEN
SEPTEMBER 1944
GUERNSEY

What a day I have had. I am still reeling and overwhelmed with emotion. There is no-one I can talk to right now, so I have returned to this much-neglected diary!

I was working in my office this morning – updating the inventory of all the medical supplies available, since we can obtain no more – when Dieter appeared at my door. He said he had an appointment with Dr Shirtcliffe, but asked if he could talk to me briefly, if I wasn't too busy. I told him what I was doing but that I could easily stop to talk to him.

He said it was timely that our hospital was requisitioning all supplies held by community doctors and residents, now that supplies from France had been cut off since June. He felt it was most uncertain when a new supply chain would commence. He wanted to know if we had met with any success. I said yes and no; mostly some aged medicines from the back of peoples' cupboards and a few tatty rags.

Dieter said he would be discussing natural remedies with Dr Shirtcliffe. He said they were working on nutritional requirements for the Islanders – indicating the folder in his hand. They were calculating the minimum number of calories required for the survival of men, women and children, according to their ages and occupations. I made some feeble joke about us all now 'living on thin air.' He said 'Yes, I know. But all our forces, the Island people and the remaining Todt workers are now in the same predicament.'

He sat down and said, 'These are times of uncertainty and we none of us know exactly how it will all end. But it will end. Your people will regain their freedom.'

I said, 'Fairly soon, I hope. The Allies must come to relieve us. It's been four months since the Normandy landings.'

He nodded.

He dug into his pocket and pulled out a piece of paper. 'I want you to have this,' he said.

I looked at it and it was an address. I was surprised. 'Is this your family's address?'

'Yes. I thought I should make sure you knew it.'

My mind was racing. Why this, why now?

I picked up my purse and put the piece of paper in my wallet. I said, 'Do you want my family address Dieter?'

'Rachel. I hope you don't mind but I have already given it to my parents! I wanted them to know how to contact you in the future if necessary.'

I was surprised. 'You have written to your parents about me?'

He nodded.

I felt fear. What next? I swallowed hard and we just looked at each other in silence.

'We should be thinking ahead. Things here could get a little crazy very quickly. I don't want us to lose contact in the very uncertain future awaiting us. I want you to be able to contact me.'

He got up. 'I should go.'

I stared at him. I was shaking. 'Are you saying goodbye to me?'

'No! No! It's not goodbye. It's just that I won't be coming to the hospital again. The Medical Planning Committee is to be disbanded immediately.'

I acted on impulse. I spun my chair around and pushed the door shut with my foot. I got up from my chair, then walked towards him. He held out his arms, I walked straight into them, and we clung to each other in silence for some time.

Then he broke free and said, 'I care for you deeply. It began soon after we first met. You were so brave. And ... beautiful. After that summer – at the beach – I began to love you. When I knew you were no longer engaged to be married, I wanted to be your love and lover. I hope that you began to feel the same way?'

I started to cry and said, 'Yes I did. Yes, I do! I do care for you too. I think about you all the time and I can't bear to say goodbye to you. I'm afraid of how this is ending.'

He whispered, 'It's not over! You will see.'

We kissed. Our first kiss and I wanted to stay in his embrace for ever, and to keep kissing him.

He said, 'I must go upstairs now Rachel. It's as you say in Guernsey only 'until the next time'. And there will be a next time. "Wir schaffen das." We will manage. I promise you! But it will be in a different time and in a different place.' His voice quavered, and he quickly left the room.

I shut the door and sat at my desk. Stricken. I was emotionally drained. My throat felt constricted and the tears welled in my eyes before cascading onto my desk.

About an hour later Dr Shirtcliffe knocked on my door and entered my room. He looked at me: 'It's been a rough morning?'

I nodded, avoiding his eyes, hoping they were not still red from crying.

He said, 'Dr Konrad has been here to inform me that the Germans are withdrawing from the Medical Planning Committee. He brought me his report on nutritional needs. While he didn't say it directly, he hinted that food shortages would get worse as they are probably going to have to supplement their own food supplies from our local sources. People are only getting 1500 calories a day already. It's stealing from the destitute!

'He went on to say that the Germans have asked the Swiss to inform the Allies that they will no longer be responsible for providing any supplies to the Islanders. Churchill has simply retorted that the Germans will be held responsible for our survival, under the Geneva Convention.' Dr Shirtcliffe was angry and added, 'That sort of posturing by our brethren won't feed us.'

Since we have already had drastic cuts in our already meagre rations it's going to get worse. Dr Shirtcliffe is afraid of mass starvation. He said that Dr Konrad personally apologised for leaving us in this state.

Dr Shirtcliffe said that he was calling an urgent meeting for those on the committee, tomorrow at 10 am in the boardroom.

As he left the room he asked, 'Will you be able to report on the supplies situation by then?'

I nodded, knowing it would keep me busy for the rest of the day.

I understand now, that if there is anything worse than unrequited love, it is mutual love that cannot be realised.

CHAPTER THIRTY-EIGHT
DECEMBER 1944
CAMBRIDGE

STELLA WAS ON THE TRAIN TO LONDON, ACCOMPANIED BY LOCAL members of the Channel Island Society, who were all going to attend a special meeting. The women were quiet and tense because on the day before there had been a V2 rocket attack on Tilbury Docks, killing many workers. Stella, who had left her baby with Alison for the day, knew that her fear of more rogue bombings must not keep her from making this important journey.

Today, a petition was to be given to the Home Secretary asking for immediate assistance for the Channel Islands. Some 9000 Islanders in the UK had signed the petition and groups of them, from all over the country, were converging on Westminster to present it.

For Stella, this journey was the culmination of eighteen months of work which had ramped up further after D-Day. The letter-writing campaign to the Home Office had increased in intensity. Many Island refugees had been bombarding their local MPs with information and questions, despite receiving few responses from these parliamentarians. The same was happening in Parliament, where two members of the House of Lords were also asking questions of the government, on a weekly basis, with negligible results.

As more information became available to the Society, from escapees from the Islands, more people had become involved in the campaign to get immediate relief sent there. The evacuees' mood was no longer of frustration, but rather of palpable anger.

Stella arrived at the Grand Hall with half an hour to spare and sought out the elderly woman who was master-minding the political campaign. Vera, who was a member of a Pacifist Society, knew that the Islanders' campaign needed to be very public and that it had to put extreme pressure on a government seemingly so reluctant to act.

Vera had arranged that letters to the editors of both the *Times* and the *Daily Mail* would be published that morning, both stating that the Islanders had no confidence in the government, that they had been totally neglected since 1940, and the government was unwilling to intervene to assist some 60,000 British subjects who were starving, only miles away from England. While the government had shown itself willing to provide food drops for those starving in Holland, their neglect of the Channel Islands was inexplicable. Both papers had responded to the letters by publishing editorials, questioning the government inaction.

Vera had planned that after the Home Secretary, Herbert Morrison had spoken, various members of the society would put questions to him which she hoped the newspapers would be interested to follow up. Stella was one of those nominated to ask a question and she was a little anxious about doing so, in front of so many people.

Vera reassured her: 'I wouldn't have asked you if I thought you couldn't do it. You are number four on the list of questioners and here is the question I want you to ask.'

She gave Stella a piece of paper with the question written in an easy-to-read script. Stella perused it quickly to ensure she understood it. Vera continued passionately, 'Herbert Morrison will have nowhere to hide by the time we have finished with him here today. This government simply must be forced to act immediately. No more obfuscation is acceptable!'

Stella found herself a seat in the centre of the hall and close to the front. She wanted to be directly in the Home Secretary's sight when she stood to ask her question. The fervent chatter in the hall ended when the minister, accompanied by his secretaries, came onto the stage with the Society Chair and the Director. After a brief introduction from the Chair, the petition was formally handed over to the minister and he was then invited to address an avid audience.

The minister was a short man and squarely built, with dark hair and black-framed glasses, one lens of which was opaque because he was blind in that eye. To hide his blindness, he always stood at an angle to his audience, so that the right side of his face and his right eye were not in direct sight. It put him at a disadvantage with his audience as he appeared to be evasive. He retained his working-class accent and the exaggerated rhetorical style he used as a former trade union leader. He was used to a sympathetic audience, as well as being listened to.

To Stella's dismay, his speech sounded exactly like the one he had delivered to the Society a year previously. It was as if nothing had changed since then. He congratulated the Society on its relief work and acknowledged the 'unstinting devotions of its helpers' and his 'hope that they would continue to give this support to those who needed it.'

He said nothing about the Islands and the people living there. He finished by assuring them that his government would consider their petition, 'in the fullness of time.'

A deep male voice from the back of the hall called: 'We want action, now, not further consideration,' and a few people clapped. The minister raised his hand. 'All in good time, my friend. We ARE working on a plan for the liberation of the Islands.'

Another voice chimed in, female this time. 'You told us that in August, Sir, and said we wouldn't have to wait much longer! Exactly what have you achieved in the past four months?'

A few more people applauded. Someone else called out: 'The Society contributed information for that plan in August 1943, sixteen months ago. It should be finished by now!'

The minister capitulated: 'Well the plan is almost completed but we have to get all the logistical supports sorted out before …'

'Not good enough!' a man called out. A buzz of muted comments sounded around the hall. People were growing restive and looking at their neighbours with alarm.

There was a loud clatter at the back of the hall as a chair fell over. An attractive young woman stalked down the aisle towards the stage, her arms folded and her high heels ringing out on the wooden floor. She stopped dramatically right in front of the minister. She had a Guernsey accent and her voice was strong.

'We don't want any more flannel, Minister. We want food and supplies to be sent to the Islands immediately to save our starving families. The government has been able to send food to the Belgians and the Greeks. It's appalling that you cannot fly in supplies today. Why won't you help your own people?

Our men made the supreme sacrifice for you. They would be appalled to know their families have been so neglected.'

The minister was now looking annoyed. In a studiously patient voice, he said, 'You must appreciate that it is more complex than that, my dear. I suggest that you don't really understand the strategic issues at stake here. Perhaps you should go back and focus your efforts on helping the needy people here and leave the government to do its job. I understand that getting Christmas presents for refugee children is now a priority for your Society.'

At that the hall erupted with catcalls and a man yelled over the rising noise: 'Bugger Christmas presents if the children aren't alive to get them.'

People stamped their feet, jeered and a hubbub of noise drowned out the minister's efforts to quell them.

A chant of 'Resign' began and spread around the entire hall. The Secretary of the Society came to the front of the stage, holding up his hands for silence. After some minutes the audience fell quiet and the Chair thanked the minister for attending.

The Secretary continued, 'These people here represent some thousands of Island refugees here in the UK. They speak for many, many, thousands at home in the Islands. We all know their needs are enormous and that they are desperate. These people are not going to wait more months whilst some great game of international politics is played out. The British Parliament must act now, or forever lose the respect of the Channel Islands people.'

At this the hall erupted with cheers and clapping and the minister and his staff hastily abandoned the stage.

Stella sought out Vera, as the audience rose, and clusters of friends congregated at the back of the hall before they spilled out onto the street. All were eager to talk about the events in the hall. 'Well that didn't go quite to script!' Stella said.

'No, but it was very powerful. I think the minister got a clear message and the press has now got a very, very good story to write up for tomorrow's papers. I can already imagine the headlines! The government won't be happy to have the Islanders, who have been so patient until now, being so assertive.'

'I'm sorry I didn't get to ask when the BBC programme for the Islands, that we made in August, was going to be aired,' Stella said.

'Don't worry! We will write a letter to the papers asking about that. We will keep the heat on, until they act.'

Stella laughed. 'You seem to know how to keep up the momentum of our cause.'

'I learned, during the First World War, from a very clever woman: Sylvia Pankhurst,' Vera retorted. 'She would not have put up with such a patronising man.'

Stella returned to the station with her friends who chatted and schemed all the way back to Cambridge. Stella then went to Alison's house to collect her six-month old daughter. At dinner, after putting Amy to bed, she recounted the details of the meeting to Mark and outlined the various tasks her group was going to be responsible for during the next two weeks.

'Vera told me it was remarkably simple for the government to act. All it needs to do is to ask the Red Cross to send its ships to the Islands with provisions. That is more important, right now, than organising to get the Germans off the Islands quickly,' she said.

When, on 14th December, Parliament announced that a Red Cross ship, the *Vega*, was to sail from Lisbon to Guernsey, Stella and Mark celebrated late into the night with other local members of the Society.

One of them said, 'I think we should get involved in the coming election campaign. We need a government that is really going to help the Islands, when they are finally liberated. I don't have faith in Churchill to do that. We need a Labour Government.'

CHAPTER THIRTY-NINE
JANUARY 1945
GUERNSEY

THE PAST SIX MONTHS HAVE BEEN SHEER HELL FOR US ALL. FIRST THE hell of realising that we have been overlooked in the advance towards Germany, without the Allies liberating the Channel Islands. Then again, by Britain overlooking, for six months, to send us food and basic supplies either by airlift from England or on a Red Cross boat. My Dad said that Churchill didn't want to feed the Germans with English food. Why did they, then, take so long to ask for Red Cross help?

We felt as if the Island was like an overcrowded lifeboat, with no provisions, little protection from the elements, and which, despite our many SOS calls, no-one was willing to rescue!

Knowing that the Germans are being forced out of most of western Europe, but that we are still under their rule, is a great psychological hardship for us. To be ignored by our so-called 'motherland', Great Britain, is emotionally devastating.

When the "Vega" arrived on 27th December the entire population was desperate for food. There had been further drastic cuts of food in the preceding two months; the Island was unable to grow winter root crops because of a fungal disease.

Food parcels were distributed to each household in quantities calculated for each resident, only in early January and then we got another parcel after a fortnight. The "Vega" came back again in early February and we got a third parcel. However, there has been no bread available since mid-month.

Water is supplied only from 5.30–7.30 am and from 6–7 pm. Electricity is not available from midnight to 5 am, nor from 2.15 pm to 5 pm. The hospital has had to borrow carbide and kerosene emergency lamps for use at night. We have only the people who are critically ill as in-patients. Community nurses in all the parishes tend to the remaining patients and we have recorded 50,000 home visits in the past twelve months. The Germans promised to find us medicines and soaps which have not materialised after three months.

Our feeding kitchens did not work out as planned. Finding energetic people to 'man' them was difficult and we were unable to obtain enough cooking implements. Local people, also, found it required too much effort to walk to them.

In January the Germans commandeered many dozens of glass houses to grow their own food. They also ordered farmers to kill some of their livestock to make them available for the troops.

Apart from our physical deprivation we are living in a state of anarchy. It has been evident for some time that the German soldiers have become undisciplined. They wander around in tatty uniforms accosting local people. Some have brandished guns and one took a farm family hostage; all to gain food.

The Commandant appears to be desperate. He keeps issuing contradictory edicts so that we cannot remember from day to day *what is now 'forbidden.' Are we still allowed to be out on the streets? Can we have outdoor recreation or not? Which beach is open today? Are we on Summertime already or not? Rumours abound and chaos results. Even in these circumstances he doesn't show compassion, with men being imprisoned for minor infractions.*

In November there was a brief resurgence of local defiance. After the British destroyer HMS Charybdis *was torpedoed and sank in the Channel, washing twenty-one British bodies onto the Guernsey beaches, a huge memorial service was held at the Foulon Cemetery. Thousands of Islanders attended in a show of patriotism, which was uplifting for local morale. Now, we are too tired and dispirited to show our disgust.*

We endure day by day. We can do nothing but wait…powerless! When will it end?

CHAPTER FORTY
MARCH 1945
GUERNSEY

TODAY BROUGHT ME ADDITIONAL PERSONAL PAIN. WHEN I arrived at the hospital, I found a note on my desk from Dr Shirtcliffe, asking me to please see him immediately. I took off my coat and went up to his office where he told me to shut the door and sit down.

He said, 'Dr Konrad has been arrested by the Germans! They have put him in Le Truchot Prison. The Germans have accused him of giving aid to the enemy... us! Apparently, he has been helping Dr Alpers. Gave Alpers drugs for some of our patients, from the German Hospital supplies. He was caught red-handed and the SS came for him.'

I was afraid and asked what would happen to him.

'We don't know. Luckily, they can't get him off the Island. But there is going to be an investigation. So far Dr Alpers hasn't been picked up, but he will no doubt be questioned. The hospital might be searched, with staff here interviewed.'

He gave me one of his long stares. 'You, my dear, were only in contact with Dr Konrad through your role as Executive Officer for the Medical Planning Committee. You had nothing to do with any arrangements with Dr Alpers. Understood?'

I felt panic. What about all the supplies the hospital received over the years? I was involved in those transactions. I said nothing but must have looked surprised.

Dr Shirtcliffe said, 'If you are interviewed you will only deal with the specific offence Dr Konrad is charged with, his recent aiding of Dr Alpers' patients. I trust all your records here are clean and that there is nothing that a search here, or at your home, could cause you trouble.'

I nodded in assent, although I felt very apprehensive for myself as well as for Dr Konrad. Dr Shirtcliffe said how he had valued my contribution over the past years and that I had always been totally reliable.

His tone changed from an official one, to one which was more paternal. 'I have something for you.' He gave me a sealed letter. He said I should read it quickly and then destroy it in the furnace room 'forthwith.'

I immediately recognised the handwriting from reports I had read. I went to my room and I did part of what Dr Shirtcliffe instructed. I read the letter. Its contents made me happy at one level, though enormously sad as well.

I could not bear to burn it! It's all I have of Dieter, except for an address which is of no use to me. I will hide the letter with this diary tonight. Should my rooms be ransacked, I am confident about *my hiding place, under the paving stones around the disused water pump. It's in a back corner of the property, which is overgrown with weeds and nettles. It would require persistence to find it. Why does loving Dieter have to be so hard?*

PART THREE

LIBERATION

8TH MAY 1945 — 14TH JULY 1947

CHAPTER FORTY-ONE
MAY 1945
GUERNSEY

AFTER MONTHS OF RUMOURS, FREQUENTLY CONTRADICTORY, hope was re-emerging that the War in Europe was nearing an end.

One rumour suggested that Hitler was dead by suicide. Another, that the Russians were now fighting against the Americans, in Berlin. An alternative said the Allies would fight a battle to free Guernsey because the Commandant vowed never to surrender. In contrast another said the Commandant with senior staff were about to flee by submarine; intending to join Hitler in South America.

It was hard to know the truth. What could be seen, though, was that the German troops on the Island were absolutely demoralised. Like the Islanders they were hungry and any faith in their cause was shattered.

Military discipline was breaking down, as the soldiers' physical health worsened. Dozens in the German Forces had deserted. Many were jailed once caught. While others, with Guernsey girl-friends, were being hidden by local people.

Marion and June often saw clusters of soldiers scavenging for nettles in the fields, just as the Todt workers had done previously. Marion was surprised to see Tobias amongst a group of dejected-looking men, in tattered uniforms, fossicking in the hedgerows for food near her house. While she felt some sympathy for him, she neither acknowledged nor assisted him.

The new German Commandant, who was a brutal Nazi, was constantly issuing edicts requiring their continued obedience. Often one day's orders were countermanded the next. The soldiers, Controlling Committee and wider population were so thoroughly confused that no-one had confidence in him. He was losing his battle for control as the Island fell into anarchy.

Towards the end of April, he had demanded Islanders attend a rally to celebrate Hitler's birthday. A large group of residents had no choice but to go to this event, but they resented the imposition more than they had on previous years. It seemed inconceivable that the local German leader would continue to give a rousing patriotic speech to his captive audience as his army's rout continued.

In a show of contempt, the crowd started to sing 'God Save the King', once the Commandant ended his patriotic tirade. He immediately retaliated by banning all future meetings of Islanders.

Although the family realised that, ultimately, they would be saved, the wait had become unbearably long. Their health deteriorated further, and fatigue and despair were endemic.

Early in the afternoon on the 8th May, Marion put Candice into her small cart in preparation for her walk to a nearby dairy farm. The little girl was wrapped up in a warm cape to protect her from the unseasonal snow flurries and biting winds. Behind Candice's back Marion had hidden away a bag of early vegetables which she would exchange for the milk they needed to supplement their scant diet.

The shops were now completely empty of food, but there was always someone wanting to trade their excess of some foodstuff with someone else's surfeit of a different kind. A local system had developed between families at Bordeaux, which the German soldiers were trying to terminate, by confiscating any food being transported between properties. Marion was hopeful that she wouldn't be searched for her contraband since Candice had been taught to start yelling when faced with a soldier.

Marion found the entire Brehaut family in their barn and was informed by her smiling neighbour, 'Churchill is just going to make an announcement.' Marion heard a crystal set on the bench emitting a screech of static, whilst Mr Brehaut fiddled with the dials.

Through the din they were able to hear Churchill's voice announcing that England was celebrating Victory in Europe. The listeners heard that a ceasefire had been agreed and that the 'dear Islands' would soon be liberated with two destroyers, already despatched, to enforce the German surrender. A fleet of cargo ships was being sent today with food supplies. The group in the barn hugged each other. 'It's almost over, thank God.'

Marion quickly traded her vegetables for a jar of milk and started home to tell the wonderful news. She passed other neighbouring houses where laughter and noise erupted when the good news was exchanged. At home Aunt Ethel was jubilant: 'We must celebrate our survival.'

'What with?' asked June.

'There's still a little brandy in the medicine cabinet. I'm sure we can afford to use it up now. And Candice can have as much milk today as she wants.'

Early the next morning Marion and June got dressed in the best of their remaining clothes. Aunt Ethel had volunteered to stay home with Candice so that the two young women could witness the momentous events at St Peter Port. They set off at 8 am on a chilly morning, following on from the preceding cold days. The sea was calm, the tide rising and the sky cloudless. The walk ahead was long, but they soon linked up with dozens of others heading, on foot, on old bicycles and in horse-drawn carts, for the harbour.

As they came around the Longstore warehouse, on its small quay, they saw dozens of ships, waiting for full-tide to enter the harbour. It was a sight not seen since the evacuation. Their excitement was growing as they hurried on to the inner harbour, where thousands had already gathered.

To the crowd's dismay the two destroyers already in the harbour started to withdraw. No-one knew why, but a rumour threaded through the mass quickly, saying that the German Commandant would not surrender and was going to blow everyone up. Some people panicked and took refuge in the streets away from the harbour, only to return to the back of the crowd when the destroyers sailed back within the breakwater.

Cheering and singing broke out when a small launch took the Commandant out to one of the destroyers. Soon after, the cargo boats, moored offshore, weighed anchor and sailed into the pier to unload goods at the White Rock. At the same time a fleet of strange-looking vessels sailed into the Old Harbour.

They floated right up to the Albert Slipway and then drove on wheels upwards, to stop by Prince Albert's statue. Marion was astonished and asked people in the crowd what these boats were. Someone said they were Amphibians. 'They were used on D-Day to land our troops in France,' she was told.

When each craft reached the top of the slipway it was parked on the cobbles surrounding the tall bronze statue on its granite plinth. Each shuddered to a halt and with loud cranking noises a hatchway opened to release British soldiers, who were immediately engulfed by the waiting crowd.

The soldiers began handing out cigarettes and chocolate to the screaming, crying people who surrounded them. Young women ran up to kiss and hug the bemused men. Older people pulled out long-hidden British flags and wrapped them around their shoulders. When the Guernsey Ensign flew once again from the States Offices, a huge cheer resonated around the harbourside.

The euphoric revelry went on through the late morning and into the early afternoon when June and Marion reluctantly left the scene for their long walk home, where Aunt Ethel interrogated them about the day's events.

The next two days were strange. They went about the same routines they had lived by for the past lean years, not yet able to think about the future, nor to fully comprehend their new freedom.

The pressure of being constantly vigilant about their physical safety was only just beginning to ease when a new danger emerged for the family at Bordeaux. Mrs Brehaut came to the house to warn Marion that there were vigilante attacks happening in the area. Young women were being terrorised for having relationships with Germans during the occupation. She recommended that Marion and Candice leave the area as soon as they could.

With phone connections now restored, Marion called Rachel at the hospital. 'You had better come and stay with me in the Catel. No-one knows you here, so you should be safer. You will need to lie low until things settle down. You and Candice can have my room and I can sleep in my sitting room. I will borrow some bedding. Just bring some clothes for you both.'

Marion and June took Candice on her cart to the bus terminal at St Sampson's town centre, where they transferred to a horse-bus going into town and then caught another going to the Catel. The town was teeming with British soldiers working to restore services for the Islanders. In the harbour, queues of German soldiers were waiting to be deported as POWs. Marion saw how emaciated, scruffy and exhausted they looked. So different to the bold troops who had marched down High Street five years ago.

That night after Candice had settled into bed, Marion and Rachel sat talking. Dr Shirtcliffe had advised Rachel that Dieter was still at Le Truchot Prison and he was seeking permission to see him there. He had asked the Controlling Committee to intercede with the senior officer of the British Liberation Force, on behalf of Dr Konrad, because of the doctor's efforts to assist the local people. He was hopeful that Dieter might be treated leniently.

'I desperately want to see him! Dr Shirtcliffe will ask the British if we may,' Rachel said.

'His health has suffered because of the poor conditions there during the past two months. I don't know if he was ill-treated by his own commanders. But there weren't any repercussions at the hospital, and Dr Alpers wasn't put into prison, as it was already full of deserters.'

'I might find out soon what happened to Fredrich. That's if his lawyer friend is still alive after all the fighting in Germany,' Marion said.

'The Red Cross will be starting work to trace people very soon. They may be able to help you find out about Fredrich. But there are millions of people missing or displaced. It's going to be a huge challenge.

'We had it tough, but compared to those places in Europe where the fighting occurred, we were relatively lucky. Our community is run-down but at least our buildings and homes are intact. Some towns and villages in Europe have been totally flattened by bombing or street fighting. It's hard to imagine how those people will be able to start life again.'

'Yes, we are fortunate that the Allies did not have to attack the Island to free us. So, we should be able to rebuild our lives relatively easily. What are you going to do?' Rachel asked.

'I will try again to see my mother. I imagine she will be going back to Paris Street. I am not optimistic that she will have changed her opinion about me though. If she still doesn't want anything to do with me and Candice, I will have to make other plans for us. What about you?'

'Well, it's going to take time for our health to recover. While I have fantasized about lovely meals for so long and would welcome a feast, I know we need to build up our diets very slowly to let our shrunken stomachs expand gradually. I also think our physical and emotional resources are totally spent, and our immune systems are weak. It may be months before we recover.

'More than that though,' Rachel continued, 'it's going to take time for us to get used to living a normal life. Learning to live with freedom from coercion and fear, will be a challenge. Also learning to trust each other again!

'I'm not confident of making any personal decisions just yet. There will be quite a bit to do with relocating the hospital again, as well as getting all the resources we need, including new staff. I won't make any decisions until next spring.'

'What about Dieter?' Marion asked.

'I don't know what will happen to him. I'm not sure that we can have any future. Certainly, not here, nor in Germany, if he gets sent back. I feel emotionally numb still, and I can't think ahead.'

CHAPTER FORTY-TWO
NOVEMBER 1945
CAMBRIDGE

DURING JULY, STELLA AND MARK HAD BEEN WORKING hard for the Labour candidate in the general election. Like most of their friends they believed that a new government was required, which would put the well-being of the working people first. They were enthusiastic about the proposed welfare provisions put forward by the Labour Party Leader, Mr Attlee, which would care for the sick, the old, the unemployed and the many families without a male breadwinner.

While Cambridge had always elected a Conservative MP in the past, they had worked to support a former schoolmaster and serviceman, who was standing for Labour. They had distributed his leaflets and organised fundraising during the six months prior to the election. They were jubilant to hear on the 26th July 1945 that their chosen candidate had won by a small margin of votes, and that Clement Attlee's party had secured a mandate to bring in new welfare and health policies.

In August, Stella and David were faced with a decision to make at home. The Guernsey school children were going to return to the Island for the start of the school year in September. The question they needed to answer was should David go home to Guernsey, or should he stay on at Harrow, to sit his Secondary School Certificate in the forthcoming academic year? He was an established part of their household and adored by their daughter Amy.

Stella's mother was very clear that she wanted David to start the term at the Boys' Grammar School in Guernsey. She was now back in her house in Rosaire Avenue, having retrieved some of her furniture and chattels from the community depot. She wanted her son back home after a five-year absence. However, Stella and Mark were not so sure that this was a good time for David to move schools. He was doing well at Harrow and his ambition to go on to study architecture in Glasgow had not changed. They decided that David needed to choose for himself.

After long discussion David decided to go back to Guernsey to live with his mother. He was also eager to see his elderly grandparents. Arrangements were made for him to meet up with his former schoolmates, when they travelled down from Glasgow to Weymouth, so that they could all return by ship together; just as they had left. David was not sure how many of them would be going on to college with him, but he was keen to see old friends and teachers again.

Stella took him up to London where he said his farewells to her and Amy. 'We will come over to visit as soon as we are permitted to. Give our love to all the family,' Stella told him.

'He is going to find that he has grown apart from some of those lads. That may be difficult for him,' she confided to Mark that evening.

'That's true but he has coped well with all the big changes so far. He's an adaptable fellow. There will be some like minds at college and the staff will be careful to blend in the kids that left with those who stayed. Being with your mother again is important for her as well as for him. As your grandparents are so frail, there may be a limited chance for David to spend time with them. He needs to rekindle his memories of them and enjoy their company.'

Three months later, on Guy Fawkes' night, Mark, Stella and Amy were aboard the boat train heading to Southampton, having secured a week's permit from the Guernsey government to visit family. With their various parents living next door to each other, it would be simple to share their limited time between them.

The train was bulging with people moving back home and whilst Stella, with Amy on her knee, was given a seat, Mark had to stand in the corridor with their baggage. Knowing that goods were still scarce in the Island they had bought presents of clothing and chocolates for their families.

As they travelled to the port, they saw fireworks being let off in back gardens abutting the train tracks. Life in England was getting back to some normalcy. At the Southampton dock the battered old mailboat – the *Isle of Sark* – awaited them.

'We need to get Amy below decks. It will be too cold above decks for her,' said Mark who went ahead to find Stella a place to sit in a forward lounge. 'Well, this is better accommodation than I had coming over to England!' she laughed.

Mark took a blanket proffered by a crew member and found a place to hunker down on the deck with their luggage. Stella and Amy slept fitfully and as the sun came in through the grimy windows, she wrapped Amy securely in a blanket and went on deck to seek out Mark.

The three of them found a place at the rail and watched as the familiar landmarks of Stella's and Mark's childhoods came into view. On the port side they could see the silhouettes of Sark, Herm and Jethou. On starboard there was the harbour at St Sampson's. 'I've got goose-bumps,' Stella confessed.

The boat moved more slowly towards the shining White Rock wharf. The rising sun was reflected in the windows of the buildings along the quayside creating a golden glow over St Peter Port. 'We are nearly there, old girl. How are you feeling?'

'Excited … a bit scared. I think we will be shocked by how everyone has aged. David was.'

'Mmm. They are scarred by what has happened to them. It might be hard to talk about their experiences. But they will all love Amy. She will help us bridge any gaps.'

There were huddles of people on the quay waiting to meet family and friends off the boat. As the passengers disembarked, they waved and called to loved ones. Mark's father emerged from the crowd as they stepped off the gangplank and grasped them all in a mighty hug.

'The others are waiting at home,' he said. 'We didn't want to overwhelm the little one with too many new faces. The journey must have been strange enough for her.'

The family reunion in Rosaire Avenue was tumultuous, but Mark's Dad, ever practical, soon had them all sitting down to a farm breakfast. 'Nothing like good Guernsey milk for you all,' he boasted.

The week passed very quickly. An important first task had been to have Amy christened, which brought all family and some of their old friends together. Amy delighted in all the attention she attracted. It was novel to have so many willing adults entertain her. She was excited to see her Uncle David again as well.

David seemed happy with his decision to come back. He and his mother had formed a relaxed relationship and his grandparents were enjoying his help. He was playing soccer for the first eleven and had made friends amongst the returning students.

Stella found the absence of her father unsettling. His death had only become real to her now that she was back in her childhood home. She found some peace by visiting his grave each day but was sad that he was not able to meet her little girl.

Towards the end of the week she met up with Rachel in her rooms, but the visit was strained at first. Each woman was wary of the other, knowing that their wartime experiences had been so different. Rachel was obviously reluctant to talk about the previous years. Stella had learned already, from family, that some topics were best not raised. Stella deftly navigated the conversation towards the safe current topics, wanting to avoid anything which could upset their now seemingly more fragile friendship.

Stella was disappointed that their easy camaraderie had gone. 'I felt like an outsider. I wasn't prepared for that,' she confessed to Mark.

'We are outsiders. We've had a different war to them. We've dealt with different things than they did. There's an air of secrecy here. Things people don't want to talk about, to those who weren't here. I've also picked up that there is a lot of anger between various people here and some want revenge on others for how they have behaved.'

'Yes, Rachel did tell me about the Barbers' Group who terrorised a number of women for some weeks. The men shaved off the women's hair. Some were physically beaten up too. It was barbaric! Marion had to leave the Island with her little girl because of the hostility. She has gone to live with a distant relation in Plymouth. She was fortunate to have some family member who could help her out with room and board. Rachel wasn't very forthcoming about Marion, but she said she was the godparent for her daughter Candice.'

'Where is the child's father?'

'He was a German officer. He went missing in action on the Russian front.'

Mark expelled a long breath. 'Well if she consorted with the Germans it is not surprising that she had to leave here, if only for her little girl's sake. The child is not to blame and should not be stigmatised.'

'You know there were multiple other disloyal things happening as well. Lots of people were keen to "dob in" friends and neighbours, according to Dad. Apparently, the Liberation Force did begin investigations into local complaints made about racketeering or illegalities over rations and quotas, but their investigations seem to have petered out without any action being taken against those accused. It was said to be too divisive.

'Dad thinks they decided these things were so widespread that half the population would be under scrutiny for some thing or other. He said it's frustrating for those who want wrongdoers to be punished but he thinks most reasonable people prefer to close the book on the recent past.'

'Let bygones be bygones, then?'

He nodded.

'Well I do find it hard to think of Marion having an affair, like that. Rachel is more tolerant of it than I expected her to be. I guess people change. You know she had to work alongside some of the Germans too. Something about getting hospital supplies. I don't really know but I guess it wasn't easy for her either. Do you know some people think that we evacuees just ran away like rats from a sinking ship? It doesn't seem to count that we did war work in England.'

'Yes, I think some people feel we let them down,' Mark said. 'People react suspiciously when they find out that I wasn't in the services. Some seem to believe that since I wasn't in the forces, I must have been a conscientious objector. Maybe in time it will become easier to re-establish our friendships back here. Feelings are still pretty raw.'

'It's been good to visit and to see everyone, but I realise our home is definitely in England. I don't think we could, again, settle down here.'

'I agree. I'm looking forward to going home to Cambridge.'

CHAPTER FORTY-THREE
MARCH 1946
GUERNSEY

I'VE BEEN PACKING UP MY FEW BELONGINGS AND JUST RELOCATED this diary, with the letter and address tucked inside it. I only retrieved it when I left my rooms in the Catel to move back to live at the new hospital some months ago. Although wrapped in canvas, the package I unearthed was damp and mouldy. It has since then dried, but the pages are warped and it smells musty. I can still read my writing, despite some smudging.

I read it through from 'woe to go' today, and it certainly has a lot of woe in it. I'm still not sure if I should take it with me when I leave. While it's a record of things that happened here, as I originally intended, it seems to be more a record of my angst. I do want to put those years behind me.

We have had nine months of freedom from occupation, but we are still adjusting to it. It took a long time before we could eat properly again as our stomachs had shrunk so much. But now I have regained my health and I don't look quite so scrawny.

My habit of thrift will take some time to change. I have bought a few new clothes, using the ration books issued from England, and I do feel more feminine wearing stockings with nice shoes. And some make-up! I also splurged on having my hair cut properly. It's growing back in a much healthier condition.

I go out with other staff and I have a social life, but I feel somehow detached from my new colleagues and I avoid conversation about things that happened to me during the occupation.

I realised at Christmas that I was just sleepwalking through my life and that instead I needed to take charge and make some changes for myself. I'm now twenty-five. After the hiatus of the past horrible years I feared I had lost any ambitions for myself. I was simply and inexorably pulled along by the tide of occupation, not by my own volition. Now I must overcome this passivity and take responsibility for my own future, which I can better control. I have energy and my mood is optimistic.

When Stella came to see me late last year, I couldn't tell her about our war here on the Island. I know she was shocked by what she had heard about the occupation and couldn't understand how we had to live beside the enemy and make things work, somehow. We all had to compromise ourselves in some way to survive those five interminable years.

Bad things have happened here, I know, but there were also examples of courage, generosity and principled behaviour as well; by Islanders and by some of the Germans. I keep hearing all these words being tossed around – consorting, collaboration, collusion, complicity. The only words that I think truly apply are complexity and co-existence.

After nine months I am going to leave here to start a new phase in my life. I am resolute about that, and this time I am going to defy my father!

I have got a job with the Red Cross and first I'm going to Geneva, for a month's training and an intense French refresher course, before I get posted to a displaced persons' camp on the Belgium border, near Liège. I feel there is nothing more I can particularly contribute to here, since more medical staff are in place and the hospital is functioning well.

I do want to help with the recovery in Europe. There is a huge task to be done with millions still suffering and I want to be involved in some way. I am incredibly grateful to the Red Cross organisation. They saved so many lives here in 1944/45. The Red Cross also seem to think my medical and administrative experience will be useful to them!

I take the ferry to St Malo, the train to Paris and then on to Geneva. I will be living in the Red Cross hostel with other inductees from around the world. One way or another I am about to travel, though not quite in the way I once dreamed I would.

I have just received a special relief passport from the United Nations, which oversees all the agencies helping in Europe and provides the money, medicines and food needed. There was another very harsh winter, all over Europe, with huge shortages of fuel and goods experienced everywhere. So, there is to be a big push this spring and summer to get the post-war crises under control before the next winter begins.

I probably should add a postscript about what happened to Dieter after his imprisonment. Dr Shirtcliffe told me that Dieter left the Island with all the prisoners of war in mid-May last year and was shipped off to a camp near Exeter. He was able to write to Dr Shirtcliffe from there, during the autumn. Dr Shirtcliffe then put together a letter signed by the Bailiff and other senior officials in Guernsey, to petition for his release from the camp because of the tremendous personal sacrifices he made, to help keep so many Islanders alive.

It seems that the letter finally found its way to a sympathetic MP in the new government, who had his situation investigated and decided that Dieter deserved clemency. The government agreed that he should be returned to Hamburg to help re-establish medical services there, rather than sitting idly in a camp. Dr Shirtcliffe heard this news from the Liberation Force here.

I haven't had any contact with Dieter since that anguished day at the hospital. I didn't visit him at the prison as I feared it might compromise him. After he left, I hoped for weeks that he would write to me; to no avail. Reluctantly, over many months I realised a letter wasn't going to materialize, coming to accept that ours was just another brief wartime connection.

However, when I saw Dr Shirtcliffe, now back in private practice, to say goodbye last week, he told me that he had finally received a letter from Dieter, who was already in Hamburg. He said that Dieter had asked after me and wondered why I had not written to him.

Dr Shirtcliffe said he investigated and has just found out that any letters written by POWs to Guernsey girls have been held back by the censors in England. He said it was apparent that Dieter had tried to write to me after all and suggested that there was not likely to be any censorship in Switzerland, if I wanted to write to him from there.

It's been eighteen months during which, I had come to terms, somewhat painfully, with the belief that he had gone, forever, out of my life. I suddenly do feel heartened, to know that he has been trying to contact me and I will write to him via his parents once I leave here.

I am now looking ahead to being in a new environment with more freedom available. I feel as if my future is a blank sheet for me to write on as I choose. I will also take my diary!

CHAPTER FORTY-FOUR
APRIL 1946
PLYMOUTH

As she had indicated to Stella after Guernsey's liberation, Marion took Candice to visit her mother. She was sure her mother would soften when she met the lively girl. Sadly, that was not the case. Mrs Le Prevost would not allow her visitors to enter the house and insisted that she wanted nothing to do with Marion and Candice.

Mrs Le Prevost said, 'I've told you before, don't come back here again. I don't want to see you or that child. You have disgraced me. Go back to your German.'

Marion had walked away with her head up, determined not to show her hurt. Her quest, for reconciliation with her mother, was impossible. She told Aunt Ethel of their stalemate.

Fortuitously, later that week Marion was offered a new opportunity and made an immediate decision to grasp it. Aunt Ethel, who had finally received a phone call from her sister Elizabeth in Plymouth, asked whether Marion could go to live with her; to start life anew away from Guernsey.

Aunt Elizabeth immediately said, 'Yes; I would be glad of some company.'

Marion and Candice left the Island on a ship filled with other young single mothers, which the British forces had organised, to stop the violence on the Island. On their exodus Marion soon learned she was one of the fortunate young women who had family to support her once she arrived. This was not possible for most of the other girls on the ship, who were very anxious about their futures.

Aunt Elizabeth was very like Aunt Ethel. She was a short and stocky woman in her fifties. She was kind and welcomed Marion and Candice into her comfortable home. Marion found evening work at a pub, which enabled her to pay Aunt Elizabeth for their food and expenses. Aunt Elizabeth was very happy to look after Candice from late afternoon and put her to bed in the evening. It seemed as if everything had fallen into place. Their smooth arrangement worked well for six months.

Then Marion's tenuous hope that Fredrich would assist her to raise Candice was extinguished. In March, a letter from Herr Drukner, forwarded from Guernsey, informed her that Fredrich had died at Stalingrad in 1943. Later that month, as Marion walked home from her job she was assaulted in an alleyway.

Twenty meters from the pub, between the church and the school, was an alley which ran down to the river. As Marion walked past it a movement caught her eye and she turned to stare into the unlit passage. A figure erupted out of the shadows towards her and grasped her right arm, twisted it backwards and then pushed her away from the street. Marion tried to wrench herself free, but her assailant pressed her arm high up her back so that the pain of it immobilised her. She yelled, but a large hand clamped across her mouth.

'Shut up you bitch.'

The man frogmarched her further into the alley and then twisted her around to face him with her back against the stone wall of the presbytery. In the dim light she recognised him from the pub. A moody, sour, middle-aged man who sat alone in the corner of the bar. Marion had served him drinks but had never stopped to talk to him. The other staff described him as a loner, who had turned up in the area during the previous year. Someone had said he was an ex-POW who was unable to work.

'I know all about you, you little whore. I've been watching you and the girl. I know your dirty little secret.'

She felt his spittle on her face as he screamed at her. She could smell the alcohol on his breath and the cheesy musk of his unwashed clothes. She tried to avert her face and to push him away, but he pressed his body against her, impeding her movements. She felt his hand pulling at her skirt, to wrest it upwards, as he tried to force his knee between hers. He muttered in her ear.

'If you can give it away to the Hun, you owe it to me. I served my country for bitches like you!'

Despite her fear, Marion's mind was racing. When she heard a heavy door being banged shut and voices of pedestrians up on the street she reacted quickly. She stopped resisting and willed her body to relax.

'Here. Let me undo my coat?' she urged her assailant.

He moved back slightly, to enable her to undo the coat's buttons. At the sound of passers-by near the alley entrance, Marion raised her leg, drove her knee into his groin and scraped her high heel down the length of his shin. As he doubled over, she began screaming. He raised his body and lifted his hand to slap her face, but, instead, hearing shouting at the top of the alley, he shoved her viciously into the wall and ran off.

Two of the young barmen, who had just closed the pub for the night, ran the few yards to where Marion had sunk down onto the cobbled way in tears and quaking. Whilst one helped her to her feet the other pursued the man down the alley.

He soon returned saying, 'I couldn't see him. He's got away amongst the trees along the river. Are you all right?'

'Yes, just shaken up. Thank goodness you came along when you did. It was that man…you know… the one who was sitting in the corner of the snug by himself. You know… the weird one.'

'Where do you live? We will walk you home,' one offered.

'You should report this!' the other suggested.

'I just need to go home now. It's only a few streets from here. My aunt will take care of me.'

The men escorted her home. 'Maybe you shouldn't be out alone so late,' one said.

'It's always seemed safe, before tonight, to walk home after the pub closed. After this I might have to consider giving up the job.'

'Or find another way to get home!' he answered.

Marion unlocked the door, thanked her rescuers and entered the hallway. She shut the door and went to sit on the bottom step of the stairs, head in hands. She felt exhausted; totally drained of strength. She stayed there a long time, until she realised how cold she had become, then crept upstairs into her room, wrapped the eiderdown around herself and fell asleep on top of her bed.

'Mummy, Mummy wake up.' Candice was tugging at the eiderdown. Aunt Elizabeth was standing in the doorway. 'She wouldn't wait any longer to see you,' she explained. 'Something's happened?' she asked anxiously, seeing that Marion was fully dressed.

Marion nodded, close to tears.

'We can talk later, when Candice has her nap. I'll make some tea. Come on Candice, let's go and make breakfast for Mummy.'

Marion lay on the bed trying to make sense of the events of last night. She wondered what she had done to provoke the attack. She certainly hadn't flirted with this man at the pub. Rather, she had ignored him. Was he angry that she was merely polite, but not friendly? Had she worn the wrong clothes? Was she the subject of local gossip?

He had told her that he had been watching her and Candice. That was scary. How had he found out about her? She hadn't revealed very much to anyone in the district. People knew she had a child, but she was thought to be a war widow, having said that Candice's father had disappeared during the war in Europe. That had ensured no further questions were asked of her.

Perhaps her attacker had found out that she came from the Channel Islands and thus assumed that Candice had a German father. If she reported him, would he reveal what he knew, to shame her?

At her Aunt Elizabeth's urging Marion reported the assault to the local constable. He said he would approach the man, who was known to the police, to warn him off. 'With luck he will leave the area,' the constable said, 'but if not, we will keep a watch on him.'

All day Marion fretted about her job. She needed the money, but she was afraid of walking home alone at night. She felt that she was going around in circles, and she could not see any way forward.

'You are in shock,' her aunt told her. 'Give yourself some time to get over what happened and then we can talk about what to do. In the meantime, I will tell the publican you are sick.'

Marion took a week off work after her assault. She continued to be gloomy and unsure about what she should do. Her expectation that all would be well for her once she settled in England had not been realised.

'I've been far too optimistic.' Marion told Aunt Elizabeth. 'I really thought I could put the past behind me when I came here. It seems as if the decisions I once made will haunt me forever.'

Her aunt shook her head. 'We are made by our past. We must accept the decisions we took, learn from them and then move forward. You must forgive yourself first! You were a young woman living in extraordinary times. Now you have a beautiful daughter whom you love and care for. You cannot be bowed down by fear or regrets. You must think ahead to the life you want for yourself and Candice.'

After much discussion during her week off, Marion decided that she needed to find another job, with better hours and more pay. She thought, too, that it might be good for Candice to be with other children, at a nursery school.

Marion realised that she must make some long-term plans to secure Candice's future. At 26 she must begin to take responsibility for herself and Candice. She needed to stop making impulsive choices and become self-reliant. Aunt Elizabeth supported her conclusions and said, 'I will ask my friends if they know of more suitable work for you. You should start looking for a nursery school for Candice.'

A couple of weeks later Marion's aunt announced: 'Mrs Giles's son, Alexander, was recently demobilised from the Navy and he is resurrecting his old law practice in the city. He is looking for a legal clerk and is willing to interview you for the job. You have all the skills necessary.'

CHAPTER FORTY-FIVE
APRIL 1946
GENEVA

Dear Dieter,

I recently heard word of you from Dr Shirtcliffe, who told me that your letters to me from Exeter were intercepted by the Army censors and not sent on, as you would have expected. It seems to be that War Office policy is not to let POWs contact girls in Guernsey.

Dr Shirtcliffe told me about Guernsey's efforts to get you released because of your generous help to so many Guernsey people. It seems that the English Military Government in northern Germany, thought that you could better serve them by leaving the camp and helping them, in reconstruction work, in Germany.

I will now try to reach you from Geneva, through your family. I sincerely hope this will work out and this letter will reach you.

I really am not sure where to start. Perhaps I should work backwards and explain what I am doing in Geneva.

I arrived here two days ago to take up a position with the Red Cross. I am involved in a month-long induction course before being transferred to a camp for displaced children in Belgium. It is in the French-speaking area of Belgium, and I am also having a French refresher course, along with many other practical classes. I am part of an international group of nurses, teachers, doctors and therapists. We are all living in a hostel and working long hours to cover the basics for our intended work.

I left Guernsey in late March and caught the ferry to St Malo and thence on via the current jigsaw of a railway system to Paris where I stayed a few days before continuing to Geneva. Many of the bridges over the Seine and Loire had been left impassable and the rail network took me on many detours.

The things I saw on my journey shocked me. I was not prepared for the ruination of lives, relationships, landscapes and property that I saw. I have no doubt you too have seen similar things. It almost made our difficulties in Guernsey seem trivial in comparison.

A man on the train told me that Normandy had eighty-five days of hell, with no water, power or phonelines. All the citizens lived in the street during that time. He said Normandy made the sacrifice for the Allies but that it had to be done!

The damage caused by carpet-bombing and street-by-street fighting has reduced towns to rubble and skeletal frameworks of buildings, with people sheltering wherever they can find cover. I was also stunned by the damage to the countryside. Denuded of vegetation, hedgerows torn apart by tanks, bomb craters, defunct military equipment abandoned everywhere and no crops in the trashed ground. It is a very sad situation. Recovery will take many years.

Suffering is all relative and I am now more equipped to understand better what the displaced children have witnessed and experienced. If it was a staggering sight for me, how traumatised must they be?

We were able to improve our circumstances in Guernsey relatively quickly after our liberation in May 1945. While food is not plentiful in Guernsey, it is now adequate. Similarly, our access to goods has improved. Gradually, our soldiers and other displaced persons are returning and mostly able to re-establish themselves in their old homes, thankfully undamaged. There is a housing shortage, but the government is managing this by letting people return only if their family can house them for six months.

Our hospital moved back to its former quarters quickly and I moved into the Nurses' Home, to free up rooms for my landlady's family. We have received many new doctors and nurses from England over the past ten months, to rebuild the medical workforce. Delayed surgery and dental services began immediately when they arrived. The longer-term effects on the health of the Islanders after years of deprivation are starting to show up, particularly when you compare the children who didn't leave the Island with those who went away. The local children are much shorter and weigh less.

Mortality amongst the elderly remains high. Most have lost their reserves of health and mental strength.

The difficulties in Guernsey after the Liberation have also been social ones. Marion, and many other young women, were forced to leave the Island because they were subjected to physical attacks at worst, and social stigma at best. Sadly, their children were also victims, which was most unfair. Other tensions flared between people over their perceived co-operation or collusion with the occupying force, or their exploitation of other Guernsey people. It became very nasty with people pitted against each other.

The British troops who liberated us were supposed to investigate war crimes, including black marketeering, but ultimately decided not to stir up further rancour and bitterness. I hope this legacy of blame and guilt can be expunged quickly, but I have my doubts, as evidenced by my father's generation holding onto their grievances since 1918.

I found this very distressing and really wanted to start my life somewhere else where I could provide post-war assistance to those still in need. Hence, I decided to write to the Red Cross and have gladly accepted their offer of a place. It was time for me to leave.

I hope you are well and recovering from your own experiences and that your family is all right too. I hope, too, you will want to write to me again.

'À la prochaine.' Till the next time.

With affection and kind regards,

Rachel.

CHAPTER FORTY-SIX
MAY 1946
NEAR LIÈGE

Dear Dr Shirtcliffe,

I am going up to the city tomorrow to buy supplies, so thought it was time I wrote to tell you what I have been doing over the past two months. My time in Europe has been a huge revelation for me about this horrific war. Life on Guernsey was hard, the bombings in the UK were destructive, but what I have seen and heard in France and Belgium has shocked me.

I have heard stories of depravity and depredation, that were well beyond my personal experience. I have heard, too, stories of simple kindness and extraordinary bravery by those who lived through utter chaos. I have felt horrified by what we humans have inflicted on others and amazement at the human spirit. Quite a lot for a little Guernsey nurse to handle!

My trip to Geneva was one of startling contrasts. As we travelled from St Malo to Paris [repeating the journey I took as a schoolgirl], I was most dismayed to see the bombed-out villages and country towns. Buildings with only one wall and a chimney left standing. Some even had intact floors, with furniture still standing as if awaiting someone's return.

There were cafés operating with no walls, surrounded by pieces of plywood and canvas to stop the driving rain. The streets, if passable, were still full of wrecked military machines, anti-tank traps and mortar holes. The countryside with all the hedgerows and forest lots pulled out, its tree-lined lanes now marshalled by ghostly tree stumps not towering greenery. I saw tanks and armaments rusting in ditches as farmers work, without proper equipment, in their fields, to meet the expected food shortage this winter. Groups of ill-clothed, shaven-headed men were scouring the lanes and fields for old ordinance, to be exploded.

The stations in Paris were festooned in noticeboards with hundreds of haunting photos of people missing. Some with heartrending requests for information about children, last seen so long ago that their photos are outdated. I saw queues of gaunt hollow-eyed men at stations and public buildings, clothed in assorted uniforms and rags. I heard someone say, 'The dead are still walking'. Sombre and tragic sights.

In contrast Switzerland appeared to be a small island of sanity on a turbulent continent. Homes are habitable, people are well clothed, and seem adequately

251

fed. Life there seemed like the old normal which we once enjoyed. For me, it felt like returning to a previous life, albeit briefly. But I've lost my innocence.

My training course at the Red Cross was excellent. Although brief it covered a lot of relevant public health and rehabilitation subjects as well as some psychology. It was challenging linguistically as my schoolgirl French hadn't equipped me with the vocabulary to include things medical!

My journey through Belgium to Liège was very much a repeat of my trip through France, but I was a bit less easily shocked by that time. It's surprising how quickly one gets inured to awful sights.

The camp though was most confronting. I was stunned at how basic and decrepit the camp was, and how few resources we had available, apart from our own determination. The first two weeks were spent doing things to make the camp habitable. We are a mixed group of nine staff from different countries and disciplines.

I think we are working well together because we all bring some different expertise to the camp. We laugh a lot as we struggle with our second languages. We undertake in-service training two evenings a week using workbooks provided by the Red Cross. Also, we have a weekly four-hour discussion about each of the children so that we are all working in concert to meet their individual needs.

I cannot describe how we felt when these displaced children arrived in a broken-down train from their German camp. We staff struggled for some weeks to manage our own feelings of horror, then anger, then grief when we first saw the forty children. As we have slowly got to know them their stories appal us.

We each have responsibility for ten children, and I have a six-year-old brother, with his four-year-old sister amongst my 'family' group. It is a slow process of gaining their trust, but we are providing stability and continuity. Our family has one classroom as a makeshift dormitory, with cubicles for each child and a large walk-in cupboard, where I sleep.

Three other classrooms are set up similarly and we use the remaining classrooms for eating, education and leisure activities. The ablution block is nearby and very basic with washbasins and toilets. We have scavenged four tin tubs for bathing the children. For them a bath is a novelty and a playtime. A makeshift kitchen has been built onto the previous office and staffroom. Our Red Cross team leader, formerly a Swiss teacher, lives there. He is in his 50s and has done similar work previously, whilst the rest of us are novices.

Right now, our focus is on the children's physical health and nutrition. We are trying to establish a safe, quiet, reliable and kind atmosphere for the children. I'm so grateful to the preparation the Red Cross courses provided me with. I have never seen children so bereft and traumatised. I would not have known how to work effectively with them without the training. I would also have struggled to cope professionally and personally.

Our camp is quite isolated. The countryside is hilly, with the slopes now bare of the forest cover they once had. Broken bridges show that the location was recently the site of a strategic battle. Once there was a thriving village community supported by a colliery. Now the school is one of the few buildings which has been salvaged and put to new use for our orphaned children.

It is somewhat eerie to be surrounded by empty and wrecked buildings, especially when the wind howls through their wreckage. Luckily, we are shielded from the worst noise and sights by a wooden fence and a copse of trees.

We have heard that some Belgian people will soon be returning here from Liège, to ease the housing difficulties in the city. We do not know if the colliery will be restarted but there is a prospect that local shops will reopen. They will be welcomed by us as we try to re-establish a new normality for the children.

Despite the difficult things I have encountered here in Europe, I am very glad to be here. I have a sense of purpose again. I feel I am learning so much each day and I am happy in our little community. It is a place for healing; not only of our youngsters!

I hope you are all doing well in Guernsey. Give my best wishes to all my old colleagues.

I very much appreciated your advice and good counsel in our dark days.

Sincere regards,
Rachel Dorey

PS. I wrote to our mutual friend via his parents.

CHAPTER FORTY-SEVEN

JUNE 1946

HAMBURG

Dear Rachel,

How happy I am to receive your letter. It has taken
a long time to get to me. I did not give up on hope,
nor give up on the good Dr Shirtcliffe to assist in our
reconnection. How much I have wanted to talk to you!
So many months and much has happened to us both.

I was sorry to hear of the great difficulties you
have experienced since I last saw you. Let us hope this
is behind us now. It appears that many of our recent
experiences, although in different countries, involve
witnessing scenes of similar destruction and hardship.

I do not want to dwell on the horrors committed over the past years of our lives. We both must learn from the madness wrought by the war, to ensure there are no more. We must foster humanism and tolerance, not nationalism and prejudice.

But first you ask about my family. My parents remain at their farm; but now with help from my second brother. He was briefly a prisoner of the British after the battle for Jutland in late April-May [just before the official surrender]. My youngest brother, who was a firefighter, was also drafted as a special force member and lost his life in a battle with the Russian forces near Kiel. This has caused much suffering and sadness for my family, which is still very raw. My own travails were nothing compared to theirs.

My time in Le Truchot prison was tolerable and relatively brief. It was a relief for me not to have caused difficulties for all my local associates. I think you all were not charged with offences because the prison was already overcrowded with deserters. I was sent to England [within days of your freedom from us] and transported to Exeter.

In the prison camp I started out doing heavy outdoor labour throughout the winter, but in January I was asked to work in the camp clinic because so many men had health problems. It rained frequently and was very cold, and in these conditions our clothes were always damp. Working indoors and living in the clinic improved my health and welfare.

I was so fortunate to have good friends in Guernsey who petitioned for my release. The agreement reached by the War Office coincided with the establishment of a welfare unit for the Military

Government in Hamburg, so in February 1946 I returned here on a British ship. Because I was bilingual, and I was not needing to be further vetted, as a war criminal, I was sent to be assistant to the Senior Medical Officer [a British man].

I can only say that I am eternally grateful for my release and repatriation by the British. They have treated me much better than I could have hoped.

Enough to say, my family were very pleased to see me and I them. However, I recognise that they find it difficult to see me working with the victor, and the new governing force. I heard somewhere that every foreign occupation is resented by those who lose aspects of their previous liberty. However well-meaning, the invaders affect the fundamentals of the daily existence of those invaded. Resentment, and hostility overtakes recognition of our common humanity. It is our turn to experience this.

Hamburg is another destroyed city, save for some of the walls and crypt of St Nicholas Church in its centre. Ten square kilometres of the city were razed by three days of bombing in 1943, which then created a firestorm. Then, during two weeks in May 1945, there was fierce street-to-street fighting, which destroyed much of the harbour and industrial areas. The result is much as you witnessed in France.

This winter was extremely harsh, and the suffering was immense for the local people, without homes, adequate food or heat. Cigarettes, even the butts, became the local currency. Money is valueless and everyone lives on 40 Marks a day.

There are thousands still missing since the firestorm, and my work involves assisting the hundreds of homeless orphans who have been living rough since 1943. They live in small groups, surviving by petty crime and squatting in derelict buildings. These buildings frequently get burned down when fires are lit in the ruins for warmth. The children are psychologically scarred and run amok.

I am amazed that once again our individual goals for the future are running parallel. I am setting up a variety of health and welfare programmes, from the basement of what was a former expensive hotel near the Elbe River. First, we installed feeding programmes, provided clothes and rehoused the children, while searching for family members to take them in. Only when this is completed can we hope to heal, educate and reintegrate these unfortunate victims of adult insanity. There is much to do.

In the meantime, the British and Russians cannot agree on priorities. One side wants to rebuild and let Germany heal itself; the other wants to destroy all German industry and punish POWs. The lunacy is not yet over.

It is good that we will have an appreciation of each other's work. We both have obligations to meet for some time but, at last, our respective countries are co-operating. I will continue to write to you through the Red Cross. I suspect letters may take some time to arrive for each of us.

With my great affection and friendship always.
Auf Wiedersehen,

Dieter

CHAPTER FORTY-EIGHT
SEPTEMBER 1946
CAMBRIDGE

Two-year-old Amy was pushing a dolls' pram around the carpeted floor of a room in the City Library, one miserably wet autumnal morning. The room was filled with excited toddlers racing around. It was noisy and chaotic. The room smelt of wet wool from the coats piled up in a corner.

Today, was the opening day for a drop-in centre, where pre-school children could play together, while their mothers shared a cup of tea and a chat, in an adjoining room. The Cambridge Council had agreed, in response to community pressure, to open a new service for mothers and young children.

The post-war housing crisis had meant that many homes were shared by more than one family, creating a lack of space and privacy. Many women who had previously been employed because of war work, had been forced to give up their jobs for the demobilised soldiers and were missing their previous social connections. Other young mothers no longer lived near to their extended family and missed the advice and help from their female relatives. Still other women were having difficulties adjusting to a husband they had not seen for years.

Stella, who was a volunteer in the local MP's office, had become aware of the social isolation and difficulties experienced by many young families when these women came to register for the new State Housing Assistance. She had realised how anxious and depressed these women were and that it was impacting on their children. She discussed her concerns with the MP who encouraged her to find a solution.

Stella talked to her long-time friend Alison and they called together the group of people who had assisted them in their canvassing during the previous year's General Election.

In February, a committee had been formed, which first drew up a schedule of the various government and council services available in the city, as well as any run by the churches or community groups. The results of this work gave them a better understanding of what services for women and children might be missing in their city.

Armed with this information, the committee then held a meeting with some of the women coming to the electorate office with their problems, who soon determined that a daily coffee morning at a central location would meet their needs for social contact and give their children a chance to play with others.

With that resolved the committee used Alison's contacts with the city council to locate a suitable place for a 'drop-in centre'. Stella's previous employment as a council librarian had helped their petition, as too did the overt support of the MP.

The council agreed to provide two large, unused rooms at the back of the library building, which was previously the Civil Defence headquarters. There was a tearoom in one corner of the smaller room to be used for the mother's morning tea and a large doorway had been inserted into the wall of the larger room for the children's play area. A back entranceway led out from this playroom into a fenced yard, once used for storage, which now sported a small outdoor playground.

The committee members had begged the local community for furniture, toys and equipment. They had raised funds for supplies, enticed husbands to undertake building and painting jobs, and established a roster of women to run the centre each morning.

While the committee was very satisfied with their efforts to get the centre established there was much still to be done to keep the centre operational. In response to the committee's request Stella agreed to act as the voluntary co-ordinator, for twenty hours a week. Alison, in turn, had offered to replace Stella in the MP's office while Amy and Alison's son Paul would attend the drop-in centre each day. By working together, the two women realised they could assist the centre to respond to emerging needs in their community.

While Mark had supported Stella's committee work in establishing the centre, he was worried about the amount of time her new role would require and its impact on their family. Mark, as an only child, was concerned that Amy should soon have a sibling, whilst Stella, who had grown up happily with a much younger brother, felt there was less urgency.

After tense discussion between them, Mark accepted Stella's wish to become the co-ordinator and to stay in that role until the centre was a viable service.

'I've got so many ideas for the centre. I feel committed to it. I know Amy and Paul will enjoy themselves playing here as well. She won't miss me at all! Let me do it for a year. Please!' she begged.

Reluctantly, Mark at last agreed.

CHAPTER FORTY-NINE
DECEMBER 1946
KINGSBRIDGE

IT WAS STILL DARK, BUT CANDICE WAS SHAKING HER shoulder and calling, 'Mummy, Mummy! Come and see.'

Marion awoke and answered sleepily, 'It's too early Candice. You know Father Christmas won't have come just yet. You need to go back to sleep till after he comes.'

'No! No. I went downstairs already, and he has been. There are heaps of presents under the tree, He drank the whisky and ate the mince pies.'

John, now awake, said, 'Well, we've been caught out! Might as well obey the summons, open one or two presents and then try to get back to bed for a while. Heavens it's only 4 am.'

'Okay Candice, we will all get into our dressing gowns and slippers and you can open two presents now and we will all go back to bed so that we can open the rest in the morning.'

Candice was happy with the compromise, and while Marion made cocoa for them all, the youngster sat under the tree feeling the presents and made the difficult decision to select only two.

The first one she selected, was the largest, wrapped in shiny gold paper. Candice had traced its outlines through the gift wrap. 'I think Father Christmas has brought me a scooter. How did he get it down the chimney?'

John hesitated, 'I expect that after he had been down the chimney with the small presents, he opened the front door to bring the large present inside. See if there is any snow in the hallway.' Candice was torn; whether to open the parcel or to look for snow. The parcel won and with urgency she stripped off the paper to reveal a bright red scooter. 'Please can I ride it. Now?'

'All right, but just once up and down the hallway and then you can take this small parcel back to bed with you.' Marion held a parcel out to Candice knowing its contents could be enjoyed by the child once she was back in bed.

With the scooter ridden up and down the wide flagstone hallway, and with her doll in her arms Candice was happy to be tucked up in bed again, able to wait for more excitement in the morning.

John fell asleep immediately but sleep eluded Marion for some time. She mused, 'I am so happy. How could we have become a contented family unit in such a short time? How did I get from barely earning enough to look after myself and Candice, to living in this beautiful home? I don't have a worry in the world! John is such a good husband and a lovely father to Candice. Our life is perfect.'

In May 1946 Marion had started a new job as a legal secretary in Plymouth, working for Alexander Giles. She found that the job, which enabled her to fully use her secretarial and accounting skills, most interesting. She particularly enjoyed her interactions with the clients rather than being in a back office.

She and Candice continued to live with Aunt Elizabeth, but Candice now went to a nursery school each day. The little girl loved having young friends to play with and was learning a lot of new skills. It also meant that Marion met some other young mothers to socialise with. Marion's life began to improve again.

One day in July a client, Mr Rideau, came to see Alexander, but was late for his appointment. He was hot and bothered because his car had broken down on the journey to Plymouth. Marion, sympathetically, made him a cup of tea and said, that because he had come such a distance, she would try to reschedule Alexander's appointments, to fit him in during the afternoon. In this way he would not have a wasted trip. The man was extremely grateful for her help.

After his appointment with the lawyer finished and the client was departing from the office, he said, 'Thank you for your assistance earlier. I much appreciated it. I hear you come from the Channel Islands! I have relatives there and visited them in Guernsey, before the war. On my next appointment I would like to talk to you about how the Islanders fared during their occupation.'

Marion nodded graciously, secretly hoping that would not happen. His relatives may know someone she knew in Guernsey. She didn't want her history told to someone else in England. She hoped Alexander had not disclosed anything about her. When she questioned him later, he confirmed that he had been discrete. However, he did say that Mr Rideau had identified her Guernsey accent, which he, Alexander, was forced to admit, was correct.

Two weeks later John Rideau was back in the office with an 11 am appointment. He came bearing gifts of fruit from his orchard for Marion and Alexander. Marion was nonplussed when he asked if he could take her to lunch at 1 pm. Having received a bag of scarce oranges and a punnet of berry fruits from him, Marion felt it would be churlish to refuse his request. However, she indicated that it would only be possible if her boss would allow it.

John took Marion to the large hotel overlooking Plymouth Hoe. He had arranged for a table on the terrace at the seafront. It had been many years since Marion had eaten such lovely food in such a beautiful setting. John told her this was the place where Sir Walter Raleigh had played bowls, before his battle with the Spaniards.

Marion, surprised, responded without thinking that Sir Walter was one of her heroes. In response to John's quizzical look, she said, cheekily, 'Any man who lays down his cloak for a woman would be my hero! Did that happen here?'

John laughed heartily and said 'No! But it would have been the ideal place.'

Marion, realising her frivolous comment might be mistaken for flirtation, quickly commandeered the conversation to ask John about the source of the oranges and berries. He said that they came from his garden in Kingsbridge. After further prompting from Marion, who wanted to avoid questions being asked of her, John gave her an outline of his life in Devon.

Marion found his story fascinating as it was so different to hers. He was a skilled raconteur, who punctuated his narrative with humorous jests about himself. He admitted that his last decade was difficult with a very sick wife who had died in 1944. She had been a good wife and they had a happy life together, but they had no children.

'Perhaps we can meet again, when I am in town, and then you can tell me about life in Guernsey,' he suggested at the conclusion of their lunch.

Over the next two months, John visited Plymouth regularly, to prepare his case with Alexander. He often asked Marion out to lunch or for a drink after work, on those occasions. John's pleasant manner won her confidence in him, and they became good friends.

In September, Marion felt comfortable enough to be frank about all the details of her life during the war. She told John about her relationship with Fredrich and the circumstances of Candice's birth. He reacted with kindness and understanding.

'It does not affect our friendship,' he said. 'Perhaps you and Candice would like to visit my home in Kingsbridge. Candice might like to pick the pip fruit in the garden.'

John came to share Guy Fawkes' night at Aunt Elizabeth's home, with Marion and Candice. All three adults and an over-excited Candice enjoyed the evening. Because John was staying in Plymouth overnight, he asked Marion to have dinner with him on the following evening. Aunt Elizabeth quickly offered to babysit Candice, allowing Marion to accept his invitation.

Marion and John returned to Plymouth Hoe that night and, before they entered the hotel, John suggested, that despite the cold they walk out to the terrace to look at the lights. He picked up a woollen cape and suggested she wrap it over her coat while they walked to the seafront. Once there he plucked the cape from her shoulders, unfurled it and lay it at her feet: 'I'd like to be your hero too. Will you be my wife?'

She laughed, 'I replaced my old hero some weeks ago! Yes, I will.'

Within the month they married, with Marion's two aunts and cousin June as her witnesses. Three old friends of John also attended, to balance their small party.

Candice, at three-and-a-half was happy to live in the big house, with John and her mother. Marion felt secure and well-loved. Today the new family were about to celebrate their first Christmas together, and form their own festive traditions in the ancient manor.

EPILOGUE
14 JULY 1947
GENEVA

Dear Dieter,

I was so happy to find your letter waiting when I got back here at midday. I've had a smile on my face all day.

It is wonderful news that you have been accepted at the University of Lausanne to complete your psychiatry residency at a nearby mental hospital. I am very happy that, finally, you can achieve what you set out to do so many years ago. There is so much work to do, throughout Europe, to help those still tormented by their experiences during the war.

From a more personal perspective, I will be delighted

to see you in another month, and to show you around
Geneva. As you will be only sixty kilometres away, in
Cerny, rather than hundreds, I am excited that we will
be less than an hour apart.

Now let me tell you what I have been up to in the
past months.

The camp at Blegny finally closed in late April, with
the last ten children [all Jewish] going off to Montreal,
which apparently has a large Jewish population willing
to give a home to these young ones. It was good to see
them leave knowing that they will go into family homes.
As well, they will finally receive a decent schooling.

However, we were worried about how some of them
will adjust, as there were four children whose only
memories are of camp life. At least their memories of
their last camp at Blegny, will be of care and kindness,
even if the facilities were very basic. I will certainly
miss working so directly with children.

The information you gave me earlier this year was
invaluable in helping us anticipate the impact of coming
changes on the children who had already been so
traumatised. It helped us to prepare them for what
lay ahead. I was able to contact a child psychiatrist
in Montreal who is prepared to give assistance to the
Jewish League which sponsored the children. Our team
were so grateful to you, as well, for sharing your
experiences of the Hamburg children, who suffered
from the firestorm there.

I finished up all the paperwork and left for Liège
at the end of May going, via Paris, back to Guernsey.
Compared to places in Europe the Island seemed
almost back to normal. The population has grown with
Islanders returning, everyone has jobs, and the economy

270

seems to be booming with fruit and flowers again being exported to England.

This summer the tourists are expected to return, and the beaches are now cleared of mines, although the gun emplacements are still there. Fresh coats of paint are being applied everywhere. I got the distinct impression that Guernsey is quickly covering up all manner of recent ugliness.

My brother is now running the farm and, with the herd numbers up, it is going well. There is still food rationing, but the farmers have a growing market to serve. My parents still live in part of the farmhouse and Dad keeps busy as the 'extra hand'. My mother is now quite well and is happy. While she didn't want me to take up this job in Geneva, she realises that with Peter married, and a baby due in December, she will have a child to dote on.

It was lovely being close to the sea again and I walked around parts of the coast every day. I went to Cobo for a somewhat chilly swim, which kindled good memories. I was surprised to realise how much I had missed the open skies and the broad vistas available there. Blegny was awfully hemmed in by gloomy forested hills, running down to the deep river valley.

In Guernsey, I visited friends from the hospital who were all interested in what I have been doing since I left. Many were surprised that I wasn't coming home to stay.

There are plans to build a new hospital in the next couple of years. It was good to see the current one well stocked and with a full complement of staff. I had a long conversation with Dr Shirtcliffe and with Matron Rabey [who is planning to retire at the end of the year].

271

Dr Shirtcliffe asked me to send you his good wishes. He was pleased to hear that we had re-connected.

I then went over to England to see Marion and Candice who is now nearly four. [You will remember that I am her godmother]. Candice is a very striking child; beautiful blue eyes and thick dark hair. She chatters away happily to all the adults she sees. She is serious but shows no shyness.

Marion is now living in Kingsbridge, in Devon, not too far from your Exeter camp, actually!

Marion has fallen on her feet! Whilst she was working in Plymouth as a legal clerk in 1946, she met a wealthy landowner who was trying to resolve some disputes about ownership of his estate. It sounded quite complex but has been resolved.

Anyway, John was a widower, some twenty years older than Marion, and with no children of his own he was lonely. Very quickly he fell for Marion and Candice. They got married within a couple of months and Marion is now happily ensconced in a beautiful home with vast gardens which are open to the public during spring and summer. The beautiful azaleas, and rhododendrons, were still in flower whilst I was there.

There is an orangery filled with citrus and other subtropical fruit as well as vast orchards because the site is protected from cold winds and frost. The house is enormous and Marion and John love to entertain in the grand dining hall. They both made me very welcome and held a large dinner party to introduce me to some of their friends.

I feared that Marion wanted to marry me off to someone in Devon. But I made it clear that I believed that neutral Switzerland was the right place for me! I told her that you were seeking a position in Switzerland! She was pleased to hear that.

Marion and John seemed to be very happy and to complement each other. Marion is building up a business on the estate, setting up a small shop and a café to supplement their farming income, whilst John manages the farm.

Marion looks as stunning as ever and decided I needed to improve my image, so we went up to Exeter to get my hair cut and re-styled. It's now quite short. She encouraged me to buy some stylish new clothes as well. It is years since I have been so self-indulgent but I'm happy with the result.

I think I told you earlier that Marion had found out that Fredrich had died at the Battle of Stalingrad. She received a small legacy from his estate, which she has set aside for Candice. Fredrich's son has recently written to Marion saying that as Candice is his only family member left alive, he would like to continue to correspond with Marion. Marion is agreeable as she wants to be open with Candice about her father and half-brother. Luckily, John supports this; he is a remarkably open-minded man!

I had a lovely visit with them and then I went to London for a few days and met up with another old school friend, Stella. She lives in Cambridge with her husband [a Guernsey man] who is a mathematician at a research centre for the university. They have a three-year-old daughter, with Stella expecting another child in October.

Their family are going off to Cambridge USA in August for Mark's sabbatical year. They will have accommodation in the staff housing complex, which, from the photos I saw, looks very modern and luxurious. Stella had been hoping to do some university study herself, but with two young children I think that might be difficult. No doubt she will find things to pursue, as she is very community minded. She has been running a women and children's centre for the past year and loves the role.

I persuaded Stella to come up to London for the day to meet up with Marion again, for the first time since she left Guernsey in 1940. It was a bit strained at first, but over lunch we three seemed to find lots to talk about and to enjoy each other's company.

Whilst we were waiting on the platform for my boat train to arrive, Marion persuaded us to sing the song we sang in our last school play. It's a silly little thing called 'Three Little Maids' which at the time, we thought was very clever and apt for our threesome. Our meeting ended in laughter; I wonder when we will all meet again.

I stayed two days in Paris going to many famous buildings and art galleries. It is a beautiful, albeit still scarred, city. Then it was on to the overnight train back here. An uneventful journey after a lovely holiday.

It's great to be back in Geneva with its long lake and distant mountain views, which both appeal to me greatly. I have been assigned a small apartment in Mt Brilliant, not far from the lakeshore. There is a tiny balcony from which I can see a sliver of the lake. It is only a couple of kilometres from Red Cross HQ and I plan to buy a bicycle to get around on. It is so flat that cycling will be easy. I promised myself that I will not be arriving at work needing resuscitation from my medical colleagues. Don't laugh!

I don't know if I told you that the Red Cross is now running all the tracking programmes for displaced persons around the world. I am going to be involved in developing disaster-relief and rehabilitation programmes. There are about twenty of us working in this programme and all of us have had Displaced Person's camp experiences, in different parts of Europe. We are to focus on practical plans, which can be implemented anywhere in the world, where emergency aid is needed. I know I am going to enjoy the work.

I must go to bed; it's very late but I wanted to write to you immediately so that my letter will be picked up in the morning post.

When we said, 'until next time' [Bis zum nächsten mal?], we really had no idea of when, or where, that would be. I think we might have found the right place. You can soon expect to have to buy me that decent cup of coffee you promised me in a different time and different place!

Take care,

Yours with great affection,
Rachel

ACKNOWLEDGEMENTS

To my friend Janet Tyson for her professional experience, guidance and support. To my cousin David Le Prevost, Guernsey, for his cover photo of the German Gun Emplacement. And to my husband Ian Calder for his help, patience and encouragement.

REFERENCES

Much of the detailed historical data is drawn from the 'Press Diary 1940-1945' published by the Guernsey Press. Other historical sources include:

1. *The History of Guernsey. The Bailiwick Story*. Revised edition updated 2001 by James Marr. Published by The Guernsey Press Company Limited 2001.
2. *A Short History of Guernsey*, second edition May 1982 by Peter Johnston. Published by Peter Johnston and printed by the Guernsey Press Company.
3. *The Country People of Guernsey and their Agriculture 1640-1840*, Published by Richard Hocart. Typeset and Printed by Ian Taylor, wwwtaylorthorneprint. co.uk,2016.
4. *The Model Occupation. The Channel Islands under German Rule 1940-46* by Madeleine Bunting. Published by Harper Collins 1995
5. *The Prey of An Eagle. A personal record of Family Life written throughout the German Occupation of Guernsey 1940-1945* by K-M-Bachman. Published by Burbridge Ltd, printed by The Guernsey Press Company Limited 1985.
6. *Aspects of War. A view of daily life during the German Occupation of the Channel Islands 1940-1945* by June Money. Revised edition published in 2011 by Channel Island Publishing Jersey.